POINT
OF
HEARTS

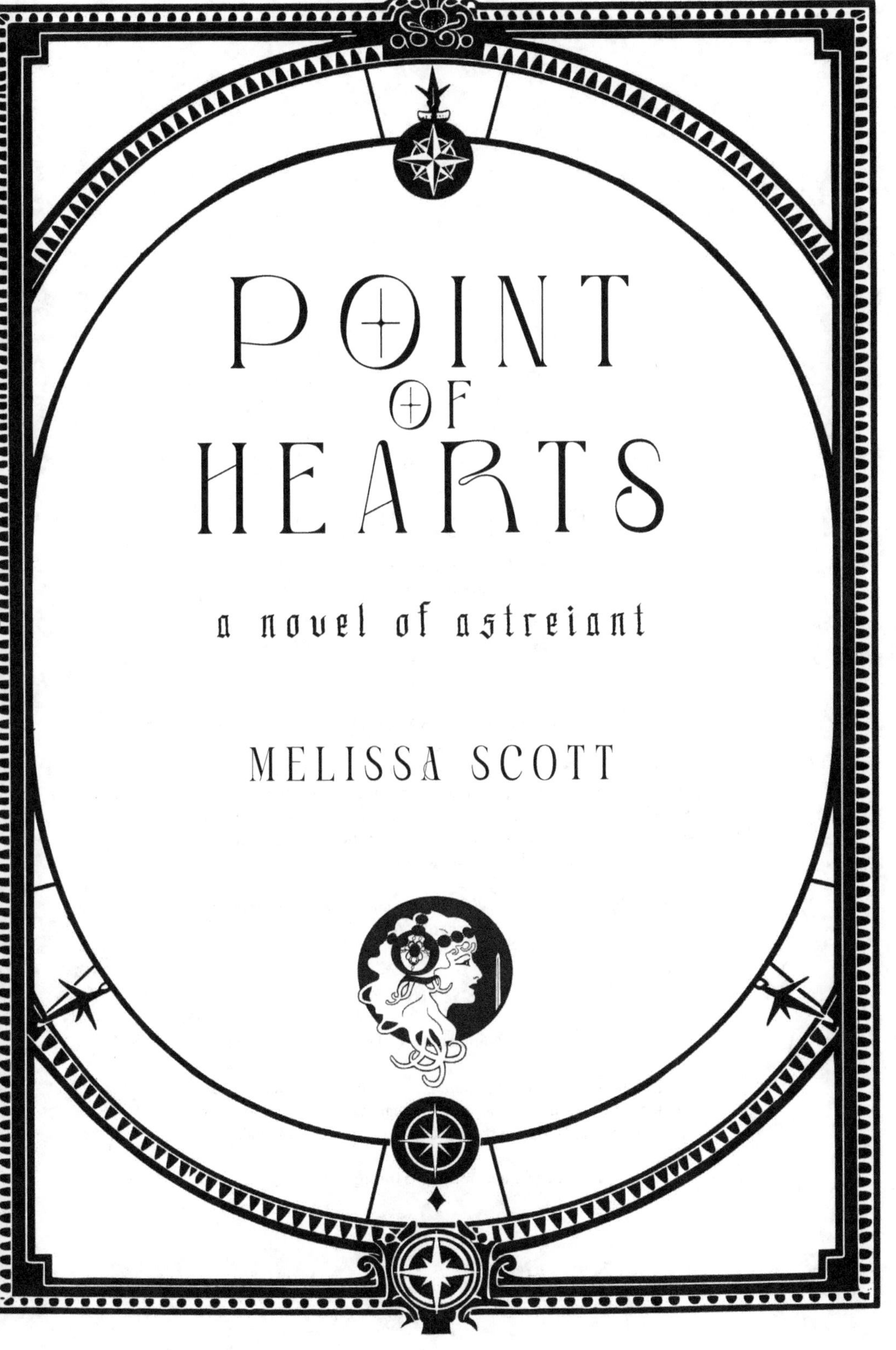

POINT OF HEARTS

a novel of astreiant

MELISSA SCOTT

POINT OF HEARTS

A Novel of Astreiant
Melissa Scott

First edition published in 2025 by Queen of Swords Press LLC.
Minneapolis, MN
www.queenofswordspress.com

979-8-9895009-5-6

Library of Congress Number (LCCN) available on request

Cover and interior design: Inkspiral Design

ACKNOWLEDGMENTS

I'D LIKE TO thank Catherine Lundoff and Queen of Swords Press for her enthusiasm and encouragement as I worked on Point of Hearts, and for the lovely new editions of the previous books in the series. A hearty thanks also to the members of the Astreiant Patreon, whose support makes these projects a rare delight.

CONTENTS

ONE

"THAT CAN'T BE right," Philip Eslingen said, and, too late, realized that he'd spoken aloud. This was most certainly not his place to speak, here in the workroom of the Surintendant of Points; he was here on sufferance and because he was the least offensive officer of the City Guard, whom the Surintendant persisted in seeing as rivals to the points' legal authority. He kept his expression neutral with an effort, but winced internally as several heads turned to stare at him. Trijn he knew well enough, the Chief at Point of Dreams where Nicolas Rathe, his leman, was the Senior Adjunct, but the neat dark woman who had been introduced as Felis Orlandi, the Chief at Point of Hearts, was a near stranger. Out of the corner of his eye, he could see Rathe frowning, and then the Surintendant fixed them all with a gimlet stare.

"That's what every woman who's heard this…judgment…has said. And yet on close examination, not a single advocate or judge has found a flaw in the argument."

Eslingen braced himself and met the Surintendant's eyes squarely. "I don't understand, sir."

"It's to do with the old laws of the Ile'Nord," Orlandi began, and the Surintendant lifted a hand.

"Allow me." Rainart Fourie was tall and thin and pale, his gray hair cropped close to his scalp, and his coat and breeches were unrelieved black, aggressively plain for his rank. "The Vidame de Castiat has been accused of failing to pay the royal salt tax—there is a small salt mine on her lands, and it had been alleged—"

"And proven," Rathe muttered, quietly enough that Fourie could ignore him.

"—that the vidame was selling some of its produce outside the legitimate markets. When she was charged with this, she came to Astreiant and in the queen's court acknowledged that she was in fact guilty. She then stated that she had full right of legal judgment within her own lands, that the crime had taken place entirely within those borders, and therefore she had sentenced herself to the appropriate fine and to imprisonment in a house which she owns in Point of Hearts. As I said, the queen ordered a thorough examination of the judgment, and it seems that everyone agrees that the vidame is in fact within her rights. She has paid the fine."

There was a long silence. Eslingen glanced sideways again, not entirely convinced that this wasn't some strange joke, but the annoyance on Rathe's face killed that hope. Finally Trijn stirred. "And has she locked herself in her cellar?"

"In the tower," Orlandi corrected. "It's a townhouse, but it has a tower." She saw the Surintendant's frown and stopped.

"She will need to be watched," Fourie said. "And that is where you come in."

"I don't have the people to spare," Orlandi said. "With this wedding coming up, every woman in the station is going to be busy dealing with that, particularly since the Levelers have chosen this moment to speak out again. We're buried in broadsheets—"

"As are we all," Trijn said. Eslingen had seen most of the new Leveler broadsheets himself, and they were a dangerous combination of genuinely funny satire, most of it directed at the Ile'Norder nobles who came to the city every winter to attend the Midwinter celebrations, and serious calls to riot against noble oppression and claim a larger share of the commonwealth. Usually the broadsheets were a nuisance; this had a sharper feel to it, and he knew Rathe felt the same way.

Orlandi went on as though the other woman hadn't spoken. "Not to mention that after Midwinter is already our busiest time of year."

"I'm well aware of that," Fourie said. "You'll borrow women from Dreams—Trijn, I know this is a relatively quiet time for you."

"Not that quiet." Trijn sighed. "Not now, given the broadsheets. But I take your point, sir. There's a fair amount of overlap between Hearts and Dreams."

"That was my thought," Fourie said. His mouth tightened for an instant, as though he'd bitten into something sour. "And I'm only too aware of the recurring Leveler problem. Given that, we will also call on the Guard to provide further assistance—with de Castiat, and possibly with the wedding, not the broadsheets. The broadsheets are points business."

Eslingen bent his head in acknowledgement, though he could only imagine what the Prince-Marshal would have to say about that. But dealing with the nobility was a large part of what the Guard had been created to do. "Of course we'll be glad to help out, Surintendant."

"I'll feel better when I hear that from Coindarel himself," Fourie said, "but I'm counting on it."

Rathe stirred then. "Can I ask exactly what's meant by watching her? Are we—or the Guard—supposed to enforce this promise of hers?"

"I doubt that'll be necessary," Orlandi said. "She's a woman of honor."

"Except as regards the salt tax," Rathe said.

Orlandi bridled, but Fourie allowed himself a thin smile. "Just so. Let's say that I prefer not to take unnecessary chances. And if both the points and the Guard are present, she will have no grounds for objection should we have to act. I trust there are no more questions?"

Orlandi looked as though she wanted to protest, but Fourie's dismissal was unmistakable. The group bowed themselves out of the workroom, an apprentice appearing from nowhere to shut the door behind them, and Eslingen followed the others down the marble stairs that led to the main hall. It was crowded—the Tour de la Cité always was—merchants-resident and venturer in their sober best mingling with advocates and judges in flaunting scarlet robes, every woman of any importance attended by a train of secretaries and apprentices and even a well-dressed knife or two as bodyguard. Orlandi scowled impartially at the crowd, and caught Trijn by the sleeve.

"The Sur can't be serious—can he? We've no remit to judge a noblewoman."

"We're empowered to enforce the law in the city of Astreiant," Trijn said mildly, and spoiled it by adding, "Besides, we'll have the Guard to back us up."

"We don't need the Guard," Rathe said, and Eslingen winced. That was an old point of contention between the two of them, that the Guard usurped some of the points' privileges by its mere existence. Certainly it didn't help that the nobles who visited Astreiant found it easier to accept the Guard's authority as deriving directly from the queen and enforced by their fellow nobles. Or at least by people who could pass for nobles: he himself was more common-born than most, a motherless man from the Leaguer town of Esling. Rathe came from the poorer neighborhoods on the south bank of the River Sier that ran through the city, but he was Astreianter born and bred, and fiercely proud of the city's independence.

"That's Leveler talk," Orlandi said. Trijn rolled her eyes, but the other woman went on unheeding. "And will we have the Guard?"

Eslingen flourished a bow. "I'm certain we will be happy to put ourselves at the points' disposal, Chief Point."

Orlandi gave him a distinctly dubious look. "Very pretty. I'll have it in writing, if you please."

"I assure you." Eslingen bowed again, and she swept away.

Trijn grimaced again, and turned more slowly toward the entrance, Rathe and Eslingen following.

"And will the Guard put itself at our disposal?" Rathe asked, after a moment.

Eslingen sighed. "Coindarel sent me on purpose. He doesn't like Fourie, but he understands our position. And he's seen the broadsheets, too. They're— concerning."

"They are that," Trijn agreed.

"He wanted me to ask: have you had any luck finding the writers?" Eslingen held his breath, hoping he hadn't pushed too hard, and Trijn sighed.

"We've found a printer or two, but all of them claim they accepted an anonymous commission, from a hooded woman who paid them too much for them to refuse. They're sitting in cells in Sighs, but so far they're sticking to their stories."

"And no doubt they'll continue," Eslingen said. "Nonetheless, the Prince-Marshal wants us to help however we can."

Rathe looked mulish, caught between doubt and wanting to agree, and Trijn paused at the top of the steps that led down to the great open courtyard. "Do you know, I think the Sur might have just done something clever? It's a precedent, after all—an Ile'Norder noble consenting to points' supervision. I wouldn't put it past him."

"No more would I," Rathe admitted, some of the tension easing from his expression. "Will she put up with it?"

"She won't have a choice," Trijn said. She reached into the purse that hung at her waist, brought out her tobacco-pouch and pipe, began filling it thoughtfully. "No, my main question now is how we're going to organize this. No matter what the Sur says, I don't have that many women to spare. Not if we're going to find whoever's writing these broadsheets."

"Yeah, I was wondering that myself," Rathe said.

Trijn flicked her striker, directing the fat spark into the waiting pipe. "Well, that'll be your next job, Adjunct Point. See who we can spare, and come up with a plan. And try to choose people who can be tactful."

"That's never been our strong suit," Rathe said, and lifted his hands in surrender. "On it, Chief."

"And I," Eslingen said hastily, "had better head back to the barracks to let the Prince-Marshal know about these new developments. Nico, I'll see you tonight."

For a moment, he thought he might have overstepped, but Rathe gave a crooked smile. "I'll meet you at Wicked's, then," he said, and turned to follow Trijn.

RATHE AND TRIJN made their way back across the Hopes-point Bridge and through the busy streets of Hopes into Dreams itself. It was always quieter in the daytime than either Hopes or Sighs, shops and taverns and eating-houses keeping hours that matched the majority of their customers, the actors and patrons of the theaters that filled the district. Now at noon, most of the shops were just opening, apprentices still setting out their wares and sweeping the steps and forecourts.

As they turned the corner to pass the Tyrseia, Rathe lifted his head at the sound of raised voices. Trijn took the pipe from her mouth, frowning, and they both turned back toward the open square. It was more crowded than it should be—the theaters were closed for several more weeks, until the next new moon—and people were gaping from the doorways at a knot of mostly men gathered around the Tyrseia's side entrance. Someone shouted, and another man lunged at the man in the center of the group, who ducked away. Rathe drew his truncheon and started toward them, Trijn on his heels with her own staff drawn.

"Here, now—"

A third man grabbed for the center man's coat sleeve, and he spun away, long hair flying. The first man swung a fist, and the center man dodged. Then there was a flash and a bang like the report of a firelock, and the attackers fell back, startled. The man in the center lifted his hand, his face bloody. "Back, now, or I'll do it again!"

"All of you, stand away." Trijn didn't quite shout, but her voice cut through the noise. "Stand away now."

Rathe flourished his truncheon at the nearest man, and the stranger took a step back, lifting his hands to show them empty.

"Pointsman! Stop him!"

Rathe swore under his breath as he finally recognized the man at the center of the brawl, and hastily moved to put himself between him and the attackers. Chresta Aconin dabbed at his bloody nose, but kept his other hand firmly closed over some small object. He was a noted playwright, better known as Aconite for his deadly pen, and seemed to be living up to his reputation as a troublemaker. He heard Trijn swear under her breath, and then she pointed at the best-dressed of the attackers.

"You. What's all this about?"

"That *poet* has slandered our soueraine," the man answered. "We intend to teach him otherwise."

Trijn shook her head. "Not in Astreiant. You can lay a charge against him if you choose, but it's not your place to administer punishment. Particularly before any judgment has been made."

She sounded like an Ile'Nord noble herself, Rathe thought, and to his annoyance it seemed to be working. The leader drew himself up. "Gladly. I will gladly charge him."

"And I'll charge him," Aconin said, still wiping blood from his nose. "They threatened my life."

"Coward," one of the others said, and Aconin rolled his eyes.

"Oh, please. Chief Point, I am done with this."

"He attacked us," the leader protested. "With magic."

"I was defending myself," Aconin said.

Out of the corner of his eye, Rathe saw his second, Lizy Sohier, pushing through the crowd, a squad from the station at her heels. "Chief."

Trijn saw where he was looking and nodded. "Good. You can make your charges at the station. Both of you will come along with me—no, just you," she added, pointing to the leader. "Sohier! Take statements from the rest of them, and from the witnesses, and then make sure this lot clears off back to their lodgings."

"Right, Chief." Sohier reslung her truncheon and pointed to the nearest of the attackers. Now that they were no longer fighting, Rathe saw that all of them wore the wreath-and-oak-leaf badge of the d'Alamenon family. They were somehow related to the de Galhacs who were marrying into the royal family: it was only to be expected that Aconin had managed to make an enemy of them.

"They're all witnesses," the leader protested. "Both to the insult and to his attack."

"They're also charged with their own attack," Trijn said. "Be glad I'm not demanding bond."

"Might not be a bad idea, Chief," Rathe said.

The leader swallowed whatever he might have said, and nodded to the oldest of the group. "Do what she says, then tell maseigne what's happened. Veusant, you'll come with me."

The group sorted itself out efficiently, an older man gathering the rest around Sohier and the junior who was taking notes. Rathe looked at Aconin. "So. What was that thing you used?" He nodded at the other man's clenched fist. "Want to let me see?"

"Not particularly." Aconin started to slide his hand into the pocket of his coat, then stopped himself. "It was a thunderflash, we use them in the theaters. It's not magistical at all, at least not within the legal meaning."

Rathe suppressed his first, profane response. "And why did you happen to have one—several?—in your pockets, given that the theaters are all closed?"

Aconin grimaced. "Because I'd been threatened, of course. These idiots seem to think I've been writing about their soueraine, though why she'd merit my attention I couldn't say. Today they were waiting for me outside the Tyrseia, and—" He put his handkerchief to his nose again, though the bleeding seemed to have stopped. "Well, you see the result."

"And you want to call the point?"

"Give me one good reason I shouldn't." Aconin's voice wasn't entirely steady, but then, he'd never been much of a fighter. Rathe shook his head.

"You won't get an argument from me. Though if you've been baiting their employer, you might want to rethink it."

"But I haven't," Aconin said. "Adjunct Point, I am, for once, as innocent as a newborn babe. Let the triteness of the metaphor be my witness! I have nothing to say about the Soueraine d'Alamenon or any of her kin. They are nothing to do with me."

"You'll still need to come to the station," Rathe said, but for once, he thought Aconin was telling the truth.

They passed through the gate at Dreams as the clock was striking the quarter hour. The courtyard and the main room were less crowded than usual, mostly with women paying fines or settling minor grievances, but the sight of d'Alamenon's men drew every eye. Trijn glared at the duty point until she looked back at her books, then pointed to the leader. "You, come with me and state your complaint. Nico, you deal with Aconin."

Rathe sighed and beckoned to the playwright. "This way."

He led the way upstairs to his private workroom, saw that the kettle was nearly empty, and called a runner to refill it. He waved Aconin to the guest's chair and settled himself beside the stove. "Right. Tell me what happened."

Aconin spread his hands, displaying elegantly painted fingers. His fine wool coat was almost certainly secondhand, but made over to fit him, and his long hair was carefully curled. "If I knew that—but none of it makes any sense. I swear, I have never had any quarrel with d'Alamenon or her people. I could care less, frankly."

"What happened?" Rathe asked again, and broke off as the runner returned with the filled kettle. He made sure that it was seated properly and the runner was out of earshot, then rested his elbows on the worktable. "From the beginning."

"I was supposed to meet with Jastinne Ybarres—she's with Izami's company these days." Aconin sounded faintly annoyed. "I had an idea that I thought might appeal to her. But she didn't keep the appointment, so I thought I'd go to the Leaguer—the midday ordinary's cheap and more than edible. But on my way, that lot accosted me. Threatened me with a beating for what I'd said about their soueraine, and then attempted to make good on their threat." He flourished his bloody handkerchief. "Not without some success, I might add. There were, I will point out, seven of them and only one of me, and I think even you might find those daunting odds, Adjunct Point. So I used a thunderflash."

"Which you just happened to be carrying," Rathe said.

Aconin's gaze flickered. "They've come in handy before now."

"So you were expecting trouble?"

"No—well, I'd heard some talk."

"What sort of talk?"

"They said I'd written a play that defamed the lady," Aconin said. "I put it to you, Rathe, they can't have been here much before Midwinter, and the last play of mine closed a month before. No, six weeks before. It's simply not possible."

"I heard you had a hand in the farce at the Bells," Rathe said, but without much hope. He'd seen that play himself, and there'd been nothing in it that could be construed as a reference to the Ile'Nord.

"A word or two here and there." Aconin waved a hand in dismissal. "But, as I'm sure you're aware, that was a city comedy, nothing to do with the nobility."

And that was the trouble, Rathe thought. He had seen both the plays in question, and would swear they were harmless. "Do you still want to press the point?"

Aconin sighed. "The last thing I need is a feud with the Soueraine d'Alamenon. If they'll admit they made a mistake and leave me alone, I'll let this go."

"You could get them banned from Dreams," Rathe suggested. This level of forbearance was unlike Aconin, and he wondered what the playwright was really thinking.

"Oh, that's tempting. But, no. They've made a stupid mistake, I can let it go."

"If you're sure," Rathe said. "But first—hand over the rest of the thunderflashes."

"I might need them," Aconin said.

"You heard the man," Rathe said. "He claims you used magic against him, and that's a serious charge. This is proof of what you actually did."

"True." Aconin reached into the pocket of his breeches and brought out a handful of dull, lead-colored objects about the size of a thumb's joint. They were shaped like a teardrop, with a heavy, bulbous base that tapered to a thin point, and when Rathe cautiously picked one up, he realized that they were dull glass rather than metal.

"You have to throw them against something hard to set them off," Aconin said. "Cobblestones will do nicely."

Rathe nodded. "One last thing, since you're here. What have you heard about these Leveler broadsheets?"

"Nothing more than you have, and quite possibly less," Aconin answered. "They're cleverer than the Broadsheet Poet was, back in the day, but she wasn't quite so bloody-minded."

"She was all for bodies in the street," Rathe said, and knew he sounded grim. The Broadsheet Poet had been the primary thorn in the points' shoes twelve years ago, when he'd been at the end of his apprenticeship. That had been the last time the Levelers had been a threat to the city: a hard winter and a meager harvest following that had left the city hungry, and discontented workers had gathered on the street corners to plot raids on the royal granaries and any house that looked as though it had food in its cellars. He had been an apprentice then, in his final year before he was made journeyman, and still remembered the blind terror of standing in the line before the doors of the granary while the queen harangued the crowd. She'd stood bare-headed in the winter weather, her troopers hidden out of sight, too far away to save her if she'd lost the crowd, and persuaded them in the end. She'd come close to emptying the granaries with her dole, gambling on a better harvest to come, but the next spring had been mild, and she'd won the wager. Rathe rubbed his chin, feeling the tug of old loyalties. He was more than half a Leveler himself, believed in the law and that everyone should be equal before it, but he'd seen enough riots to think that was not the way to win that goal. Which made him, in the end, no real Leveler at all, and he still felt guilty about that.

"She wanted a fight, and she wanted to see the nobility brought low," Aconin said. "And there were one or two she made a good case needed hanging. But this— 'burn it all down' isn't even particularly clever."

"No."

"It's not me writing them," Aconin said. "Not that I love the nobility, but they're what we have for patronnes. I'll make a mock of them as I please, but I don't want them dead."

Rathe nodded. "Are you sure you won't let me call the point?"

"I can't afford it," Aconin said.

"Let me know if you change your mind," Rathe said, and let the other man out of his workroom. He watched Aconin down the stairs, then glanced down the hall to see the door to Trijn's workroom still firmly closed. Sohier had returned, and now came to join him, a sheaf of papers under her arm.

"I've got the rest of the gang's testimony for the chief, but the leaders are still in there. Did Aconite say anything useful?"

"Not really. And he decided not to call the point." The kettle had been boiling. Rathe sighed and moved it to the hob, then began fixing a pot of tea.

"Which argues he's not as innocent as he claims," Sohier said. "What a surprise!"

"He said they accused him of slandering their soueraine in one of his plays," Rathe said. "And that it was unexpected—that he hadn't written anything that qualified."

"Not recently," Sohier said, visibly considering. "Something older?"

"Remotely possible," Rathe said. "But then how did they hear about it? If it was scandalous enough to make it all the way to the Ile'Nord, it would have been an even bigger scandal here."

"A broadsheet, maybe?"

"Aconin has more sense than to put his name to slander," Rathe said. "And anyway, I haven't heard of anything, have you?"

Sohier shook her head. "Nor I. What did the Sur want, anyway?"

"Ah." Rathe couldn't suppress a wry smile. "You've heard about the Vidame de Castiat?"

"Astree's tits. They're not serious, surely?"

"They are. And we'll be helping ensure that she stays under—I suppose you'd call it self arrest."

"I hate the nobility," Sohier muttered, and added hastily, "Not in a Leveler sort of way, just—"

"The ordinary way," Rathe suggested, and won a laugh.

ESLINGEN MADE HIS way across the city on foot, partly because it was all but impossible to snag a low-flyer in the busy streets outside the Tour, but also, if he was honest, because he wanted some time to think about how to present this new problem to the Prince-Marshal. Coindarel and Fourie had hated each other on sight, and he still wondered why no one had thought to compare their natal horoscopes before they'd been expected to work in harness. Probably because there was no one else the queen could have trusted to command the still-new City Guard: Coindarel was a Prince-Enfant, her close cousin, and had proved his utter loyalty on the battlefield. And, just as much to the point, there was nothing anyone else could offer him that he would want, at this point in his career. Still, things would have been easier if the two men could tolerate each other.

The plaza around the Pantheon was also busy, more than a dozen horses held waiting at the base of the steps that surrounded the circular building, and a busy pack of children squatting on the steps and in the shade of the nearest vendors' stalls, hoping for their turn to earn a demming. A merchant-venturer or her agent, still in riding dress, shook the worst of the dust from her skirts and started up the stairs, followed by two men with expensive firelock muskets and a third with an ironbound casket under his arm: the temple of Areton acted as banker to most of the kingdom, and also provided safe storage for the gunpowder weapons technically outlawed in the city. A pair of merchants-resident, elegant in dark wool that provided a background for their exquisite lace, drew back out of the way, while behind them a boy and a slightly older young woman seemed to be taking advantage of their mothers' inattention. More power to them, Eslingen thought, and turned to go widdershins around the circle.

The edges of the plaza were filled with broadsheet sellers, some with well-built stalls that were almost tiny houses, some with just a table and a stack of papers, and everything in between. Most had raised a pole from which the most recent printings fluttered like flags, and he scanned the block-lettered headlines as he passed. Many of them had to do with the upcoming wedding between the Castellan of Feramis, daughter and heiress of de Galhac, the most powerful of the Ile'Nord families, and the queen's great-nephew the Sousenfant Prince Loreten. He'd already read the astrologers' commentary on the chosen dates, an auspicious conjunction of Seidos and Metenere in her exaltation, and saw nothing new among the offerings. Of course, it was always legally tricky to comment more directly on the marriage's prospects; surely someone would soon enough, but at the moment, no one was taking the risk. There were also a selection denouncing the new Levelers in no uncertain terms, and reminding the city of the last time the Levelers had been active, but no sign of any Leveler writings themselves. He hadn't expected them: any sensible woman would keep such potentially seditious documents well out of sight, and sell them only to women she knew and trusted. Probably there wasn't a single Leveler sheet in the entire plaza, though he wouldn't bet against one or two of the dealers having a private selection at their other shops.

He stopped at one of the smaller stalls to consider the bundles of tight-rolled weekly prophecies. He chose one marked with Seidos's horse-head for his signs of the Horse and the Horse-master and tucked it into his cuff for later reading. He would as a matter of common courtesy have bought one for Rathe as well, but Rathe didn't share his stars with anyone. It wasn't precisely a point of contention, not anymore, but it still felt enough like distrust that Eslingen didn't like to think too much about it. He paid his demming for his own prophecy, and started toward the Guard's barracks on the edge of Manufactory Point.

The Guard had taken over the remains of a failed caravanserai, converting the stables and paddocks for their horses, and refurbishing the two small houses on the far side of the working ring for barracks and working space. The larger of the two was officially Coindarel's residence, as well as the company's headquarters, and in recognition of this there were two troopers casually on watch at the scarlet-painted door. They straightened into a salute at his approach, and the page who had been sitting on the top stop leaped to her feet.

"Shall I tell the colonel you're back, Captain?"

"Yes, thanks, and the major-sergeant." Eslingen let the girl dart ahead of him, hoping he'd have time to raid the basket of winter fruit that Coindarel kept waiting in the long hall, but before he could do more than pluck a single tiny orange from the pile, the workroom door swung open and Patric Estradere looked out.

"Vaan Esling. Good. The colonel wants to hear what Fourie had to say."

Eslingen tucked the orange into the cuff of his coat and followed dutifully. Coindarel wouldn't like anything he was going to hear; hopefully Estradere's presence would smooth over some of the difficulties.

The workroom was pleasantly warm, a fire crackling in the painted stove and a kettle simmering on its hob. Eslingen relaxed in spite of himself, and the Prince-Marshal scowled at him from where he sprawled on the low couch. "Well? What new folly are we expected to abet?"

"Have you heard about the Vidame de Castiat?" Eslingen said cautiously, and Estradere spread his hands.

"I told you that would be it."

He was, as well as being the Guard's major-sergeant, Coindarel's leman, and could get away with saying things like that. Coindarel sat up sharply. "Why haven't they gotten the judiciary to overturn her judgment?"

"Apparently the consensus is that it's correct," Eslingen said. "She is the ultimate authority in her own lands, and she's admitted her guilt and sentenced herself to imprisonment."

"In a lovely jewel-box of a house in Hearts," Coindarel said.

"She's agreed not to leave without royal permission," Eslingen said. "Also— she's agreed to let us and the points set a watch on her."

"Has she, now," Estradere said softly.

Coindarel pursed his lips. "I'll admit that's a surprise. What does Fourie say to that?"

Quickly, Eslingen ran through the proposed plan, and was relieved to see that Coindarel was nodding. When he had finished, Coindarel looked at Estradere.

"We were already planning to send patrols into Hearts. Will that be enough, or do we need to rework the roster?"

"We were?" Eslingen said, in spite of himself, and Estradere sighed.

"It's this Dis-damned wedding."

Coindarel made a warding gesture. "Never say that, we need it to come off. It's the best chance in a generation to make peace with the de Galhacs now that the rest of the family has come around to supporting the Palatineur."

"I didn't realize de Galhac was a man," Eslingen said, startled.

"Dariela de Galhac died five years ago, never having married and without an heir of her body," Estradere said. "Her brother Martin inherited the title, and his daughter—he was married to a merchant-resident, conveniently now deceased—became Castellan after him."

"Andariel's relations were none too happy to see the title go to him," Coindarel said, "but they seem to have resigned themselves."

"They've all come to Astreiant for the wedding, anyway," Estradere said.

"I'm sure they're glad of the excuse," Coindarel said. "And for the Palatineur to foot the bills."

"And we're expected to be in the middle of this," Eslingen said.

Coindarel's smile was not entirely pleasant. "Because that's our job, Captain vaan Esling: to keep the nobility from disturbing the city's peace. Which these days seems more important than ever—I assume you've seen the broadsheets?"

Eslingen nodded. "A fair few of them. They're—concerning."

"That's one way of putting it," Coindarel said. "What does Rathe have to say about them?"

"He doesn't like them," Eslingen said. Most people knew Rathe had Leveler sympathies; if this was Coindarel's way of asking about Rathe's loyalties—but it wasn't like the Prince-Marshal to play games. "They—Dreams and all the stations—are hunting for the writers, but they haven't had any luck. No one's pleased about that. And it means none of them have women to spare to watch de Castiat."

"Which brings us back to my question," Coindarel said. "Patric. Do we have the troops?"

Estradere glanced again at the sheaf of paper waiting on the table. "We should. If we're backing the points and not going it entirely alone."

"That was the request," Eslingen said carefully, and Coindarel sighed.

"Then I'll leave you to it."

TWO

THE MAIN SUN had set and the Winter-Sun was barely a finger's-width above the horizon by the time Rathe made his way to Wicked's. The tavern had once been a temple of some sort—Wicked had gotten both her nickname and the tavern's name from the conversion—and the courtyard wall and the building itself were constructed of solid stone. Even the kitchens and the flagged backcourt that held the privies were stone-built, and there was a generous cellar that presumably had once been the crypts. The main room was long and open, wheel-candelabra hanging from the central beams, and there was an enormous fireplace as well as a series of semi-enclosed tables at the back that each had their own tiny stove, and Rathe paused just inside the doorway to let his eyes adjust to the relative darkness. It was crowded, as it always was for the evening meal—Wicked's ordinary had earned an enviable reputation—but one of the waiters saw him and paused, tray in hand.

"Adjunct Point. The captain's waiting in the back corner."

"Thanks." Rathe threaded his way through the tables, relieved not to see anyone he knew. He was not an unsociable man, but it had been a long day.

Eslingen had claimed one of the small tables against the wall, and lifted a hand at his approach. "Nico. Wicked says the beer's off, so I've ordered wine for both of us."

"It's been that sort of day." Rathe took the seat opposite, working his shoulders.

"It's certainly been interesting," Eslingen agreed.

"Did you talk to Coindarel?"

Eslingen nodded. "He'd already been planning extra patrols in Hearts thanks to the wedding, so he didn't complain too much."

"That's a change."

"That's why he sent me to the meeting," Eslingen said. "Or why Estradere did."

"Not a bad idea," Rathe admitted. Fourie had reason to be jealous of the points' privileges, as he had fought for decades to establish that the points did in fact have jurisdiction over everyone within the city, noble as well as commoner. They had all worried that the City Guard would interfere with that, but so far it had been possible to avoid any serious conflicts. A good deal of that was thanks to Eslingen, who as the most experienced of the four captains had made it clear that the points should generally take precedence, but the intense dislike between the Surintendant and the Prince-Marshal added unnecessary tension to the relationship. Personal as well as professional, Rathe added silently, but they weren't talking about that if they could avoid it. And he trusted Eslingen, that went without saying. But the situation remained awkward.

A waiter circled toward them, balancing their pitcher and cups along with a tray for another table, and they took the opportunity to order the ordinary. As the waiter moved away, Rathe poured them each a cup, and Eslingen leaned back against the wall. "It's going to be a busy few weeks. And the astrologers are predicting snow to come."

"It'll be pretty for the wedding, I suppose," Rathe said.

Eslingen shrugged. "Myself, I'd rather have dry feet. But I suppose the nobility don't have to worry about things like that."

"Do them good if they did," Rathe muttered.

Eslingen lifted an eyebrow. "Dare I ask?"

"Aconin's managed to get himself crosswise with the Soueraine d'Alamenon's household." Rathe gave a quick explanation, and Eslingen shook his head.

"What in Seidos's name did he say?"

"He says he didn't say anything," Rathe said. "And for once I believe him."

"It's not like him to refuse a fight," Eslingen said. "But he doesn't lie about them, either." His eyes slid past Rathe, and Rathe turned to see Gavi Jhirassi heading toward them. Jhirassi was their upstairs neighbor, an actor with Gasquine's Women, so it wasn't unusual to find him at Wicked's. But it was unusual to have him seek them out like this. Rathe glanced back at Eslingen, who lifted his shoulders in a fractional shrug.

"Nico." Jhirassi sounded both nervous and determined, never a good sign. "Have you got a minute? I have a question for you."

Rathe glanced past him to see another table full of actors, all carefully not looking in their direction. That was another bad sign, and he suppressed a sigh. "Have a seat."

"I won't be long." Jhirassi drew a stool away from the table and settled himself, elbows on the tabletop. Eslingen lifted the wine pitcher, but Jhirassi shook his head. "Thank you, no. It's by way of a legal question. Can the players be charged with slander just for reciting someone else's lines?"

Rathe blinked. As far as he knew, the question had never been raised, so he didn't have an answer, but he didn't think it was good that Jhirassi was asking. "I don't know. You'd need to ask an advocate."

"But I can't." Jhirassi leaned forward slightly, adjusting his voice so that it didn't carry beyond their table.

"I know several women who wouldn't charge you," Rathe began, and Jhirrasi shook his head.

"If it was just a matter of paying for advice, we could take up a collection. No, it's—the whole thing is a bit touchy."

"Do we want to know why?" Eslingen asked.

Jhirassi's smile was wry. "Most likely not. It's about the review, you see."

"Of course it is," Eslingen said.

Rathe nodded. It was an open secret that the actors of Dreams took advantage of the theaters' Midwinter closure to put on a review in one of the private theaters in Hearts, parodying the major events of their past season. As an unlicensed performance, it was technically illegal, but Hearts and Dreams always turned a blind eye. But if there was something in this year's performance that was forcing Hearts to pay attention, it might be better to know in advance. He said, "Tell me anyway. Hearts has never seemed to care before this."

"They don't, generally," Jhirassi said. "But this year, with the wedding—

every petty noble and her half-sister are in town for the ceremony, and they've all got allies and enemies. They've lined up into factions and they're determined to read every line as political and usually as a slur against their side, and—well, you can imagine how badly a parody is likely to go over."

"I thought the performance was private," Eslingen said.

"Except for patrons, special friends, and the occasional investor," Jhirassi said. "And of course all the factions have been competing to be those as well."

Rathe frowned. "And what does Aconin have to do with this?"

Jhirassi looked alarmed. "How did you—no, never mind, I can guess."

"You let him write it," Rathe said. That might well explain the complaint from d'Alamenon's people.

"Not *let* him, exactly," Jhirassi said. "But he and Bayard Dielz are feuding with the Galenon, and the two of them together wrote a parody of their new all-singing performances, and—honestly, it's brilliant! But it insults *everybody*, and the women from the Ile'Nord are going to take offense."

Rathe gave Eslingen a meaningful look. "Sounds like I need to have another word with Chresta."

"I'll help," Eslingen said. "In the meantime—Gavi, have you talked to Matthie? Surely she's sensible enough to see the problem."

"Matthie is directing this year," Jhirassi said.

Rathe swore under his breath. Matthie Gasquine was generally a voice of sanity among the theater managers, and if she was actively working to make it happen—but maybe that meant it wasn't that bad after all.

Eslingen said, "Aconin swore he hadn't written anything about d'Alamenon, right? So what are they complaining about?"

"They've taken it into their heads that this is a *code*," Jhirassi said, with loathing. "Both factions agree on that, though the Old North and the Young South disagree on the precise meanings. And they're both absolutely certain that the other one is behind every insult." He leaned forward again. "But it's not. It's about Perse and the Galenon, and nothing to do with them. There's a dragon—all right, it's a northern dragon, but that's where dragons come from. Anyway, this dragon is attacking villages, and the only person who can stop it is the drunken son of the local landame who is a deadly warrior when he's drunk enough. The other gentry persuade him to attempt it by promising him that a noble lady will marry him, and in the end the boy kills the dragon by kicking it—er, under the tail, but instead of the noble lady, he's given to the local brewster who thinks he's pretty and, more importantly, is the only person who can afford his drinking habits." He paused. "There's a lovely tenor aria, 'Sure my stays will bust with sobbing And my heart quite crack with throbbing. My poor eyes are red as ferrets, And I ha'n't a grain of spirits.' Only Aconin would rhyme ferrets and spirits."

That was probably true, Rathe thought, but was hardly the relevant part. "You could argue that this involves a political wedding," he pointed out, "not to mention the slaying of a northern dragon."

"One can see why the Ile'Norders might take this amiss," Eslingen said.

"But it's nothing to do with them," Jhirassi said.

"I assume you've said as much?" Rathe asked.

"We have, I swear," Jhirassi said. "Which brings me back to my question. Can the players be charged if we didn't write the lines?"

"I don't know." Rathe considered. "I think first you'd have to prove defamation, which means showing the statement was made knowing that it's false, and in this case it sounds like you'd have to prove that this code existed and meant what the factions claim it does. It's the sort of case that buys advocates new houses."

"So what should we do?" Jhirassi asked.

Rathe looked at Eslingen, hoping for rescue, but the other man spread his hands. "Cut it out of the review."

"We can't do that," Jhirassi said.

"Then don't invite the factions."

"We have to," Jhirassi said. "At least some of them."

"Gavi, those are the only things that are going to help." Rathe reached for the wine pitcher, feeling that he'd earned another drink. "Tell Matthie I know a good advocate if she needs one, but that's about all I've got."

Jhirassi fluttered his eyelashes. "You'd contribute to my bail, surely?"

"You're part of this?" Rathe lifted his eyebrows.

"I'm the drunken son," Jhirassi admitted. "It's a wonderful part."

Eslingen laughed, and Rathe shook his head. "Of course it is. Gavi—" He stopped, shaking his head again. "I've given you all the advice I've got. If the factions want to demand a point, it'll be up to Hearts to deal with them."

"Well, it was worth asking." Jhirassi pushed himself to his feet. "Thanks, Nico."

Rathe watched him walk back to the rest of the actors, then looked at Eslingen. The Leaguer shook his head. "I feel Chresta has been…insufficiently forthcoming, one might say."

"One might," Rathe said. "Help me track him down tomorrow?"

"Gladly."

THE MORNING DAWNED cold, with a white haze to the sky that gave weight to the astrologers' predictions of snow. The wind had a damp edge to it, too, and there was ice in the shadows that looked unlikely to melt even in the doubled warmth of both suns. Returning from handing Sunflower over to the weaver for his day's boarding, Eslingen passed a runner from Dreams on the stairs, and suppressed a sigh. One way or another, the day's plans had just changed.

Rathe was busy with the toasting fork, and Eslingen automatically fetched butter and cheese, setting them on the table beside the teapot. "I take it we're not going to talk to Aconin this morning?"

Rathe plucked a piece of bread from the fire and set it on the table. "Trijn says that Bartelmane—that's d'Alamenon's head knife, though he wouldn't thank me for calling him that—he's claiming that Aconin used magic against them, so I'm to go interview whoever it is who makes the Dis-damned thunderflashes and make sure they're technically within the law."

"Do you want me to go with you?" Eslingen began buttering the warm bread, taking the next slice from the fork.

Rathe shook his head. "Someone needs to talk to Aconin before he has a chance to think up a new excuse."

"I can do that," Eslingen said.

Accordingly, he wrapped himself in his second-best coat and a hat that would shed the elements, and made his way to the stage door of the Tyrseia. The theater's doorkeeper hemmed and hawed, but finally admitted that Aconin had been there, and had gone on to Hearts. Eslingen lifted an eyebrow.

"Brave man."

"He'll be all right, he's gone to the Lilies." The chatelaine winced, and Eslingen sighed.

"Which is where the review is to be held? No, don't bother, I'll find him there."

It was a cold walk across the bridge and along the riverfront, but once he was into Hearts proper, the tree-lined streets and walled gardens blocked much of the wind. He had to ask directions to the Lilies, but the woman who ran the tea shop where he stopped knew the place. Amusement lurked in her eyes as she explained the best route, and Eslingen braced himself to face an expensive resort-house.

Even so, the place was a surprise. It was really two houses, or perhaps a house with an equally large second wing set perpendicular to the main house. A stable big enough for half a dozen horses stood opposite, and there was a broad graveled courtyard between the wing and the stable, separated from the street by a wrought iron fence badged with brightly painted lilies. There was a guard's box beside the half-open gate, and as Eslingen approached, a burly man stepped out of its shelter.

"Can I help you, master?"

Eslingen smiled cheerfully. The guard wasn't in livery, though coat and breeches were well-made, and the buttons, as he came closer, were clearly marked with the house's flower. "I'm looking for someone."

"Her name?" The guard glanced back into the box, where a runner was waiting beside a brazier. A book was propped on the ledge beneath the little window, its pages weighted with a piece of cobble.

"I'm looking for Chresta Aconin," Eslingen said.

The guard's expression shifted, hardening. "Sorry, master, we don't do that sort of business."

Behind him, a door opened in center of the jutting wing, and a pair of actors came down the low steps, to stand fanning themselves. Eslingen nodded toward them, then tapped the silver gorget half hidden by his cravat. "I'm with the Guard. I need a word with Aconin about an—incident—yesterday." He was willing to bet that Aconin had complained vociferously about his adventure, and he was unsurprised when the guard sighed.

"And he swore he was the victim, too."

"There have been charges made on both sides," Eslingen said, deliberately vague. "So I need a word with him."

The guard beckoned to the runner. "Fetch Mistress Gasquine. She can deal with this."

Eslingen suppressed a sigh, but the runner returned quickly, Matthie Gasquine at his heels looking annoyed.

"Captain. You wanted to talk to Aconin?"

"That's right."

"I knew there was more to it," Gasquine muttered. "Right. We're on a break at the moment—Tyrseis save us from over-complicated stage machinery—so you might as well get it over with."

"This is a theater?" Eslingen fell into step beside her as the guard closed the gate again behind them.

Gasquine nodded. "There are a fair number of private houses like this in Hearts. The owners like to be able to provide a wide range of entertainment for their patronnes."

I imagine they do. Eslingen swallowed the words, and followed her up the stairs into the foyer. It was considerably smaller than the lobbies of the Bells or the Galenon, but even more ornately decorated, with false columns dividing the walls into segments that were filled with painted plaster wreathes—lilies, again— liberally touched with gilding. "Someone's spent a few hundred crowns on this."

"Oh, you should see the stage," Gasquine said, and pushed through a door faced with quilted leather. Eslingen blinked once as his eyes adjusted, and then made out a series of terraces running down to meet the stage. The terraces were set with couches rather than individual seats, and when he followed Gasquine down the central aisle, he could see two tiers of curtained boxes to either side of the stage. There were more boxes on the back wall, also well-curtained; the stage itself was small, but he could see the troughs and trapdoors that hid the stage machinery. The arch that held the curtain was as elaborately painted as the foyer, and even pulled back for maximum access, gold fringe dripped from the curtains.

"Most impressive."

"Overdone," Gasquine said. "But, give him his due, he spent just as much on the machines." Before he could ask who she meant, she lifted her voice. "Chresta! You're wanted on stage."

There was a scuffling from the wings, and the playwright appeared, tugging at his lapels as though he'd just put on his coat. "Yes—oh, it's you."

"You're lucky it's not Rathe," Eslingen said mildly. "You weren't entirely forthcoming yesterday, Chresta."

"And that's my cue to exit," Gasquine said briskly. "Chresta, I do want you later, so try not to get yourself arrested." She turned to the stairs that led up to the stage, and vanished into the wings.

Aconin hesitated, then climbed down to join Eslingen. "I don't know what you're talking about."

"Chresta."

"I don't!"

"You told Rathe that you hadn't written anything that would cause the Soueraine d'Alamenon's men to attack you," Eslingen said. "Then we find out that you have in fact written a short play that features a northern dragon, a noble wedding, and a drunken bridegroom. We feel you need to clarify matters."

"It's a joke," Aconin said. "And nothing to do with d'Alamenon or de Galhac or this Dis-damned royal wedding. It's about the Galenon."

There was genuine frustration in his voice, and Eslingen gestured to the nearest couch. "Let's sit, then, and you can explain this to me."

Aconin seated himself, arranging the skirts of his coat carefully on the velvet. Seen at close range, there were rubbed patches and the wooden frame showed scratches and chips, but even so, it remained impressive. "They're putting on all-sung performances at the Galenon—barely a skit of a plot, eked out with interminable musical flourishes. Five minutes of scales, to say 'I love you' or 'I hate you,' and then another ten while the chorus embroiders the tune. I ask you, who stays awake for that? So Bayard—Bayard Dielz—and I put together a parody, based on 'The Dragon-hunter.' That's a ballad that was popular, oh, five or six years ago."

"Before my time," Eslingen murmured.

"As you say. But that's all this is. They're running mad here in Hearts."

Eslingen sighed. "Don't be disingenuous, Chresta. There is a royal wedding with a northern bride and a fair amount of tension on all sides. Of course someone is taking this amiss."

"But it's not reasonable," Aconin said. "For once, I'm not to blame."

"This must be the first time," Eslingen said, and Aconin rolled his eyes.

"Very amusing. But I dislike being set upon in the streets."

"Most people do," Eslingen said. "But in this case, I see their reasoning. And you left all of this out of your conversation yesterday with Rathe. He takes it poorly."

Aconin looked away. "I suppose he might. But I swear, everything I said was the exact truth. There is no code, and I don't give a fig for the Soueraine d'Alamenon."

To his sorrow, Eslingen believed him. He said, "Cancel the review."

"We can't do that!" Aconin gave him a look of real horror. "This is our way of thanking our best patronnes, the ones we rely on through the year. We simply can't cancel."

"Remove your skit, then," Eslingen said.

"Why would we do that?" Gasquine reappeared at the edge of the stage, frowning. "It's hilarious—one of Chresta's better pieces, though I say so who shouldn't."

"Too kind," Aconin murmured, and sketched a seated bow.

"Because there's at least one Ile'Norder noble whose servants are willing to assault playwrights in the street over it," Eslingen said. "Or are you looking to start a riot?"

"It won't come to that," Gasquine said. "D'Alamenon has more sense—and if she doesn't, the Palatineur certainly does. A word from the Guard should set things right." Eslingen lifted his eyebrows at that, and Gasquine had the grace to look embarrassed. "Well, you know what I mean. You people have the authority there."

"It would be easier if there were fewer provocations," Eslingen said, but he knew it was a losing battle. "I don't know whether to suggest you hire some knives of your own, or pray you don't."

"Amorin keeps a quiet house," Gasquine said. "And has the patronnes to make it stick. We'll be fine here."

Eslingen looked at the playwright. "Are you sure you won't reconsider? I don't hear any promises being made about your safety."

Aconin gave a wry smile. "No. But then, I can always rely on the points and the Guard, can't I?"

"We can't be everywhere," Eslingen answered.

"Is that a threat, Captain?" Aconin rose gracefully to his feet.

"It's a warning," Eslingen said.

It took most of the morning to track down the workshop that manufactured the thunderflashes Aconin had used, but finally a friend of Jhirassi's directed him to a street of artificers on the southern edge of the city. The buildings there were more like farmhouses, squat and stone-built, and set at a distance from one another in wide fenced yards. A few still had fields out back, fallow now for winter, or cold frames propped against outbuildings, but the majority were small manufactories, and the air was sharp with coal smoke. The Sign of the Star was one of the smaller holdings, the main house that served as a workshop and a couple of outbuildings set well back against the wall that marked the end of the property, but the sign above the door was newly painted, and even had a touch of gilding on the narrow rays. The narrow courtyard was swept clean of leaves and the stone doorstep had been washed that morning.

Rather pushed open the main door, and heard a bell jangle somewhere in the shadowed back. The shop itself was crowded, cluttered, even, something of a surprise after the empty courtyard, its walls lined with glass-fronted cabinets and four good-sized tables piled with boxes and baskets and odd bits of carved wood and glass and metal, none of which he recognized. Mage-lights hung from the ceiling, striking sparks from a casket of what he assumed were glass gems, and an oil burner sweetened the air with notes of lemon and lavender. Beside it lay a pile of metal rings too large to be bracelets and he glanced curiously at them, remembering a street juggler who'd performed with just such a set, joining and separating the apparently-solid rings as though by magistry. He picked one up, but there was no obvious seam.

A door opened in the back wall and a young woman came through, wiping her hands on a coarse canvas apron. "Can I help you, master?" She saw his truncheon then, and her mouth tightened, but she managed to keep her tone even. "Are you interested in Oriane's Rings, then?"

"Is that what they're called?" Rathe set the ring back in its place with mild regret. "I saw it done once, and always wondered how."

"You won't see the trick in our rings, not unless you look a good deal closer," the woman said. "You can pass them around the hall, and unless they know the secret, there's no one who'll be able to find it." She paused. "But I don't think that's what you're here for."

"No. Do you make thunderflashes for the theaters?"

The woman gave him a wary glance. "We do. Is there a problem?"

"One was used in a street fight yesterday," Rathe said. "One of the participants claimed magistry was involved, which, as you know, is against the law inside the city. So my chief's sent me to get a statement of how they're made."

"That's our secret," the woman said doubtfully. "I'll have to fetch the mistress."

"Thank you." Rathe watched her disappear into the back, then looked around the room again. Now that he looked more closely, he could recognize many of the objects as belonging to the theaters, both the big effects that graced the stages of the Tyrseia and the Bells, and smaller devices used for private performances. One cabinet even seemed to contain articulated figures that were probably automata—a dancer, a horseman holding out an oversized cup, a third, smaller figure that when he stepped closer proved to be a boy pissing into another large cup. He lifted his eyebrows at that, imagining Eslingen's reaction, and knocked his foot against a low cabinet that gave off a growl like thunder. It looked more like a case for a virginal, but when he touched it again, it rumbled softly.

"I see you found the thunder box."

Rathe turned to see the door close behind a tall woman in a leather apron, her graying hair confined by a neat cap. "Is that what it is?"

She came to join him, and tipped the box sharply. It moved on a hidden hinge, producing a startling realistic peal of thunder. "We make them for most of the major houses, and for some of the smaller ones. Betts said you were from the points? With a question about one of our devices?"

"I'm Nicolas Rathe, adjunct point at Point of Dreams. And I need to know about your thunderflashes." Quickly, he explained what he had told the journeyman, and when he had finished, the woman grimaced.

"Don't tell me, it was Aconin himself who set it off, wasn't it? I told him that's not what they're meant for. Though I'll have to see one to be sure it's ours, of course." She paused. "I'm Lavanet Aurelis, by the way. This is my shop."

Rathe reached into his purse, brought out the thunderflashes he'd taken from Aconin. "These are what he used. I didn't see a maker's mark."

Aurelis plucked one from his palm, turned it over in her fingers, then weighed it thoughtfully in her hand. "I'd say that's ours. And if it was Aconin—"

"Which it was," Rathe said.

"Then it's almost certainly ours. He buys them now and again, when he's feeling put-upon."

That was one way of putting it. Rathe said, "He's annoyed the household of the Soueraine d'Alamenon, who's in the city for the royal wedding. So they're not particularly familiar with city ways."

"Evidently not, if they took this for magistry," Aurelis said.

"So you'll swear there's no magistry involved?"

Aurelis hesitated. "None in the use. There's some involved in the making, to hold the powder in suspension."

Rathe sighed. It was no more than he'd expected, but it did complicate the question. "Can you explain it to me—I don't need your secret details, just a statement you'd be willing to swear to so that we can take this business off our books."

"Let me think." Aurelis turned the thunderflash over in her fingers, her eyes focused on nothing. "I suppose—come out back, and I'll walk you through it. You're lucky this is a quiet day, I've time for this."

Rathe followed her through the door and into a hall that gave onto a parlor on one side and a dining room on the other. Stairs led up to the main living quarters, and then they passed through the busy kitchen and out into the rear yard. Smoke was rising from one of the two outbuildings, smelling strongly of sea-coal; the journeyman was standing in the doorway, wiping sweat from her face with a dirty rag. The other building was closed and shuttered, and Aurelis frowned.

"Still no delivery?"

"Not yet," the journeyman answered, and Aurelis swore under her breath.

"Right. Well, that's for another day. You wanted to know about thunderflashes." She held up the glass teardrop, balancing it between thumb and forefinger. "It's ultimately a simple thing. We make the glass casing, add suspended powder—that's where the magistry comes in, you need a magist to create it—and then seal it with a bit of wax." She twirled it so that the pointed end was facing Rathe. "You see it there?"

Rathe nodded. "I do. So how's it used?"

Aurelis turned, flung the teardrop expertly at a line of paving stones. The glass shattered with a flash and bang, and Rathe flinched, though the journeyman never moved. "Break the glass and you get that."

"Maybe I shouldn't be carrying them in my purse," Rathe said, and she grinned.

"It's always good to be cautious, Adjunct Point. But, to be serious, it takes a hard blow to break the glass—they're meant to be thrown down hard onto stone or iron, we make them that way for safety's sake. You don't want them going off every time someone drops one on a wooden stage."

Rathe hauled out his wooden tablets. "Tell me that again, if you would."

Aurelis obliged, and Rathe made notes, digging his stylus into the wax. It would, he thought, be enough to quash the Ile'Norders' complaint of magistry, and he put the tablet away with a certain satisfaction. "And you'll swear to that if necessary?"

"To that much, and no more," Aurelis said firmly. "They're a specialty."

"Do you sell many?" Rathe asked curiously. He didn't remember seeing the effect all that often, and Eslingen dragged him to most of the season's plays.

"Most of the theaters keep some in stock," Aurelis answered. "And when they do need them, they need a lot, for rehearsal as well as the performances. It takes practice to use them well." She paused. "Just as well we're at the Midwinter break, we're running low on our stock, and the powderers haven't sent our usual supply for us to make more. I don't know what their problem is, but I hope they fix it soon."

"I hope so, too," Rathe said, and let her see him out. In the street, he hesitated, momentarily tempted to try one of the thunderflashes he had left, but better sense prevailed. Besides, he told himself, Eslingen would want to see as well.

THREE

ESLINGEN LINGERED ON the steps of the Lilies' private theater, hoping to see someone else he knew who might be able to tell him more about what was sounding more and more like an ill-advised performance—Jhirassi, perhaps, or Verre Siredy. Siredy at least was technically a Master of Arms rather than an actor, and might be amenable to reason, though given that he was currently Jhirassi's favored lover, that might be asking too much. A pair of actresses appeared, but swept past him with only a quick and sidelong glance, and disappeared into the main body of the house. He sighed, and turned toward the gate, but turned at the sound of footsteps behind him.

"Captain." The speaker was a young man a little past apprentice-age, blond and visibly well-muscled even in the Lilies' neat livery. "Master Bonamy would like a word if you have a moment."

Not the name he was born under, I'll wager, Eslingen thought. *I'm sure he's been a good friend to many ladies.* He said, "I have time."

The young man bowed. "If you'll come with me?"

Eslingen followed him up the well-scrubbed stairs and into the main part of the house. It was as elegant as the exterior promised, with polished parquet floors and brocade panels set into the hallway walls, and the air was sweet with the odor of the glasshouse flowers. The door to the main parlor was partly open, offering a glimpse of a pleasant, well-lit room with more brocade panels and a suite of chairs and couches covered in the same pale-green shade. A handsome dark-haired man was standing by the fireplace, one hand resting gracefully on the mantel, his attention on someone hidden by the half-closed door. Behind a second, closed door, someone was playing a lute or a cittern, embroidering a tune that Eslingen almost recognized.

The young man led him past the stairs to the back hallway, still neatly furnished but without the expensive fabric, and tapped on a door that probably led into a smaller parlor—or a counting room, Eslingen thought. The passage under the stairs would lead to the kitchens. There was a murmured response, and the young man pushed open the door.

"Captain vaan Esling, sir."

A man rose from behind the long worktable, came forward with a practiced, affable smile. He was handsome still, though there were wings of gray at his temples and his sober pine-green coat and paler green waistcoat were cut to flatter a fuller figure. A tiny spray of enameled lilies was fastened to his cravat, and there was good lace at his cuffs: a man of wealth, however, discreet, Eslingen thought, and not one to trifle with.

"Captain." The man's voice was lovely, deep and resonant without being affected, and Eslingen wondered if he'd been an actor before taking up a career in Hearts. "I'm Amorin Bonamy, and the Lilies is my house. It's a pleasure to welcome you here."

"Master Bonamy." Eslingen accepted his hand and let himself be bowed to the guest's chair. There was a pitcher and an array of expensive glasses on a tray at the end of the worktable, and Bonamy turned toward it, clearly preparing to draw out the ritual. Eslingen decided to take a leaf from Rathe's book. "I should say right now that I'm not here for anything involving you. I wanted a word with Aconin."

Bonamy blinked, but didn't seem to relax. "What's he done now? No, I suppose it's none of my business."

"He was set on by some of the Soueraine d'Alamenon's people," Eslingen answered. "Both sides are demanding someone call the point."

"Of course they would," Bonamy murmured. "Though that's not why I wanted to speak with you, Captain. There's another matter that's been concerning me—and some of my neighbors as well. We could use your help."

"If I can," Eslingen said. "It's likely to be Point of Hearts' business."

"They're busy with the wedding," Bonamy answered. "I'd like at least to report it to someone who can listen."

"I'll do what I can," Eslingen said again.

Bonamy glanced at the pitcher again, and visibly decided not to pour. "It's the carts," he said.

"Carts?"

Bonamy nodded. "Carts. They come through Hearts late at night, not carrying lanterns or mage-lights, or at least not more than the smallest possible. They're heavily laden, and the folk who've seen them up close say that they're well-guarded—knives with swords on the box with the driver, not just someone with a club. But the cargo is always well-covered, and the wheels are well-greased and the horses' hooves are muffled. That's not the behavior of an honest carter."

"Smugglers?" Eslingen asked. That would have been the answer in most other cities, but Astreiant's questionable cargos were more likely to come by water, and travel blamelessly in daylight once they'd come ashore.

"That's what I thought at first, but…" Bonamy hesitated. "I know most of those who buy and sell around here, and they're just as bothered. No, it's nothing we can think of, and that makes us nervous."

"And who's 'us'?" Eslingen asked.

"Those of us who keep resort-houses," Bonamy answered. "And the better sort of taverns and eating-houses. We like things calm here in Hearts, it's best for business that way."

"Do these carts do anything? Besides disturb your sleep."

Bonamy sighed. "Not yet. But they're—out of the ordinary. Whatever they're carrying, it's not right."

Eslingen paused, considering. He couldn't help wondering if it had something to do with de Castiat's illegal salt-selling, though cartloads seemed overly ambitious, particularly when she was self-imprisoned practically under the queen's nose. But at the same time, there would need to be some evidence of an illegal act before anyone could act. "You know this is properly points' business, not the Guard's. Unless you have some reason to think one of the nobility is involved?"

Bonamy made a warding gesture. "Seidos forfend. No, I've told you everything I know—and before you ask, that's everything I suspect, as well."

"There's not much I can do with that," Eslingen said. "But I'll pass the word to keep an eye out for them."

"That's all we can ask," Bonamy said, in a tone that made it clear he would have liked more, and rose gracefully to show Eslingen to the door.

Eslingen made his way back toward the Hopes-point Bridge, wondering exactly what Bonamy expected him—or the Guard, or the points, for that matter—to do about these mysterious carts. Though if it did have anything to do with de Castiat and her salt, maybe the resort-house keepers would want it stopped before it drew attention to any other parts of their business that might skirt the edges of the law. Either way, though, it fell outside the Guard's responsibility, and he'd be more than happy to hand it over to the women at Hearts.

"Philip!"

He looked up sharply, surprised and then pleased to see Rathe coming off the end of the bridge. He lifted a hand in answer, and Rathe moved easily through the crowd of shoppers, fetching up at his side with a grimace for the muddy gutter.

"Did you find Aconin?"

"I did. Did you get what you needed about the thunderflahses?"

Rathe nodded. "And now I could use a drink—I imagine you could, too, if you've been spending time with Chresta."

"He was moderately forthcoming," Eslingen answered. "I could also stand a meal."

There was a teahouse two streets from the bridge that served a decent ordinary as well as better-than-average tea. It was also generally less crowded than the larger taverns and teahouses closer to the markets, and attracted fewer of the working boys. It was late enough that there were plenty of empty tables, and the waiter apologized insincerely for being out of everything but bacon pie and the stew. They split a bacon pie and a pot of the smoky stone-growth tea that came from the southern coast, and Rathe fished in his pocket to produce a teardrop half the size of his thumb.

"That's a thunderflash."

Eslingen prodded it gingerly. "I gather I shouldn't drop it?"

"The maker says you have to throw it hard against a hard surface, metal or stone for preference, but—I'd still take care."

"Did she say what powers it?" Eslingen turned the glass bead over in his fingers. It was heavier than he'd expected, and cool to the touch, in spite of having come from Rathe's pocket. "It isn't magistry, I assume?"

"She says not." Rathe held out his hand, and Eslingen returned it. "There's suspended powder in it, she said, and that was all she'd say about the specifics. Takes a magist to make the powder, but the rest is ordinary handwork."

Eslingen flinched in spite of himself. He'd seen suspended powder in use at the siege of Gislaer, prepared by the queen's magists in bunkers on the far outskirts of the besiegers' camp and carried in tiny packets through the ranks to be handed over to the sappers. They'd brought down the wall as promised, but three of their own had died in the process, hit by falling stones. "Chancy stuff," he said, and was pleased his voice was steady.

"She said the glass contains it, makes it stable and reliable. And there's not much of it anyway, so it's safe." Rathe gave a sudden grin. "And I expect it would have to be, if she's selling it to actors."

Eslingen laughed in spite of himself. "All right, yes, I can't see most of our friends taking the care our sappers did."

The pie arrived and they cut into it. Rathe said, his mouth full, "So what did Aconin say?"

"Very much what we expected." Eslingen took a drink of his cooling tea. "He swears up and down that this playlet of his has nothing to do with the royal marriage, it's all a jab at the Galenon."

"Swears on his mother's bones, in fact," Rathe murmured.

"He would if he had one. But Gasquine agrees that they can't cancel." Eslingen quickly ran through what he'd been told, and when he'd finished, Rathe sighed.

"So, Gavi gave us the meat of it. Not that I expected otherwise, but it's unlike Aconin to run this much of a risk."

"It's for a play," Eslingen said. "There was one other thing, though. As I was leaving, the Lilies' owner asked for a word, and complained about mysterious carts traveling through Hearts in the dark of night under armed guard. I'm not sure what to make of it."

Rathe frowned. "That is a strange thing. There's a curfew in Hearts and generally the resort-houses and the taverns work together to keep things quiet. And it's not like Hearts is on the way to anywhere. Carts get noticed."

"I wondered about de Castiat," Eslingen said. "Though why she'd risk bringing her salt into the city…"

"Because she couldn't keep control of the business any other way?" Rathe said doubtfully. "I suppose it's worth asking if there's been any changes in the salt business. Or, more precisely, getting Hearts and the rest of the stations northriver to ask. I think we'd have heard if there was anything happening on the south bank." He paused. "We should talk to Annechon."

Eslingen hesitated. He'd only met Rathe's friend once before, and he wasn't entirely sure how he felt about her. Certainly she'd known him since they were both children—she'd been Rathe's child-minder, in fact—and that gave her certain privileges, but it made him uneasy to watch Rathe revert to a younger self in her presence. He wasn't jealous, or at least he was mostly sure he wasn't; it was just that she knew too many of Rathe's sore spots, and her teasing wasn't always kind. He said, "Do you think she'll help?"

"If Bonamy's worried enough to raise the question with you," Rathe said, "Annechon will know all about it. And no one in Hearts likes to draw the points' attention."

There was nothing to be said to that. Eslingen nodded, and poured the last of the tea.

Annechon's current residence was small but lovely, a delicate jewel box of a house set between two much larger buildings. The wrought iron gate gave onto a pebbled walk that ran between two well-tended flower beds, and the steps and the painted trim shone pale against the darker brick. This was a relatively new house for Annechon, Rathe knew; she had parted with a long-time patronne less than a year ago, and bought or rented this place in search of a fresh start. It had been an amicable parting, as those things went—or at least that was the story she gave out—but she had not seemed entirely happy the last time he'd seen her. Still, afternoon was a good time to approach her: it was before she opened her doors to more important visitors, but still close enough to that moment that it was incentive to answer his questions and get them gone before they became inconvenient. He frowned a little at the thought. Surely Annechon would be willing to help, both for old times' sake and for the sake of peace in Hearts. Hearts had always valued its privacy.

He climbed the gleaming steps and rapped sharply on the door. It swung open to reveal a page of about apprentice-age in a plain brown coat, who looked nervously from him to Eslingen.

"Nicolas Rathe, to see Annechon."

The page hesitated for an instant, then stepped back, opening the door wide. "Of course, Adjunct Point. And—Captain?"

"Captain vaan Esling," Eslingen said.

The page inclined his head, not the bow he would have given a social superior, but more acknowledgement than Rathe had been expecting. "If you'll come with me."

He brought them into what Rathe suspected was the second-best parlor, a pleasant room with silk-hung walls and furniture that was only slightly worn at the edges. There was no fire in the fireplace, but wood was stacked ready for the evening chill. The afternoon light was filtered by pale curtains—the least expensive muslin, Rathe noted—and there was rush matting instead of carpets. But even with these economies, the room still had style, and comfort to spare. It was unmistakably Annechon's taste, he thought, and was smiling as the door opened again.

"Nico." Annechon swept forward to take his hand, resplendent in an afternoon gown of good silk brocade. Clearly she was not economizing on her wardrobe. Rathe submitted to being kissed, and then released, aware of the familiar smell of lilacs. Annechon had worn that scent since she was a girl, and it suited her. "And your black dog."

"Madame." Eslingen sketched a bow, his face set in a blank smile.

Annechon waved vaguely at the couches. "Do sit. Then you can tell me what brings you to my house."

"Old times' sake," Rathe suggested, seating himself on the nearest couch, and Annechon snorted.

"If it were that, I'd have seen you months ago. Or hadn't you heard?"

"I heard you'd parted," Rathe admitted. "Word was, you'd parted friends."

"And so we did, but it was a parting nonetheless." Annechon's voice was perhaps sharper than she'd meant, and she managed a flat smile. "But that's neither here nor there. What have I done to be favored with a visit from the points? And the Guard, of course." She nodded toward Eslingen.

"Amorin Bonamy at the Lilies told me an odd story," Eslingen said, "and Nico thought you might be able to shed some light on it."

It wasn't like Eslingen to be so direct. Rathe saw Annechon flinch, and wondered just what she was trying to hide. She recovered herself in an instant, and waved her hand as though she held a fan.

"What sort of odd story? I'm sure he has plenty to tell."

"Carts," Eslingen said. "Mysterious carts with armed guards, traveling through Hearts in the dead of night. He wanted the Guard to look into it."

"He did?" Annechon fluttered her hand again, and Rathe thought there was a note of real fear in her voice before she controlled herself. "How very unlike him! He generally has no use for the Guard, unless they're in the prime of their youth and willing to oblige a lady. Or for the points, either." She gave Eslingen an overtly speculative glance. "As I'm sure you'll discover, Captain."

"Annechon," Rathe said. She looked at him, and he met her gaze squarely. For a moment, it hung in the balance, and then she looked away.

"There's been talk," she admitted.

"Just talk?" Rathe cocked his head.

"Well."

"Have you seen them?" Rathe wasn't sure that was the right question, at least not yet, but she nodded.

"Once. Maybe twice."

"And?" Out of the corner of his eye, he could see Eslingen sitting utterly motionless, a hunter waiting to pounce, and willed him to stay silent.

"What Amorin said. A cart, loaded full, with an armed man beside the driver—armed with a firelock, I mean, not sword or cudgel. Going through the streets as fast as they dared after curfew, only one lantern showing."

"After curfew?" Rathe asked.

"Or as close to it as makes no difference," Annechon said. She shrugged. "I was coming home from visiting a friend, and I'd stayed later than I meant. So I was keeping to the shadows myself, which is probably why they didn't see me."

"And they were carrying firelocks in the city," Eslingen said.

She cut her eyes sideways at him. "Patently illegal, yes, Captain. But I could see the match glowing—it was the only light besides their lantern."

"Just the one cart?" Rathe didn't dare take out his tablets, but he was sure he'd remember the details.

"Yes. Not a big one either, about the size of a brewster's dray, the kind that carries one big barrel, or two small ones, with the load under a heavy canvas. It looked like it might be barrels, too, but I couldn't say for certain. The top was rounded, like so." Annechon sketched a graceful arc.

"Where were you when you saw it?" Rathe asked.

"On Vintners' Row, just past where it crosses the bottom of Taddeis Square."

Rathe nodded. Not one of the major roads, but big enough to take a cart, and it would put them in position to make for either Temple Point or for the edge of town. "And it was going—which way, into town or out?"

"Definitely in," Annechon said. "If they'd stayed on the Row, they'd have come out behind the Embroiderers' Hall."

Rathe nodded again, though that made less sense. "And the other time?"

"One cart again, and it came past the house—not the main street, the one that runs behind us. It's not really wide enough, and they were going slow, but you couldn't miss them." Annechon paused. "That was a week ago, maybe ten days? I don't remember exactly. The other time was a couple of days ago—no, I tell a lie, it was three days, the moon was full."

"And your friend?" Eslingen asked.

"She wasn't with me."

"And I daresay she'd lie for you anyway."

"She's not that good a friend yet," Annechon said primly. She looked back at Rathe. "Truth, Nico, Amorin's right, there's something going on here. Those carters can't be up to any good."

"I can't argue," Rathe said. "But you know this is properly Hearts' business."

Annechon snorted. "They wouldn't be hauling carts through the streets if someone there wasn't fee'd to look the other way."

Rathe sighed. That was also all too true, and meant he'd have to move carefully. "We'll see what we can do. But you'll have to keep us informed of any other sightings."

"I can do that," Annechon said. "If you'll keep my name out of it."

"As far as I can," Rathe said, and took his leave.

Eslingen followed him silently out through the yard and down the dusty street, holding onto his hat as a gust of wind swirled between the buildings. Rathe glanced sidelong at him. "Does that match with what Bonamy told you?"

"Well enough. She had a bit more detail, but the story was much the same." He hesitated. "Nico. Did it strike you she wasn't her usual self?"

"What do you mean?"

"I know I've only met her the once, but she flirted more, and teased. Hard. Today she seemed, I don't know, subdued."

Rathe's instinct was to deny it, but he had to admit that Eslingen had a point. "She's still getting over her lost patronne, that's enough to sober anyone."

Eslingen shrugged. "More to the point, what can we do about this? I'd lay money she's right about Hearts being fee'd."

"So would I," Rathe said. "That wasn't a bad idea you had. About the salt, I mean."

"Thanks. Though I can't say I know where it takes us next."

"I'll need to make some inquiries about salt, but not today. I'll need Trijn to tell me who I should talk to." Rathe looked for a tower clock, found none in sight, and squinted at the sky instead. "We've a bit of time before first sunset. Do you know where de Castiat's house is?"

Eslingen reached into his sleeve and produced a slip of paper. "As it happens, Adjunct Point…"

Rathe glanced at the directions. "The house of the gargoyles, on Lector Street beyond the Charity Fountain. The way Annechon described them going—you could get there easily enough, especially if you were trying to keep to the side streets."

"There's no point in looking for tracks," Eslingen said, "but surely our people would have noticed a cart. Or carts."

"Unless it came in by daylight? We haven't had reason to look for one yet," Rathe said. "Which is something I intend to change directly."

THEY MADE THEIR way up Lector Street and through the narrow plaza that held the Charity Fountain. Eslingen eyed the practical spouts and solid basin, topped with a statue depicting three donors dispensing alms. From their clothes, the fountain had been erected at least a century ago, and the plaque that displayed the donors' names was deeply weathered. Rathe saw where he was looking and shrugged.

"Merchant-venturers buying luck," he said. "Or so the story goes."

"Did it work?"

"Not well. The last of the families died out before I was born. But the fountain's still good."

Eslingen stopped to drink from the cup chained to the nearest spigot, and had to acknowledge that the water was sweet and cool. It was, he thought, a very Astreianter story.

The house where de Castiat had imprisoned herself looked more like a country manor than the taller buildings around it. It was built of stone, not brick and only two stories high, with gabled windows poking out of the slate roof; a squared tower rose from the western end, three stories beneath the pointed roof. A stork's nest crowned the very top: that was counted lucky in Esling and the north generally, but he didn't know how Astreiant felt about the birds. The wall surrounding the house was a mix of brick and tall iron bars, through which he could see that the courtyard was larger than average, with a separate low side building that probably served as a stable.

"Plenty of room for a cart in there," he said, and Rathe nodded.

"Though again it's not exactly discreet."

"Unless there's a back way in."

"We'll ask," Rathe said, and nodded to the young man sitting in the concierge's box beside the main gate. "Toller. How are things?"

"Quiet, sir." The journeyman rose to his feet politely.

"Have there been many visitors?"

"Not to speak of." Toller fumbled in his pocket for his tablets, glanced quickly at the wax. "Her dressmaker, some tradesmen—all for the kitchen, they were— and a lady who gave her name as Framboise. Not really a lady, that one, the cook says she has a house two streets over that maseigne used to frequent."

"Useful," Rathe said, though Eslingen had his doubts. "You've made friends with the staff?"

"They're mostly hired local," Toller said. "The vidame only brought her steward and her personal maid from up-country."

"Interesting," Rathe said. "Has anyone in the household been complaining about carts?"

Toller looked blank. "No, sir."

"Let me know if they do," Rathe said. "Is Sohier about?"

Toller tipped his head sideways. "There's a tea garden opposite, one house down. It's a lively place of an evening, but quiet enough by daylight. Easy to watch from."

Though it only covered the front of the house, Eslingen thought. But there was probably someone else watching the back alleys, and Sohier was more than competent. He followed Rathe across the street to the tea garden, where Sohier sat alone beside a crackling stove. It was an expensive-looking place, with a wide platform dotted with little stoves and sets of tables and chairs. A bright blue canopy kept off the weather, and there were screens to cut the wind, but even so the air was chill. The only other customers at this hour were a pair of elderly women, retired shopkeepers by the look of them, who gave the newcomers a cheerful smile before they saw where they were going.

"Sohier." Rathe settled himself in one of the open chairs, and Eslingen copied him.

"Adjunct Point." There were empty cups waiting. She filled three of them, then topped up the pot from the kettle simmering on the stove. "I can't say I've anything useful to report."

"You've got a good view of the place," Eslingen said.

Sohier made a face. "Not as good as you'd think. Oh, I can see anyone who goes in and out the front door, but the vidame can keep an eye on me just as easily. She's in the tower, the third floor, you can see her at the window sometimes, and I don't doubt she has her maid watching the rest of the time."

Eslingen glanced casually toward the house, picked out the window. The suns were behind the main house, and there were no lights within, but even so he imagined for a moment that he saw something move behind the glass.

"Everyone likes to keep an eye on things here in Hearts," Sohier said, with some bitterness.

"What's it like round the back?" Rathe sipped at his tea, and nodded. "That's quite nice."

"They offered me a discount, being as we're keeping things quiet," Sohier said.

Rathe lifted a hand. "Nothing meant, it's good tea."

Sohier nodded, mollified. "There's an alley for deliveries, though most of the trades come in the front gates. It's trash and the nightsoil men at the back. Perrie is watching there today."

"Anything?"

"You talked to Toller," Sohier said. "That's pretty much what we've seen so far. Tradesfolk come in and out, and some of her friends come to visit, though the women here say a lot of them have stayed away since she admitted her guilt." She tipped her head toward the interior of the building. "They were expecting the vidame to bring more business, so they've been willing to talk. At least a little." She paused. "Speaking of which—"

In the same moment, Rathe said, "Have you heard talk—"

They both stopped, and then Sohier said, "These carts?"

"What have you heard?" Rathe asked.

"A lot, but I can't make anything of it," Sohier said. "Carts with armed men beside the driver—firelocks, not swords—sneaking through Hearts after curfew. On Vintners' Row, specifically, though I haven't managed to talk to anyone who's seen them herself. I've got a few more names to try."

She hesitated, and Rathe said, "What do they say at Hearts?"

"Nothing helpful," Sohier answered. "They said the talk was exaggerated, that they'd had people out watching and never saw a thing. Their Adjunct suggested it was a way to complain about all the disruption of the wedding without actually having to speak against the queen."

"Not likely," Eslingen said, in spite of himself, and Rathe gave him a wry smile.

"It sounds more like someone's being paid to look the other way, doesn't it?"

"Hearts has a reputation that way," Sohier muttered.

If Point of Hearts was being paid to ignore the carts that were rumbling through their streets in defiance of the curfew, they were also going against the wishes of a great many of the locals, Eslingen thought. He said, "Maybe that's why Bonamy spoke to me. He knew Hearts wouldn't do anything."

"Or suspected it," Rathe said.

"Not to mention that this can't come cheap," Eslingen went on. "It's not just looking the other way, it's going against what the important women want. So what are they moving?"

"Smuggling," Sohier said, and shook her head. "But what? What would you bring through Hearts? There are plenty of better ways in and out of the city, even northriver."

"One immediately thinks of salt," Eslingen said. "Being as the vidame is right here. But if you haven't seen any sign of them—"

"—and we haven't," Sohier interjected. "And I'm damned sure none of our folk have been fee'd."

Eslingen dipped his head in acknowledgment. "Then that seems unlikely."

"And yet. It does make you wonder." Rathe gave him a crooked smile. "You know what this means."

Eslingen sighed. "You want to go cart-hunting."

"Stalking, I was thinking. But yeah, I'd like to see what we could turn up."

"When did you have in mind?"

"No time like the present," Rathe said.

FOUR

"I'M STILL NOT sure why you think they'd come this way," Eslingen said.

They were waiting in the shadows of a shop doorway, the building itself locked up for the night behind them. It was one of the few that was not also the shopkeeper's residence, a small brick structure notable only for the steps leading up to the arched entranceway. From its shadows, Rathe could see down Vintners' Row as well as into the Fountain Court opposite, and it was quiet enough that they'd hear the sound of a cart approaching. It was also nearly half an hour past Hearts' curfew, so they were also listening for the sounds of any patrols. Rathe hoped they would be focusing their attention on the houses closer to the river, where trouble was more likely to break out, and not on the empty side streets. "Vintners' Row was mentioned more than once," he said, matching Eslingen's low tone. "Annechon said she saw them here, and so did Sohier's informant. It's as good a place as any to start."

"We need more people."

"If we don't see anything, and I grant you there's every chance we may not, I'll try to get our night shift to spread out to keep watch," Rathe said. "But if Hearts is being fee'd to look elsewhere—"

Eslingen sighed. "Then the more people, the more chance Hearts will realize we know something's going on. I know. I just don't love these odds." He smiled suddenly, the expression just visible in the light of the waning moon. "Not to mention I miss my own bed."

"So do I," Rathe said dryly. Given a choice, he would far rather be back in Dreams, settled comfortably between Eslingen and Sunflower. "However—"

He stopped abruptly, hearing a sound in the distance, and Eslingen melted back into the shadows. Rathe cocked his head, and the sound came again, not the rattle of wheels on cobbles, but the sound of booted feet. "Points."

Eslingen nodded, and pulled his dark neckerchief up over most of his face. Rathe did the same, and they both stood frozen, listening. The steps came closer: two women, by the sound, walking without any attempt at concealment. A moment later, Rathe saw the flash of a lantern, and a voice said, "—all quiet."

A man answered, an unintelligible mutter, and the lantern flashed again. Rathe held his breath. Not that it would be more than an embarrassment if they were found, but the longer he could keep from having to deal with Hearts' fees…

"Never anything along here," the man said, and the lantern's beam swung across the entrance to the Fountain Court.

"And a good thing, too," the woman answered. They moved on, the sound of their boots fading into silence. Even so, Rathe counted to a hundred before he lowered his neckerchief.

"They're gone."

Across the archway Eslingen copied him. "So now what? If they're patrolling here, presumably the carts are going elsewhere."

"Not necessarily," Rathe said, though he had to admit that it was a long shot. "They might come through, make sure everything's quiet, and then not look back when the carts follow."

For a moment, he thought Eslingen would protest, and scrambled for further arguments that might be more convincing, but after a moment Eslingen just shrugged. "No harm in waiting a while longer."

Rathe leaned back against the cold bricks, hoping he wasn't making a mistake. If Hearts was taking fees to let the carts through, it would mean most of the night watch was involved—well, maybe not that many, if the carts came through when one particular team was on duty, but even so, it was too many for it to be much of a secret around the station. The problem was that most points didn't see anything wrong with taking fees, and even in a case like this, they'd prefer to look the other way than to question their fellows. At Dreams, Trijn kept fees to the minimum, but that was all she could do. Sohier and one or two of her juniors followed his example and didn't accept any fees, but she was in the minority.

Eslingen straightened suddenly. In the same moment, Rathe heard the distant sound of horses' hooves, moving east on Vintners' Row. Not just hooves, he amended, but the rattle of cartwheels, and he couldn't suppress a quick grin.

"Second time lucky," Eslingen said, and pulled the kerchief up over his face.

Rathe did the same, pressing himself back into the shadows as the cart came closer. He could see the faint glow of a lantern now, and then the cart itself came into view. As Annechon had said, it wasn't very large, barely big enough to hold the pair of barrels lashed to its back, and the horse was pressing hard against the harness to keep it moving even on the level street. There was a man beside the driver, in a broad-brimmed hat that shadowed the upper part of his face and a dark stock wound high enough to hide his mouth and chin; he rested a firelock casually against his shoulder, the end of the slow-match glowing gold through the dark. The driver wore an old-fashioned hood that concealed most of his face: neither man was taking any chances on being identified. Rathe watched them pass, then fixed his eyes on Eslingen.

"They're going on down the Row," Eslingen said, his voice barely above a whisper, nothing that would carry even in the quiet night. "And they're turning— to the left, onto the next cross street."

"Stone Lane," Rathe said. He closed his eye, visualizing the way the streets crossed and twisted. "Come on."

He slipped out of the doorway without waiting for Eslingen's answer and started up the street, still careful to keep to the shadows. At the intersection, he peered cautiously around the corner of the nearest building, and saw the cart three houses ahead of them. He put out his hand to warn Eslingen, and felt rather than saw the other man stop at his shoulder. "Turning again," he began, and paused. "No, they're stopping."

Eslingen shifted uneasily, but knew better than to try to see for himself. The street was very quiet without the sound of the cart, and Rathe could hear soft voices. He strained to make out the words, but could make out only the hiss of a curse and then the rattle of wood against wood. He risked a glance, and saw the driver heaving at the closer of the two barrels. The cart moved, and the driver swore again, snatching his hands away as the barrel shifted. The knife said something, sounding impatient, and the driver dragged the canvas cover back over the barrels and climbed back into his place. He chirped softly to the horse, and the cart jerked into motion.

"They were checking the barrels," Rathe said softly. "And—yes, they're turning. Right this time."

He eased forward again, still keeping to the shadows, Eslingen at his heels. At the crossroads, he peered around the corner, but there was no sign of the cart. He swore under his breath, and Eslingen said, "They turned?"

"Looks like." Rathe hurried toward the next intersection, less careful now to stay out of sight, but when he reached it, the cart had vanished. He swore again, trying to guess the most likely destination. De Castiat's rented house was to the left, not quite half a mile away, but he believed Sohier when she said none of her people had seen any sign of a cart. To the right was back toward the river, and that seemed almost as unlikely: if you were smuggling something by water, it would be far easier to take the river the entire way, and avoid the trip through the city. Unless the goods were coming from the city, but even then there were safer loading places upriver that didn't require a trip through the streets of Hearts. "We'll try to the left."

"You go ahead," Eslingen said. "I'll catch up."

He turned back without waiting for an answer. Rathe hesitated—what was he after?—but there was no time to waste. He took the cross street, hurrying now, squinting in the moonlight to try to pick out the tracks of the cart. He could just make out a few marks in the muddy patches where the cobbles had been lost, marks that seemed to point straight through the next two intersections, but then the street opened onto another fountain square. It was empty, the water glittering in the moonlight. Rathe picked his way around the edge of the square, hoping no one was wakeful in the rooms above the shops, but the streets that fed into the square were just as empty. He turned back, and saw Eslingen emerging from the cross street. Rathe stopped, stepping back into a patch of shadow, and waited until the other man was in earshot. "I lost them."

"This whole district is a maze." Eslingen shook his head. "Nico, it's not salt."

"What?"

"I thought I saw that some of the cargo had spilled, where the cart stopped. It's gunpowder." Eslingen reached into the cuff of his coat and brought out his handkerchief. He unfolded it carefully to reveal a smear of mud and coarse black grains like cracked peppercorns.

46

"You're sure?" Rathe shook his head in turn. "No, sorry, of course you are."

"What quality it is, I couldn't say," Eslingen said. "Nor if it's for weapons or blasting or some manufacturing process I don't know about. But I'd give my oath it was powder."

"But why in Tyrseis's name would you be smuggling gunpowder into the city?" Rathe asked. "You can buy it from the Powderers—"

"Unless you were supplying a company of your own," Eslingen said. He paused. "Or I suppose there might be some benefit to not paying taxes on it? I assume it's taxed?"

"No more than any other import," Rathe said. "And if you want to avoid that, buy from the Powderers. I don't like this."

"No more do I," Eslingen said. "I'd hate to think that d'Alamenon was arming her people."

"Astree forfend." In the distance, a clock struck the hour, and Rathe grimaced. "There's nothing more we can do tonight. I'll have a word with Sohier in the morning."

"And say what?" Eslingen asked. "She's already on the lookout for the carts, and if it's gunpowder, I doubt it has anything to do with de Castiat—"

"No, but I can't exactly ask Hearts, can I?" Rathe scowled. "At least not yet. Can't your lot do something?"

"Right now, we don't have a night patrol," Eslingen answered. "Though I think I can persuade Coindarel to change that."

"It's a start," Rathe said. "Come on, let's go home."

COINDAREL WAS AT breakfast when Eslingen arrived at the barracks, and looked distinctly displeased at the interruption. Not that Eslingen himself was feeling particularly cheerful: it had been a long night, and he'd not gotten nearly as much sleep as he would have liked. Estradere was looking a little worn, too, and Eslingen wondered if there was more going on than he'd been told.

Coindarel waved a hand at the empty chairs. "Sit—eat if you haven't, it's damnably early. And tell me why you're here at this gods-forsaken hour."

"Rathe and I were trying to track down a rumor that's spreading in Hearts," Eslingen said. "People are complaining of carts coming through after the curfew, with knives who carry firelocks openly. We were lucky enough to see one, though we weren't able to track it to wherever it was going." He went through the rest of the story in more detail, pleased to see that both Coindarel and Estradere were paying close attention, and finally brought out his handkerchief. "We thought at first it might be de Castiat smuggling salt—"

Coindarel made a rude noise at that, and Estradere rolled his eyes.

"—but what I found in the road was gunpowder." Eslingen unfolded the cloth and slid it across the table. Estradere examined it, his eyebrows rising, and passed it on to Coindarel, who frowned.

"Have you had an alchemist look at it?"

"Not yet. I wanted to report to you first."

"It's powder, right enough," Estradere said.

"I want proof," Coindarel said. "The sort of proof that will stand in court. You'll see to that, Philip."

"Yes, sir."

"What does Hearts say about this?" Estradere asked.

Eslingen hesitated. "We haven't spoken to them yet, except in generalities. Rathe's second asked about the rumors, and their adjunct said it was just rumors— maybe a way to complain about the wedding disruption without seeming to speak against the queen."

"That's thin," Coindarel said, but Estradere shrugged.

"Not impossible, though. I imagine it hasn't been that good for business."

"What does Rathe think?" Coindarel asked.

"He thinks they're fee'd to look the other way," Eslingen answered.

"Also not impossible," Estradere murmured. "In fact, not unlikely."

"And—what else?" Coindarel cocked his head, smiling tightly. "You've got that look, Philip. What do the points want from us now?"

"To add a night patrol, if we can," Eslingen said.

Coindarel frowned, and Estradere said, "That would require coordinating with Hearts. Which seems as though it might cause problems if they're being fee'd."

"We hadn't discussed the details," Eslingen said. "Just that it might be useful."

Coindarel kept looking at Estradere, who shrugged. "It could be done. But, as I said, it draws attention."

"Not right now, then," Coindarel said. "Tell Rathe I want some better sort of plan—or a better excuse, I'd take that, too. But I don't want to get involved with the points' internal business."

Fair enough, Eslingen thought, and nodded. "Very good, sir. There was one thing more."

"Yes?" Coindarel lifted an eyebrow.

"The Soueraine d'Alamenon's people are still threatening to cause trouble for various of the actors in Dreams. For once, I think Aconin is telling the truth, and he's not working to cause trouble." Eslingen paused. "I thought it might be worth asking the Palatineur to have a word with his cousin."

Coindarel's eyebrows rose further. "What sort of word?"

"A reminder that everyone needs to keep the queen's peace," Eslingen said. "There's already been one brawl, and both sides are threatening to press the point."

"Better they do that than fighting in the streets," Estradere said. "Particularly with these Leveler broadsheets in circulation."

Coindarel nodded. "That's a fair request, as long as you can also assure the Palatineur that we—and the points—are taking d'Alamenon's people seriously."

"The points are investigating," Eslingen said, "but they don't expect to find anything. D'Alamenon's people are complaining that Aconin used magistry, which he demonstrably didn't, and that Aconin's satire somehow has to do with d'Alamenon, which it also demonstrably doesn't."

"As long as you can say they're investigating." Coindarel sighed. "Very well, I'll warn the Palatineur to expect you. If you'd see to that, Patri?"

Estradere nodded.

"And find out for certain if that is gunpowder," Coindarel went on. "That's a worrisome thought if it is."

"It does raise the question of why someone would be bringing barrels of powder into the city," Estradere said.

Coindarel lifted an eyebrow. "Certainly. And if you have any suggestions, I'd be glad to hear them."

Estradere shrugged. "Factions arming their households—there's too many Ile'Norders in the city for my taste just now, and plenty of unsettled feuds. The queen would most certainly not approve, so they're doing it in secret."

"A lovely notion." Coindarel looked at Eslingen. "And your thoughts?"

"That was mine, also," Eslingen said. "Someone arming their knives. Failing that, we wondered if there were some spectacular robbery planned, something that involved bringing down a wall or opening a strongroom. But I can't see how you'd get away with that inside the city."

Coindarel said, "Well. First prove that it is powder, then we can worry about the rest. And keep me informed."

"Of course," Eslingen said, and made his bow.

He made his way to the deadhouse, the handkerchief tucked safely into his cuff. Strictly speaking, it wasn't really their sort of work, but Fanier and his people were all alchemists, and Eslingen was happy to take advantage of Rathe's connections in the city. To his relief, it seemed to be a slow day: several of the apprentices were kicking a ball around the narrow courtyard, and all the carts were tucked neatly into the stables. The journeyman who answered the bell looked hopeful, seeing him, but she was polite enough to deflate only slightly when he admitted he hadn't brought a body.

"Fanier should have some time to spare," she said. "Wait here, Captain, and I'll let him know you're here."

Eslingen murmured his thanks and settled himself to wait. As always, the deadhouse smelled of nothing much at all—soap, perhaps, but only faintly, and the tiles that covered the floor and rose knee-high up the walls were scrubbed spotless. He always felt vaguely as though there ought to be more sign of the alchemists' work, but then, that would be disrespectful to the dead. The staff paid no heed to rank or riches, but they were meticulous in their devotion to those they served.

The door opened again, and the journeyman beckoned. "This way, captain. He says he can see you."

Eslingen followed her down the equally well-scrubbed corridors, though for once they did not turn right into the well-lit rooms where the bodies were examined. Instead, she brought him to a warren of smaller rooms, a few with doors open on cases of books, one with a jumble of what looked like astrologer's gear piled on a table, and tapped on the largest of the doors. "I've brought the Captain," she said, and stood back to let him through.

Fanier was dressed more neatly than usual, a sure sign that he hadn't been working, though a battered fisherman's jersey was slung over the back of a chair. The alchemist rose to his feet at Eslingen's entrance, taking one pair of spectacles off his nose and replacing them with the pair that had been tucked into his mop of gray curls. "Philip! Welcome. What can I do for you?"

"Slow day?" Eslingen reached into his cuff and brought out the folded handkerchief. "I'm afraid I'm not going to enliven it by much."

50

"Something's better than nothing," Fanier said, and then made a warding gesture. "Not that I wish for work, Dis knows we've had enough this winter, but it's been two days since we've had a body. What have you got for me?"

Eslingen set the handkerchief on the table and carefully unfolded it. "Coindarel wants to know for certain that this is gunpowder."

Fanier lifted an eyebrow. "Running short?"

"Not exactly." Eslingen hesitated, but there was no reason not to explain. "There have been carts passing through Hearts after the curfew, and one of them was carrying this. We wanted to be sure we could say in court that it was powder."

"Easily enough done." Fanier switched spectacles again, then reached for a larger, hand-held lens. "Certainly looks like powder." He licked his forefinger, then touched the cloth, his eyes fluttering briefly closed. "Feels like it, tastes like it, but..." He frowned, wiped his hand on a rag, and rummaged through the clutter on his worktable until he found a slip of what looked like ivory. It was covered with delicate lines that might be alchemical symbols, and Fanier murmured something before he touched it to the grains of powder. "Huh. That's interesting."

"It's not gunpowder?"

Fanier shook his head. "Oh, no, it's powder, all right. A fairly standard mix, I'm afraid, nothing to give me a hint of who made it. But there's salt in it. I can't think of any reason to mix salt and gunpowder. Unless you can?"

"Fireworks?" Eslingen said, doubtfully. "It seems to me I've heard that some salts will color the flame when it explodes?"

"True enough." Fanier touched the cloth again, finding a different spot. "But this is just—salt. Or it could be contamination, I suppose. What was it carried in, did you see?"

"A barrel," Eslingen said.

Fanier spread his hands. "Maybe the barrel carried salt and wasn't properly cleaned? Could be anything."

Salt. And that brings us back to de Castiat again. Eslingen said, "Could be. But you'll swear that it's powder? As well as salt, of course."

Fanier nodded. "Oh, yes. Do you want something in writing?"

"If you wouldn't mind," Eslingen said, and tucked the cloth back into his cuff.

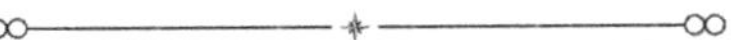

Point of Hearts was not at its best early in the morning. Most of the houses were still closed, shutters pulled tight against the suns' light, the streets still drifted with the debris of the night before. The shops were closed, too, and the only market square was just starting to open, merchants from outside the district hastily piling their merchandise onto trestle tables while a handful of yawning servants stood in line to get their pick of the goods. In Hopes or Sighs, the market would be half sold out already.

Rathe skirted the square, seeing no one he knew nor any sign of Hearts' people, and made his way along the wider avenue that ran perpendicular to the river and would take him to de Castiat's house. It was, if anything, even quieter along the avenue, gates locked and the little shelters where the houses' watchmen kept an eye on the customers emptied and folded away. A few pieces of crumpled paper blew past, propelled by the fitful breeze, but Rathe could see that they'd been used to wrap some greasy snack from the night before. An older woman staggered out of an alley, stopped to brace herself against the nearest wall. She looked half-drunk, tendrils of gray hair spilling out from under a grubby cap, but she gave him a grin that showed a missing tooth.

"A fine morning, young man."

And not a sober one, if you're coming on to me. Rathe said, "Certainly, dame."

"Don't suppose you'd care to have breakfast with me," the woman began, and Rathe swept past her.

"Sorry, I have an appointment."

"They always do," she said, sadly, and he pretended he hadn't heard.

Sohier's teahouse was closed, but a food-seller had set up her cart on the corner by the locked gate, and a small crowd had gathered around. Rathe could smell bacon and hot oil and the tang of charcoal, and joined the line to order and pay. Three demmings bought him a ball of fried sourdough stuffed with cheese and bacon, and as he worked his way clear of the crowd, he was unsurprised to see Sohier perched on the low wall across from the teahouse. She lifted a hand in greeting, and he moved to join her, perching on the worn stones to unwrap his breakfast.

"Any news?"

Sohier shrugged. "Ranic saw one of your carts last night. It came down the alley behind de Castiat's house, but it didn't stop. He tried to follow, but he was in a bad place, and by the time he could move without them seeing him, he'd lost his chance."

Rathe grimaced. "One cart, two men—one of them with a firelock? One horse?"

"That's what he said."

"We saw them too, Philip and I. And lost them." Rathe shook his head. "Anything more from Hearts?"

"I sent Lish over to ask about the carts," Sohier admitted. "I thought maybe she'd get something, innocent as she looks. But she got the same answer I did: not real, just a way to complain without blaming the queen. That was before Ranic saw one." She paused. "I'd lay money they're being fee'd."

Rathe nodded in agreement. "But to what end?" He finished the last of his pastry, said, indistinctly, "Philip picked up what he thought was spilled gunpowder."

"From the cart?" Sohier sounded shocked, and Rathe nodded again. "That can't be good."

"Philip suggested one of the landames is arming her people," Rathe said. "I've no desire to see a pitched battle in our streets, but it seems like a lot of powder, even for a small war."

"That's an ugly thought," Sohier said. "But if not for their knives, what?"

"To blow something up?" Rathe said. "Though I can't quite see what good that gets anyone. Set off a barrel or two of powder, and you'll knock down even a countinghouse wall, but you'll also bring the points down on you faster than the wall fell."

"And I can't see Hearts overlooking something that big," Sohier said. "Regardless of the fee." She hesitated. "I suppose it could be politics?"

"Again, to what end?"

"The Levelers?" Sohier gave him a wary look. "I know you hold with some of their ideas, but the Broadsheet Poet was all for hanging the nobility. They never did catch her, did they?"

Rathe shook his head. "She fled the city, so we were told. I was new at Hopes then, Pheris—she was Chief Point then—she had us spend a moon-month hunting up and down Printers' Row even after the riots were stopped, trying to get someone to name the person who paid for the printing. We never got so much as a name."

"That was before my time," Sohier said.

Rathe nodded. There had never been anything solid to hang the point on, and the handful of printers they'd managed to catch swore they never knew the woman and kept to that story. The broadsheets had stopped, though, so everyone had eventually assumed that either the Poet had fled the city or she'd been frightened to silence. "Why now?" As soon as the words were out of his mouth, he could guess the answer. "Because of the Dis-damned wedding, I suppose. So many nobles in the city, and high nobility, Ile'Norder palatines and soeuraines who never need to visit Astreiant because they're very nearly queens in their own domains. It would be a temptation."

"And someone like the Poet could plausibly fee Hearts," Sohier said. "Or at least the adjuncts. Or they might have sympathizers in the station."

"That's more likely southriver," Rathe said. "Hearts profits off the nobility. But you're not wrong." He pushed himself to his feet. "It's worth looking into, that's for sure." He closed his eyes for a moment. Pheris had retired not long after, but Monteia had been an adjunct point, and would surely remember the details of the investigation. If that failed, there were the archived daybooks in the Tour de la Cité. "If Philip comes looking for me, tell him I've gone to Hopes. If I've left there, I'll leave word."

"Right," Sohier said, brushing crumbs off her skirt. The teahouse was starting to open up, and the fried bread woman was closing up her cart before anyone asked if she had a license to be there. "Anything else I should know?"

"We might be getting the Guard to do some night patrols, but that's not decided yet. Send for me if anything turns up."

"You know I will," she answered, and Rathe turned away.

Somewhat to his surprise, Monteia was already in her workroom when he arrived at Hopes, and professed herself willing to see him. "As long as you haven't anything too appalling to drop on me," she added, drawing a snort of laughter from her own senior adjunct, and shut the workroom door behind them.

"The Levelers," Rathe said, and Monteia blinked.

"I suppose I should have seen that coming, I've read the broadsheets. But why me? Have you got anything to link them to Hopes?"

"Not specifically," Rathe said. He quickly outlined the story of the carts, and Eslingen's suspicion that they were carrying gunpowder, and his own concern that this might be connected to the new broadsheets. When he had finished, Monteia shook her head.

"It's not impossible, I'll give you that. And of course everyone who's read these new sheets is thinking of the Poet. But why would she come back now?"

"Because of the wedding?" Rathe spread his hands. "That would be my guess, anyway. There haven't been this many of the high nobility in Astreiant in—well, I can't remember the last time."

"It's been fifteen years at least," Monteia said. "And, yes, if anything would bring her back, it would be so many northern families in town. She truly hated the Ile'Nord, that was clear."

"I thought she hated everyone," Rathe said, and was surprised at his own bitterness. But she had made it all but impossible to make a case for even the mildest reform.

"As I remember, you weren't exactly unsympathetic to the cause," Monteia said.

"I thought—I still think that the nobility ought not to be above the law," Rathe said. "And it seems the Sur and the queen agree, which is why we've got the Guard. But I don't hold with murder, and that was what the Poet was after. Otherwise..." He stopped, not wanting to finish the sentence. Otherwise, he would have found it very hard to do his duty, and he was grateful he'd never had to make that choice.

Monteia grunted. "The broadsheets just stopped. After we raided that printer in Customs Point, which we all agreed was a good sign the woman was guilty—"

"No conviction," Rathe said, in spite of himself, and Monteia glared.

"She had an excellent advocate. And she deserved every demming of the fine."

Rathe nodded. "No, you're right. But she kept to her story, and we couldn't prove otherwise."

"And wasn't Chief Guisbert furious. But, no, there was never any solid proof. Except that the broadsheets stopped."

"And then the talk went round that the Poet had fled the city," Rathe said. "Was there ever proof of that, or was it just wishful thinking?"

Monteia frowned. "There was a circular from the Surintendant," she said, after a moment. "That was where the idea came from, I think. But I don't remember exactly what it said. Hold on a moment." She went to the workroom door. "Katri! Go down to the cellar, fetch out the daybooks from Lepidas twelve years ago— everything from the first of the month to the mid-month, don't bother with the end." She fished under her skirts and handed over a ring of keys. The woman who answered the call took them and disappeared. "The Sur let me hire a clerk to keep the records. Things were getting out of hand."

Rathe nodded. Even when he'd been an adjunct here, it had been hard to keep the records up to date; if he suspected some of the confusion was deliberate, an attempt to disguise fees received, there were other districts that were worse. "There were never any accomplices identified either."

"Oh, everybody and her sister had a name for us after the granary riots," Monteia answered. "Particularly when the Regents put up the reward."

"But most of them were paying off old scores," Rathe said. "I remember that, all right. At least it was generally easy to spot those."

"A waste of time and effort," Monteia said. "And the Poet was laughing at us the whole time, I'm sure of that." She paused. "Mind you, there were one or two that I wondered about, but none of them ever panned out."

Rathe frowned, an old memory tugging at the back of his mind. "Wasn't there someone in Point of Hearts? An actor or something?"

Monteia rolled her eyes. "Oh, that went nowhere fast. Someone swore that her sister's hobby-horse knew more about the Poet than he was saying. Hearts looked into it, but they never made a connection. Said it was jealousy when the sister wouldn't share."

"Are we sure of that?" Rathe asked.

Monteia shrugged. "I don't remember there being any reason to question it. I know, you're worried they're taking fees now, but at the time they didn't have any worse a reputation than any other district."

"It seems to me it's gotten worse under Orlandi," Rathe said cautiously, and Monteia's mouth tightened.

"I wouldn't argue with that, but you didn't hear it from me."

The workroom door opened, and the clerk appeared, clutching three enormous ledgers to her chest. "Are these the ones you wanted, Chief?"

Monteia took them, checked the dates, and nodded. "Yes, thanks. That'll be all for now." She flipped through the first book, then, more slowly, through the second, stopping at last two thirds of the way through the book. "Here's the Sur's notice." She turned the book so that Rathe could see the paper glued to the page facing the day's reports. Shorn of its formal phrasing, it announced that the absence of broadsheets for the last month would be held to confirm the report that the so-called Leveler Poet, or Broadsheet Poet, had left Astreiant for a safer haven. The points were expected to continue to watch for any recurrences, and to report any further Leveler talk, but for the moment the case was to be considered closed.

"He doesn't give a reason," Rathe said.

"No." Monteia grinned suddenly. "You could always ask him."

"Astree's tits." Rathe shook his head. "Not without considerably more to go on, thank you. It's just that it would have been nice to eliminate a Leveler connection."

"And you can't," Monteia said. "Not quite." She sighed. "And I can't say you're wrong to worry, either. Powder and shot—it's just the kind of thing the Poet was suggesting. I'll have our people keep their ears open. If we hear anything, I'll let you know."

"Thanks," Rathe said. "Oh. What was the name of the man in Hearts?"

Monteia flipped back through the book. "Amery—no, Amorin Bayart. A ladies' friend of impeccable reputation, at least at the time. I'd be surprised if he's still around, it's a wearing profession."

"You never know," Rathe said, and took his leave.

FIVE

ESLINGEN LEFT THE deadhouse with Fanier's sealed report tucked into his cuff, and checked the nearest clock tower, squinting up into the watery sunlight. There had surely been enough time for Coindarel to have informed the palatineur to expect his visit—and if not, he couldn't think it was a bad thing to put de Galhac on notice that the Guard was taking an interest in d'Alamenon's troublemaking. He made his way back to Point of Hearts, taking the route through the Horse Fair that brought him to the edge of the Western Reach. This was where most of the queen's court lived, year in and year out, and as he crossed the wide avenue that ran north through the Royal Gate, he could just see the pennants flying from the towers of the queen's palace, bright against the pale sky.

The Palatineur de Galhac had been given a mannorie just within the Western Reach, one of the crown properties that the queen reserved for favorites and favored visitors. This one was one of the largest, with a main house that rose to three stories, and a range of outbuildings that included a bakehouse and laundry as well as stables and a workshop. De Galhac's banner of three rising ravens, black on a white ground, flew over the gate, and the watchman at the gate wore an old-fashioned short tabard with the same heraldry over otherwise ordinary shirt and breeches. Eslingen nodded to him.

"Captain vaan Esling, to see the palatineur. I'm with the City Guard." He put on a slight smile, copying a twelve-quarter noble he'd once served with, and hoped that Coindarel's messenger had indeed preceded him.

"Of course, Captain," the watchman said, and put two fingers to his mouth to whistle sharply. A page boy, also in a de Galhac tabard, came running and skidded to a halt just inside the gate. "This is Captain vaan Esling. Bring him to the steward, please."

For an instant, Eslingen considered protesting, but reminded himself that this was protocol in a noble household. Should he tip the watchman? No, but the page should get a demming, he reminded himself. He bent his head, and the page made a scrambling bow.

"This way, please, Captain."

Eslingen followed him across the courtyard, careful not to stare at the bustling retainers. There were at least a lunar dozen of them, mostly men but some women as well, the majority at work by the stables, where there was already a considerable manure heap, the rest scattered throughout the compound. As he watched, a young woman emerged from the laundry carrying a loaded basket, and vanished into a side entrance. Another woman came to the doorway and called sharply to one of the men, who dropped his pitchfork and turned his attention to the woodpile. Washing day, Eslingen thought, and wondered how many people the palatineur had brought with him from the north. But that wasn't something he could ask: if he were in fact as nobly born as his assumed name implied, he would know. Instead he followed the page up the wide, well-washed stairs to the main door.

It opened at their approach, a footman in a white livery coat bowing them in, and the page said, "Captain vaan Esling. To see the steward."

The footman bowed again, closing the door gently behind them, and the page stared down the wide hall. The chairs that lined the hall were a bit out of fashion, though their cushions looked new, and there were tapestries on the walls that bore more of de Galhac's ravens. Those must have come with the palatineur, though surely the furniture had been provided with the house; even so, the baggage wagons must have rivaled the train of a small army.

They passed open doors that revealed what looked like a largely unfurnished ballroom, and another to the right that seemed to be a formal parlor, then passed under the stairs to a smaller room behind the ballroom. The page knocked twice, and opened the door.

"Captain vaan Esling, maseigne."

The steward had been sitting at a worktable wedged awkwardly against the windows, but rose to her feet at their entrance, stepping carefully around the end of the table. The room was more normally a pantry, Eslingen guessed, used to set up refreshments before they were brought into the ballroom. "Captain. I'm Ferandisa de Pal, hereditary steward to his excellency."

And clearly I'm expected to know her rank: higher than mine, anyway, though it can't be much above a landame. Eslingen swept off his hat and made a polite bow, equal to equal. "Maseigne. I believe you've had a message from the Prince-Marshal."

"We have," de Pal said.

Eslingen reached into his pocket, flipped a demming to the hovering page. "If his excellency could spare me a few moments, I'd be grateful."

"His excellency asked me to bring you to him as soon as you arrived," de Pal said. "But if I may mention—we are all very much occupied with the preparations for the wedding."

"Of course," Eslingen said. "My errand won't take long."

De Pal looked doubtful—as well she might, Eslingen thought; anything that demanded the City Guard's attention was likely to be time-consuming as well as unpleasant—but gave an abbreviated curtsey. "Thank you, Captain. This way."

He led them up the main stairs and through another well-furnished withdrawing room, to emerge at last onto a gallery overlooking the ballroom. There was another row of chairs against the wall, old-fashioned but neatly painted and gilded, and a bright carpet stretched the length of the space and ran down the stairs at each end. Voices rose from the space below, and Eslingen glanced curiously over the railing.

Half a dozen people were gathered at the end of the room almost directly below the gallery. One woman was obviously an Astreianter merchant, her assistants hovering with tablets and an armload of fabric, but the others were clearly of the nobility. The graying man had to be the palatineur, elegant in black and silver; the young woman in rich emerald brocade shared the same sharp chin and wide-set eyes, which should make her the young Castellan, the soon-to-be bride. And that meant that the equally elegant young man in gray was likely the queen's great-nephew, the Sous-Enfant Prince Loreten. He was grinning widely, clearly about to break into mischievous laughter, and the Castellan slapped his shoulder lightly.

"Wicked creature! You mustn't say things like that."

Loreten mimed apology, still grinning, and the Castellan turned to her father. "But, really, Papa, is there any reason we *couldn't* replace the banners with bunting? We could still use our colors—and the royal colors, too, that would make everyone happy."

"The banners are traditional," de Galhac said, but he sounded more indulgent than censorious. "Not to mention considerably less expensive."

"But we could recover the bunting and use it for livery-wear," the Castellan began, and the steward hurried down the stairs to interrupt.

"Your pardon, Excellency, but Captain vaan Esling is here. You asked me to let you know at once."

Both the Castellan and Loreten looked up sharply at that, and Eslingen felt himself flush under their combined stares. He bent his head politely, hoping they couldn't see the color, and de Galhac nodded.

"Excellent, thank you. Sylla, discuss the matter with Dame Julin, and bring me a number. Then we'll see. Ferandisa, stay and advise them, please." He started up the stairs without waiting for an answer. Behind him, the Castellan gave Eslingen a last curious look, then returned her attention to the merchant and her swaths of cloth. The Palatineur reached the top of the stairs and Eslingen swept a deeper bow.

"Excellency. I'm grateful that you could see me."

"When the Prince-Marshal requests a favor, it's wisest to obey," de Galhac answered. Seen up close, he was somewhat older than Eslingen had thought, perhaps in his late forties. But he was still comely enough, and the lines that bracketed his dark eyes had been carved by laughter. "And also—tales of your exploits have reached even into the north. The man who saved the queen! And rescued the city's missing children! I was curious to meet you."

Eslingen bowed again in acknowledgement, hoping his blush wasn't too obvious. "I'll endeavor not to disappoint, Excellency."

"I'm sure that's not possible," de Galhac said, politely. "Though I would have been glad to meet your partner."

"Perhaps we can find an opportunity." Eslingen took a deep breath. "Excellency, I don't want to keep you—"

"Yes, I'm sure Ferandisa made a point of that," de Galhac said. "But truly, I am happy to speak with you."

"I believe the Soeuraine d'Alamenon is your kin," Eslingen said, and de Galhac frowned.

"She is my cousin, a close cousin, and Sylla's heir until Loreten gives her a child. What has she done?"

And that was an interesting question, Eslingen thought. He said, "There has been some trouble between her household and some of the actors in Point of Dreams, culminating in a fight. Points have been sworn, charges and countercharges, but at this moment, it seems to have stemmed from a genuine misunderstanding. If you would be willing to have that word with her—"

De Galhac was already nodding. "Yes. Gisela can be—well, her people can be overzealous in her defense. You say the Guard agreed this is a misunderstanding?"

"We do," Eslingen said. "The points investigated, and we've confirmed it. I spoke with Aconin myself."

"Aconin." To Eslingen's surprise, de Galhac smiled. "I've not seen as much of his work as I would like, but he is a clever man. And sharp-tongued. I see that might lead to…misunderstandings."

"He's not interested in politics," Eslingen said. "Or, rather, the politics he cares about are the politics of the theater. He has a quarrel with one of the other theater companies, and the soeuraine's people mistook his meaning."

"I understand," de Galhac said. "I'll make sure she takes them in hand."

Eslingen bowed a third time. "Thank you, Excellency."

He made his way back to the barracks in the afternoon sun, delivered Fanier's report to Estradere, then begged a late meal from the company kitchen before Coindarel summoned him to report on the visit to de Galhac. Eslingen summed up his visit, a wary eye on Coindarel, and relaxed to see him nod thoughtfully.

"Martin's a sensible sort, and d'Alamenon will have to listen to him. He's head of the family, even if he is a man."

"She would have claimed the palatinate if she could," Estradere said. "I think we'd do well to keep a closer eye on her."

"Did I say we shouldn't?" Coindarel gave him a sharp glance. "I'll leave that to you, then, Patri. Philip, make sure the points know we're backing them in this."

"I will," Eslingen said, and made his escape.

He took a low-flyer back to Point of Hearts, but to his disappointment found that Rathe had gone back across the river on a series of errands. There would be no tracking him down at this hour; his best bet was to head home, collecting dinner on the way, and wait for Rathe to find him there.

He barely had time to build up the fire and set the stewpot on the hob to warm before Rathe arrived. He was carrying a bag of his own, which proved to contain a couple of loaves of bread and a jug of the harsh red wine they drank hot and spiced. Eslingen turned his attention to brewing that, rasping sugar into a bit of water, then adding the wine and spices and the last of the winter oranges he'd brought from the barracks. By the time Rathe had changed clothes, everything was ready, and Eslingen doled out bowls and cups while Rathe put a portion of the stew aside for the dog. They ate in silence, until finally Rathe pushed his bowl aside. Sunflower lifted his head, then bustled over as Rathe set the bowl on the floor for him.

"Any news?"

"I spoke to Fanier—Coindarel wanted a report we could take to court if need be—and then he sent me to de Galhac."

"How'd that go?" Rathe asked.

Eslingen shrugged. Rathe's bowl, licked clean, hit his foot; he collected it, and set his own down for the dog to clean. "I told him d'Alamenon's accusation was founded in a misunderstanding. He said he would speak to her about it."

"Will he?"

Eslingen blinked, considering. It had not occurred to him to doubt de Galhac, and even now he thought the man had been sincere. "I'd say so. He struck me as an honest man. Preoccupied with this wedding, the whole house was busy with it, but I think he'll do what he promised."

"She's some kin of his, isn't she?"

"A cousin. She's next in line to the palatinate after the Castellan." Eslingen paused. "I don't think he's entirely happy about that."

"Would you be?" Rathe asked, and Eslingen shook his head. "What did Fanier have to say?"

Sunflower had scooted the second bowl halfway across the room, and Eslingen rose to retrieve it. "He said it was gunpowder, and contaminated with salt, but where that gets us I couldn't say. I gave the report to Coindarel."

"We should take another look at de Castiat." Rathe topped up their cups. "How much powder do you need to arm a household?"

"It depends on how many men you have," Eslingen said, frowning. "But those weren't small barrels. If one of the landames is arming her people, she's expecting to need a well-armed company, and that doesn't seem likely in the city. On the way back to the Ile'Nord, maybe, that would make more sense, but then why not store it outside the city until you need it?"

"Agreed. I wondered about some sort of robbery, using it to break into a strongroom or such—"

"Not exactly subtle," Eslingen said.

"No. Not to mention that the banks and countinghouses all have guards of their own, day and night. And of course we have to consider the Levelers." Rathe's smile was wry. "Which is awkward."

Because Rathe was known to have Leveler sympathies. Eslingen kept his face expressionless, said carefully, "Has there been any progress with these new broadsheets?"

Rathe shook his head. "Less even than we found the last time, and that wasn't much. But they have the sound of the Poet, and she advocated the overthrow of the crown and the abolition of all titles of nobility, to be followed by the redistribution of noble lands, and hanging for anyone who disagreed. These aren't that different."

"You said the last time it was a starving winter," Eslingen said cautiously.

"It was. And that certainly helped the Levelers get recruits. No one's going hungry now, thank Heira. But this is the first time in a decade that there have been so many of the high nobility in the city, thanks to the wedding."

It was a grim thought, and Eslingen shook his head, trying to set it aside. "But what would Levelers do? Recruit their own army and storm the palace? That's hardly something you can keep secret for very long."

"I know," Rathe said again. "But the ideas never went away."

"So what do we do about it?" Eslingen asked.

"I spent part of today looking up old records," Rathe said. "We never had much to go on. But there was a man in Point of Hearts, a ladies' friend, called Amorin Bayart. He was supposed to have some connection with the Poet. I'd like to know if he's still around."

Eslingen lifted his eyebrows. "The man who runs the Lilies is Amorin Bonamy. And that's where the Dis-damned review is being held. It's not a common forename."

"Interesting," Rathe said. "I wonder if Annechon would tell me if it's the same man?"

"We can always ask," Eslingen said, though he wasn't eager to pay another visit, and Rathe nodded.

"Tomorrow."

IT WAS AFTERNOON before Rathe was able to free himself from routine business at Dreams and collect Eslingen for their next foray into Point of Hearts. Both suns were out, and the day was warmer than it had been, something Rathe was grateful for as they crossed the river. The district was beginning to awaken as they made their way through the streets, and Annechon's house was more crowded than it had been the last time they'd visited. A maidservant met them at the door, her hair brightly hennaed and her eyes rimmed with kohl. She gave them a wary look but clearly didn't dare refuse, and brought them down the long hall to one of the smaller parlors. Music was playing in the room next door, a trio of viols, and Rathe recognized the tune from the Galenon's latest production.

Eslingen had recognized it, too, and his smile was wry. "It seems Chresta's dislike isn't universal."

"They usually have their finger firmly on the pulse," Rathe said, and nodded to the maid. "Madame's throwing a party?"

The maid gave him a quick, unreadable look. "She has any number of friends. All of whom are welcome here."

"I only need a brief word with her," Rathe said. "We don't want to interrupt."

The maid's mouth tightened. "I'll let madame know you're here," she said, and closed the door gently behind her.

"Somehow I doubt we'll be offered refreshments," Eslingen said.

"We're not exactly good for Annechon's business," Rathe said. "Decorative as you may be."

"'May be'?" Eslingen lifted an eyebrow, and Rathe grinned.

"Are, then. But I doubt you're what her friends are looking for." His smile faded at the thought. If Annechon was offering the services of a resort-house without the requisite licenses—at best, it made things very awkward. But of course it was Hearts' business, and in Hearts discretion mattered more than facts. There was no law against holding parties, and if in the course of them arrangements were made, the law would look the other way. But it was a step down for Annechon, and that was hard to bear.

The door opened softly and Annechon appeared, elegant in a plum-colored gown trimmed with an impressive show of lace. Eslingen would know to the demming what it would cost; Rathe could only assume that either she hadn't suffered too great a financial reverse from her recent parting, or her dressmakers were still granting credit. It was probably the latter: the cut was unusual, and Annechon had a name for leading fashions. To his surprise, a second woman followed her in, a square, stocky person in unflattering rose-colored satin: expensive material, but a conservative cut, and Rathe wondered if she was bidding to become Annechon's next protector.

"Nico." Annechon came forward with both hands outstretched, but there was a faintly wary note in her voice. "Captain."

Rathe accepted the half-embrace, saw Eslingen sketch a graceful bow. The woman in rose eyed them with disapproval. "I don't know what business the points have here, particularly the adjunct from Point of Dreams. Or the Guard, for that matter."

Annechon gave a swift look over her shoulder, mouth curving into a practiced smile. "Nico is a very old friend of mine, Renae. I'm in no trouble—am I, Nico? And of course his leman is always welcome here."

"I don't like to see you bullied, my dear."

Something flickered in Annechon's expression, but her voice remained light and easy. "Nico, this is the landame d'Oreilles, who has been kind enough to become one of my good friends."

"Maseigne." Rathe made an effort to hide his instant prickle of dislike. "As Annechon says, she's in no trouble. I came to her in the hope she might be able to give me some advice. We won't keep her long."

D'Oreilles looked at Annechon. "Only if you're certain, my dear."

"I assure you." Annechon's smile was steady. "If you remind Titone to be sure the parlor's ready, I'll join you in a moment. That will be enough, surely, Nico?"

Rathe nodded. "It should be."

D'Oreilles hesitated, but turned away. "I'll come back for you in a bit," she said, and closed the door behind her.

There was a little silence, and then Rathe said, carefully, "What should I think of her, Annechon?"

Annechon snorted. "She presumes on favors I haven't yet granted. And yet—she's very rich, Nico. I literally can't afford to offend her."

"She doesn't seem like your usual sort," Rathe said. Annechon's previous protectors had all been careless, generous women, fond of music and good food as well as of Annechon herself. None of them had been averse to sharing—or if they were, they'd hid it well—and they'd all seemed genuinely happy with what Annechon offered.

"She is being remarkably generous," Annechon said. "And I think she means well. Now, what do you want to ask?"

'Means well' was hardly ringing praise. Rathe put aside his worry with an effort, and said, "You remember the trouble with the Broadsheet Poet?"

Annechon grinned, and the expression took him back to their shared southriver childhood. "She gave your lot fits, and then some. You must have had fun, Nico."

"It wasn't the easiest thing to deal with," Rathe said. "But the main thing—there was talk, nothing we could prove, then or now, just a rumor that she had a man in Hearts called Amorin Bayart. Is that the same as Amorin Bonamy who owns the Lilies?"

"I can't answer that," Annechon began, and Rathe quickly lifted his hand.

"I swear I'm not looking to call a point on him—or at least not for that, he's up to his neck in the trouble we're having with this private production, and if there's a point in that, I will call it."

"Call one on Aconite first," Annechon said.

"It's actually not his doing this time," Eslingen said.

Annechon snorted. "I'll believe that when the sun goes retrograde. He and Bayard Dielz have worked up a feud with Cleonie at the Galenon—mostly because she wouldn't risk Aconite's last city comedy—and they'll do anything to make her look small."

"Philip's right," Rathe said. "Don't look at me like that, Annechon, for once he's the one who's being attacked in the street."

"Not without desert," Annechon said.

"Not this time," Rathe said again, and she sighed.

"That was a bad business. The Poet, I mean."

Rathe nodded. "It was."

"No one needs a return of that trouble. These broadsheets are worrying enough."

"Agreed," Rathe said. "And I meant it, I'm not looking to call a point here, that's old business that can stay buried as far as I'm concerned. But once the question's been raised, I'd like to eliminate any Leveler angle if I can."

"And your captain?" Annechon tipped her head toward Eslingen.

"I'm with Nico," Eslingen said. She studied him for a long moment, then finally bent her head.

"Yes, he's the same man. He chose Bonamy when he bought the Lilies—for obvious reasons, he's been a 'good friend' to so many. But I don't believe he had anything to do with the Poet."

"That's helpful." Rathe paused, and decided it was worth one further question. "I don't suppose you've had any dealings with the Vidame de Castiat?"

"What's she got to do with this?" Annechon's voice was sharp. "That's the one who put herself under arrest, isn't it? No, I've nothing at all to do with her. That's too chancy a business for my taste."

"I just wondered," Rathe said, startled. "You know most people in Hearts."

"Not her," Annechon said. "And if you don't want Renae barging back in, you'd better be on your way."

There was something false in her voice, in the vehemence of her denial, but he knew she was right that d'Oreilles would be back at any moment. "I'll likely be back."

"And of course I'll do what I can," Annechon said, and opened the parlor door.

They didn't speak until they were back on the street and out of sight as well as earshot of Annechon's house. Rathe made a face, not sure what to do next: he believed Annechon about Bonamy, but there had been something off in her disclaimer about de Castiat. Beside him Eslingen slowed, looking back at the house.

"What was that about de Castiat, do you think?"

Rathe sighed. "Pretty obvious, wasn't it? Surely she's got more sense than to go hunting a patronne there."

"One might think," Eslingen said. "Still, that was useful about Bonamy."

"I suppose." Rathe shook his head. "No, it's good to know. I'm just not sure what I want to ask him."

"It might be incentive not to host the review?" Eslingen sounded doubtful even as he spoke, and Rathe shook his head again.

"We can't do that. No, for that, I think it would be better if Trijn had a word with Matthie Gasquine, see if she can't be persuaded to calm things down."

"It might work," Eslingen said. "So what do we do now?"

Rathe looked around, saw no neighborhood clock, and squinted at the sky. "We've still got daylight. Maybe it's time we made the Vidame's acquaintance."

"And what exactly do you plan to say to her?" Eslingen asked, his eyebrows winging upward.

"I'll think of that when we get there," Rathe said.

It wasn't a long walk to de Castiat's rented house, and Rathe was pleased to see that Sohier's people had the property under close observation. He stopped at the teahouse long enough to alert Sohier to their visit and to receive her report—nothing happening out of the ordinary, just a few visitors and a greater number of trades-folk calling at the alley door. The latter had proved willing to gossip, but had nothing useful to say.

Rathe made a point of taking them to the street door, where de Castiat's gatekeeper shared the keeper's shelter unhappily with one of the junior points. She greeted Rathe with a cheerful salute, but the gatekeeper scowled impartially at both the newcomers.

"Please state your business."

"Adjunct Point Rathe and Captain vaan Esling, to see the Vidame," Eslingen said.

"Do you have an appointment?" The gatekeeper's scowl deepened.

"We're here on the Surintendant's authority," Rathe said. "To ensure that the Vidame is keeping to the terms of her agreement."

Out of the corner of his eye, he saw Eslingen frown, and the gatekeeper drew breath as though for an angry retort, but then controlled himself. "I'll inform maseigne's chatelaine," he said, and stalked away across the narrow courtyard.

Rathe looked at the waiting point. "She'd better see us."

"Oh, she'll see you," the woman answered. "At least she always has when we've made our checks. She'll keep you waiting as long as she dares, but she'll see you in the end."

"Does she get many visitors?" Eslingen asked, and the pointswoman shrugged.

"More than I expected, to be honest. It's all by ones and twos, maybe three to make up a card party."

"What sort of people?" Rathe asked.

"A mixed bag. Women of leisure from the houses around here, some minor nobles and merchants-resident, once or twice a kinswoman. Sohier has the list."

Rathe nodded. "Anything you'd note about any of them?"

The woman shook her head. "If maseigne wasn't under self-arrest, I'd think she was auditioning for a new lover."

"That's one way of passing the time," Eslingen said.

The gatekeeper returned, and jerked a thumb toward the door. "Maseigne will see you when she can."

"I'm sure she will," Rathe said.

The door was, of course, shut, and it took a few minutes for someone to answer the knock. Rathe braced himself when it finally swung open, but to his surprise, they were greeted by a neatly-dressed woman with the chatelaine's bundle of keys dangling at her waist.

"My apologies, Adjunct Point, Captain. Maseigne is presently engaged, but will see you as soon as she's free. If you'd come with me?"

DE CASTIAT'S HOUSE was not very different from the other houses Eslingen had seen in Hearts, smaller than the wealthy merchants-residents' houses in Manufactory Point or even in Sighs, with only the thee-story tower tacked on to the end of the hall to distinguish it. The main door opened onto a broad hall with a glossily polished floor, with two parlors to the right and a ballroom to the left. A stairway soared at the end of the hall, lit by an arched window; beyond that would be a dining room and the hall that led to the kitchen. The chatelaine led them into the smaller parlor, where a fire was newly kindled in the tiled fireplace, and gestured to the row of waiting chairs. "If you please, sirs. Maseigne will see you as soon as she's able."

Eslingen nodded. Rathe said, his tone clearly doubtful, "Of course."

The chatelaine bent her head, refusing the bait, and closed the door gently behind her.

Eslingen glanced around the room. It was comfortably furnished, but not fashionably so, and some of the upholstered pieces were showing subtle signs of wear. Brought from de Castiat's holdings, he guessed, for when she attended the queen's court: presumably she hadn't been planning to confine herself here, or she would have brought better. Or maybe the best pieces were now in her tower. He tipped his head toward the painted door set discreetly into what would have been the outer wall. "The tower, I presume?"

"I'd guess so." Rathe glared at it. "It'll be interesting to see how badly she wants to insult us."

"That seems like a foolish choice," Eslingen said, carefully, and Rathe shrugged.

"We'll see."

Arguing would only prolong Rathe's annoyance. Eslingen settled himself in a chair where he could get the good of the fire, and after a while Rathe came to sit opposite him. There wasn't much to say, or at least not much that he wanted to risk saying here in de Castiat's own parlor. He heard the sound of a distant tower clock striking the quarter hour, echoed a bit later from a case clock somewhere in the house. Outside the long windows, the sunlight was fading to the mellow gold of late afternoon, and he bit down hard on his own anger. If de Castiat was doing this on purpose, he wouldn't give her the satisfaction—and it still made no sense for her to antagonize both the Points and the Guard. It seemed odd that a woman clever enough to have thought of placing herself under arrest to avoid worse punishment, and clever enough to have gotten it through the courts, should thumb her nose at the law she was using so adeptly. He glanced at Rathe, but the other man's set face told him this wasn't the time to raise the question. Nor was it wise, where they might easily be overheard; he would wait until they were more private.

The clock struck twice more before the tower door finally opened. A woman stalked out, flinging her cloak around her shoulders, and strode across the parlor before Eslingen could catch more than a glimpse of her features. She was older than he, perhaps in her early forties, and well dressed: too old and not striking enough to be one of Hearts' ladies of leisure, but her clothes weren't as expensive as he would have expected if she were of the nobility. He looked back at the door to find a younger woman waiting, a loose flower-embroidered house-gown open over a plain skirt and bodice. Plain but well cut, he amended, and the fabric was the best wool. Her dark hair was wound into a coronet of braids, with an expensive lace cap perched on top for propriety. Rathe rose to his feet, and Eslingen belatedly followed.

"Adjunct Point." Her voice was deeper than he'd expected. "And Captain vaan Esling. Please accept my most sincere apologies for keeping you waiting. I was unfortunately detained by matters of business."

That was not at all what Eslingen had been expecting, and from the look of him, neither had Rathe. They both managed to murmur a polite response, and de Castiat waved vaguely toward the room behind her.

"Won't you come in? As you're well aware, I'm pledged not to leave the tower."

Rathe nodded, and Eslingen shook himself back to attention, managed to make a polite bow. "Thank you, maseigne."

As he'd suspected, the tower room was better furnished than the parlor, with a new-looking painted stove and an expensive woven carpet over the polished wood of the floor. Chairs and a divan had been drawn up by the stove, and a tea service sat on the little table between them.

"Please, make yourselves comfortable," de Castiat went on. "Or perhaps I could offer you some wine?"

Eslingen felt his eyebrows rise: after the studied rudeness that had kept them waiting, this excess of courtesy came as a surprise. Or maybe it genuinely had been business that kept them waiting; the woman who left had had the look of an upper servant.

"Or I could send for more tea." De Castiat gave a wry smile. "I wasn't expecting you—but of course I understand that's the point."

"Nothing for us, thanks," Rathe said, and Eslingen nodded in agreement.

"Then you'll forgive me if I indulge?" De Castiat didn't wait for their answer, but moved to the sideboard and poured herself a generous glass of wine. She took a swallow, and waved again at the chairs. "Please, do sit."

Rathe settled himself, looking faintly wary, and Eslingen copied him. De Castiat came to join them, taking another long drink of her wine.

"As you see, I'm here, as promised. Is there anything else I can do for you?"

"There's a question or two I'd like to ask," Rathe said, "about an entirely unrelated matter. Since you have less to distract you than many other women—"

"Because I have fewer entertainments available?" De Castiat waved her free hand in apology. "But of course I'll help if I can."

Eslingen leaned forward. "You may have heard talk, perhaps from your servants? About mysterious carts traveling through Hearts in the dead of night."

To his surprise, de Castiat hesitated, licking her lips. "I've heard something of the sort? Some talk, at any rate. My chatelaine assures me it's nothing of consequence."

"Then you haven't seen any such thing yourself," Rathe said.

"No, nothing." De Castiat shook her head.

"Has anyone in your household seen one?"

De Castiat shook her head again. "Not that I know of. Though they might not mention it to me, of course. My chatelaine would know better than I would."

"You won't mind if we asked her, then," Rathe said.

"Not in the least." De Castiat gave him an uneasy look. "Are they suspected of something, Adjunct Point?"

"They're an oddity," Rathe said. "And things are already unsettled enough with the wedding. And the recent broadsheets."

De Castiat inclined her head in what was meant to be gracious agreement, but lines of strain showed around her mouth. "I'm afraid that having so many noble families in Hearts and at the court at the same time has led to extra work for everyone."

"It's led to the occasional street fight, and maybe more," Rathe said, bluntly, "and we're determined not to let that escalate."

De Castiat hesitated. "If you're referring to the playwright, Aconite——"

"He is, for once, the injured party," Eslingen said.

"Truly?" De Castiat licked her lips again. "I'm glad to hear so, for his sake."

"I believe you're related to the accuser," Rathe said. "The Soeuraine d'Alamenon."

"We're cousins," de Castiat said. She forced a smile. "But that doesn't make her right."

"Are you a follower of the theater, then?" Eslingen asked, and she gave him a startled glance.

"As much as I can be, when I'm only here in the city in the winters. I only know the man by reputation."

And that was a lie, Eslingen thought. He looked at Rathe, and saw the same knowledge in the other man's expression.

"The Soeuraine needs to keep her people in check," Rathe said.

"I'm sure she'll do so," de Castiat answered. "Like all of us, she's sworn to keep the queen's peace."

"We've spoken to the Palatineur," Eslingen said, "and he has promised a word with her."

"That's likely to be more effective than anything I could say," de Castiat answered. "D'Alamenon is my cousin, yes, but on my father's side. And of course she's of higher rank than I. I'm not sure what I can do for you, Captain."

"Put in the good word," Eslingen suggested, his voice dry, and de Castiat bent her head.

"If you think it would help—of course." She emptied her cup. "And if that's all?"

A wry smile flickered across Rathe's face. "We'll still want a word with your chatelaine, maseigne."

"Of course." De Castiat reached for a bell that stood ready beside the teapot, rang it twice. "Tell her that I said you could speak to anyone in the house."

"Thank you, maseigne." Rathe pushed himself to his feet and Eslingen copied him. "We appreciate your time."

"That was the agreement," de Castiat said, and Eslingen was certain he saw her shiver.

SIX

T HE CHATELAINE ARRIVED in answer to the bell, and Rathe followed her from the tower, slowing once the door had closed behind them. "I'd like a word."

The chatelaine gave the door a fleeting glance, but bent her head. "If I can help, Adjunct Point."

"These carts," Rathe said. "What do you know about them?"

Her mouth tightened in disapproval. "Prentice tales. And servants' gossip, though not in this house, I'm pleased to say. Our people know better than to waste time with such nonsense."

"They've been seen by reliable witnesses," Eslingen said, cocking his head to one side.

The chatelaine shook her head. "Not by anyone in this house. And if you'll excuse me, sirs, I do have work to manage."

"From her tone, her people had better not have seen anything," Eslingen said, when they were back on the street. "Do you think it's worth trying to talk to the rest of the household?"

Rathe considered. Part of him wanted to insist on it, if only to annoy the chatelaine, but that wasn't the most effective way to get the information he wanted. "Sohier must have some contacts among the kitchen staff. We could get her to ask."

Eslingen nodded. "And then there's de Castiat. Why was she so nervous, if she didn't know anything about the carts?"

"Nervous about that and d'Alamenon," Rathe answered.

"I suppose she might just be worried about falling into more trouble," Eslingen said doubtfully. "As she said, d'Alamenon's her cousin, and she outranks her—de Castiat, I mean. If d'Alamenon was demanding support?"

"But for what?" Rathe shook his head. "D'Alamenon's got plenty of knives of her own, she shouldn't need de Castiat's help. And it didn't look as though de Castiat brought much in the way of bodyguards."

"I didn't see any signs of such," Eslingen said. "Her manservants could probably all wield a cudgel if they had to, though."

"Not the same," Rathe said. The house servants might fight for their employer if they were attacked, but they were likely to balk at being asked to attack a random poet. Particularly if they were hired in Astreiant and not brought with her from her estates.

"No," Eslingen said. He paused. "I still think she knows more than she's saying. I just don't know how to pry it out of her."

"Agreed," Rathe said. "Let's see what Sohier has to say."

Sohier was still at the teahouse, though she'd moved into the shelter of the main building as the suns dropped below the rooftops. She had chosen a corner table where she could still keep an eye on the house but not be easily overheard, and they joined her there, hunching together over the teapot on its little stove.

"We've talked to the servants," Sohier said, "and they've certainly heard about the carts, though I don't think anyone claims they've seen them. The chatelaine keeps a close watch on them, and they all say she doesn't want to hear a word about it."

"That seems a bit odd," Eslingen said.

Sohier shrugged. "It's not a big household. In fact, I'd say de Castiat was trying to save money. There's an older woman who lives there with her son when the vidame is on her own lands, but gets bed and board only. Not to mention she's getting frail, and the boy isn't what you'd call capable. He's good with the garden, they say, and not much else. Most of the rest of the staff was hired locally— she's always done that, leaves everyone except her chatelaine, her cook, and her favorite maid back in the Ile'Nord while she comes to Astreiant. The chatelaine doesn't much care for the city, the kitcheners all say she hates being here. But she's absolutely loyal to the vidame."

Not surprising, but not particularly helpful, either. Rathe said, "Who was the woman who was there before us?"

Sohier fished beneath her skirts and came up with her tablets. "Toller just reported. That was Dame Ylvare, one of d'Alamenon's household. Some sort of senior steward."

"Interesting," Eslingen said, and Rathe nodded.

Sohier glanced at her notes again. "She's been here a few times. The first time, she brought a book—one of the Nightside romances, Barra says. After that, it's just been visits. I think she's making sure de Castiat keeps her word. Toller's been talking to one of the housemaids, she says de Castiat's always upset after Ylvare visits."

Eslingen looked up sharply. "As we saw ourselves."

Rathe nodded. "That's a connection worth pursuing. I wonder if d'Alamenon has any connection to the salt trade? Any other visitors of interest?"

Sohier looked at her tablets again. "Mostly tradespeople and a few ladies of leisure."

"Ardrene did say she was acting as though she was auditioning for a new lover," Rathe said.

"It looks a bit that way." Sohier paused. "One of them—I think you know her, Nico? Annechon."

Rathe froze. He'd thought Annechon had been a little too quick to deny any knowledge of de Castiat, but there hadn't been any reason to press her on the question. "Yes. Tell me about her visit."

"Visits," Sohier said. "We've seen her four times, first for a card party and then twice more by day, alone, and then for an evening. She went home alone, though, after curfew."

Those did sound like the visits of someone feeling out a possible relationship, Rathe thought, and it wasn't like Annechon to keep her protectors secret. Eslingen said, "She said she was coming home after curfew when she saw the cart. Do you think that was the same visit?"

"It's possible." And if it was, did it point to a connection between the carts and de Castiat? Rathe grimaced. "Seems I'll need to have another word with her. But that's for tomorrow." He pushed himself to his feet, and Eslingen copied him.

Sohier nodded. "We'll keep looking for the carts."

"Thanks," Rathe said, and led the way out of the teashop.

The clouds had closed in while they were eating, and the twilight was thickening. Rathe started toward the river, and Eslingen cleared his throat. "Maybe we should drop in on Annechon tonight?"

"She was entertaining," Rathe said. "You saw."

"She might be more willing to talk if she needed to get back to her guests."

He wasn't wrong, but Rathe shook his head. Annechon might have lied, but she would have a good reason for it. Or she might know something that would cause trouble for de Castiat, and that would take delicate handling if he was to persuade her to share what she knew. "I'd rather talk to her in daylight, when we're not likely to be interrupted by any of her protectors."

Eslingen nodded. "All right. But it's odd she didn't speak out. There's no reason not to say she's courting de Castiat's favor."

"Except that she had other possible protectors in the house," Rathe said. "Including that d'Oreilles."

"Who seemed more possessive than she had a right to be," Eslingen agreed. "All the same, Nico—"

"We'll talk to her tomorrow," Rathe said, more sharply than he'd meant. Even in the twilight, he saw Eslingen recoil, and shook his head. "I know her, Philip. I've known her since I was a boy."

She still lied. The words hovered, unspoken, and then Eslingen looked away. "Tomorrow, then."

"Thanks," Rathe said, softly enough that they could both pretend he hadn't spoken, and Eslingen touched his shoulder lightly.

They turned onto the broader street that would bring them to the Hopes-point Bridge, the mage-light lanterns and flambeaux hanging at the house gates providing a better light. They would pass the Lilies, Rathe realized, and wondered if they should try for a word with Bonamy. No, he thought, the same argument applied as had applied to Annechon. Better to wait until daylight, when there were fewer distractions for the man, real or feigned. He could hear voices rising from that direction, and hoped Bonamy was keeping a firm hand on his visitors. In the same moment, Eslingen lifted his head, his step faltering.

"I hear it, too," Rathe said, and Eslingen shook his head.

"Not that. I mean, I hear it, but—I thought someone was following us."

Rathe quelled the reflex to look over his shoulder. "Are they?"

"I'm not sure." Eslingen had his hand on his knife anyway, and Rathe gave his truncheon the twist that loosened it in its holder. "I thought so, but—if they were, they've stopped."

"They realized you heard them." The noise ahead of them was growing louder, taking on a note that meant trouble, and he looked around to see if there was anyone he could send for the nearest points. The street was empty, but the nearest house had a watchman's box at his gate, and as he looked, the watchman himself stepped out, looking worried.

"What's going on?"

"I don't know," Rathe answered. "Send to the points—do you have a runner?"

"I do," the watchman said, and disappeared into his box. A moment later, a girl darted away from the house, and the watchman retreated behind the house's gate, dragging it closed with a scraping of iron-shod doors on the stones of the street. The sounds from the Lilies were growing louder.

"This isn't good," Eslingen said.

"No." Rathe lengthened his stride, and came around the corner to see the gates of the Lilies forced back and a crowd milling in the courtyard. He caught a glimpse of one or two familiar faces, actors from Dreams, struggling to get to the theater door, and drew his truncheon. "Here, now—"

The nearest man turned on him, swinging a fist the size of a small ham. Rathe ducked, doubled him over with a punch to the gut. Eslingen swept him aside, drawing his knife, and Rathe saw the doorkeeper cowering in his box, one hand to his bloodied mouth.

"Go for the points," Rathe said, but the man shook his head, shrinking back into the doubtful shelter. "Get the points, damn it!"

"I sent our boy—"

Someone came up behind him, and Rathe ducked, blocking a blow with his truncheon. The courtyard was full of struggling people, women and men alike, some with clubs and knives, the people from the house with buckets and rakes and other improvised weapons. They were gathered in a knot around the stairs that led to the main door, while another group, actors, mostly, were pressed against the wall of the private theater. One of the attackers stumbled back, and Rathe caught him by the collar, planting the truncheon in the small of his back and spinning him away from the fight.

"Go home, man, you're drunk." It wasn't much use, but it was the best he could think of in the moment. The man stumbled free—he did look drunk, and for an instant Rathe hoped this was just an ordinary riot. At his side, Eslingen swore breathlessly, knife in his left hand, a club in his right, and from the front of the crowd a bell began to ring. The attackers raised a cheer, and a woman's voice rose above the crowd.

"Bring it down! Bring them all down!"

That was an old Leveler cry from thirty years before, in the famine years at the end of the old queen's reign, and it drew another cheer from the crowd. Other voices picked up the call, and a gang rushed the stairs, driving the household's defenders back.

"We need the Guard," Eslingen said, and Rathe nodded. The Guard or the points from Hearts, enough to quell the riot—

There was more movement behind him, and the sound of running feet, and he turned, hoping it would be Hearts coming to the rescue. Instead, a stranger crowded into him. He blocked the attack, turning his shoulder into it, and something struck him hard on the back of the head. Lights exploded across his vision, and he staggered sideways, the strength going out of his legs. He reached for the side of the doorkeeper's box—if he went down in this melee, he was lost—but there was nothing there. He stumbled again, and fell into darkness.

ESLINGEN HEARD THE rush of movement behind him, and swung to face it, sweeping the club blindly before him. The attackers fell back—the men who'd been following them, he guessed, searching for livery marks even as he fell into a defensive stance. The nearest man lunged at him, his knife clearly longer than the legal limit. Eslingen ducked and slashed at his face, driving the man back into his neighbor. Out of the corner of his eye, he saw Rathe take a glancing blow to the shoulder, and in the same moment a second man swung for Rathe's head. Rathe stumbled sideways and went down, crumpled awkwardly against the doorkeeper's box. Eslingen lunged left-handed for the attacker, driving his knife deep into the man's kidney; the man went down without a cry, but the knife caught, wrenching the hilt from Eslingen's hand. Eslingen let it go, spinning to block another man, laying about him with the club until he could place himself over Rathe's body, back to the wall of the doorkeeper's box. The mob at the stairs was still shouting—*bring them down, bring them down*—but they weren't making much progress. The actors weren't doing as well, but he could barely spare them a glance before the next man attacked. He parried, wishing for a sword, or better still his pistols, and then at last he heard shouts from the street. His attacker fell back, and Eslingen seized the moment to snatch up a kitchen knife someone had dropped. Then the gates burst open, and a stream of points poured through, truncheons at the ready.

He flattened himself against the doorkeeper's box, all too well aware of how little it would take for one of them to hit out at him by accident, and felt Rathe moving against his legs. "Stay still," he said, not daring to take his eyes off the fight, and felt Rathe brace himself, pulling himself up so that he was sitting against the wall. "Keep still," he said again. "You took a nasty hit—"

Another group of points rushed through the open gate, Sohier in the lead. She skidded to a stop, seeing Rathe, but waved the others on. "Is he all right?"

"I'm fine," Rathe said, though he didn't sound it. "Shut this down."

Sohier hesitated, but Eslingen nodded, and she started after the rest of her people. He went to one knee at Rathe's side, supporting him with the hand that still held the club. Rathe grimaced and leaned away. "Don't, I'll be sick."

"I wouldn't doubt it," Eslingen said, tilting Rathe gently so that he could see that other man's head. There was blood, but only from a cut where he'd been hit, not coming from his ears, and Eslingen risked putting down the club to examine Rathe's scalp more closely. It was badly swollen as well as cut, the bruise already the size of a goose egg, and Rathe flinched away from him.

"That hurts."

"Sorry." There wasn't much they could do here, Eslingen knew. What he needed was to get Rathe to bed, let him rest in a darkened room for a day or so until his wits settled in his head—and get a doctor to him, though there wasn't much even the best women could do about such an injury.

The courtyard was crowded now with points, herding the rioters by the lunar dozen into corners where they could be penned and questioned. One or two were already being let go, to slink off into the shadowed street, but most were being held. *And should be,* he thought. He wondered if d'Alamenon's knives had been behind this riot, too, though he hadn't recognized any of them from the previous encounter.

Rathe leaned more heavily against him, eyes closing, and he prodded him gently. "Here, stay awake for me, now—"

"Philip." That was Sohier, appearing out of the crowd, her hair pulled loose from its queue and her truncheon still in her hand. "Philip, there's trouble."

"What do you mean?" Eslingen looked around quickly for more rioters, and she shook her head.

"They're saying this was a Leveler riot, that there were Levelers leading it, and Nico's name is being mentioned."

"What?"

"One of the points from Hearts swears he was here, leading the riot." Sohier glanced over her shoulder. "And their adjunct seems inclined to listen."

"We didn't get here until after the fighting started," Eslingen said.

"Did anyone see you?"

"I doubt it." Eslingen scowled. "As I said, the fighting was well underway before we got here—that's why we never got further than the gates."

"I believe you," Sohier said, but she looked worried. "I'm just not sure the adjunct will. Is he all right?"

"He took a nasty blow to the head," Eslingen said. "He needs to be home in bed, not—are you saying Hearts wants to call a point?"

Sohier had the grace to look ashamed. "They're sounding that way."

"I won't have it," Eslingen said.

"I can't stop them," Sohier said. "I haven't the rank, and this is their territory."

"They'll seriously toss him in the cells with the rest of this lot?"

"Probably not with them," Sohier began, and shook her head. "I don't like it, either."

"He needs to be under a doctor's care."

"They'll call one to him, especially if you pay. Though you might not want to be seen, they might want to call a point on you as well—"

"Not going to happen," Eslingen said. He looked past her at the points, still milling around trying to get the last of the rioters under control. They were all focused on the main house and the alley that led to the back gardens; the side doors of the theater were open again, actors hovering there and at the windows, and he jerked his head in their direction. "Help me get him up. Nico, you're going to have to walk."

Rathe mumbled something that sounded like agreement. Sohier gave them both a doubtful look, but helped Eslingen draw his leman to his feet. "Are you sure he's all right?"

"He won't be any better for spending a night in the cells," Eslingen answered, and Sohier grimaced. She moved to Rathe's other side, taking part of his weight, and together they moved slowly toward the theater. Rathe's eyes were closed again, his feet slurring in the dirt, and Eslingen caught him around the waist. "Come on—"

"Wait, who's this?" That was one of the points from Hearts, barely out of apprenticeship by the look of him, and Eslingen prayed he didn't follow the broadsheets.

"I don't know. One of the actors, I think. He's hurt—"

Someone shouted behind them, and the journeyman looked away. "Go on then."

Eslingen hauled at Rathe's unresponsive body, trying to hurry without hurting him further. On Rathe's other side, Sohier had tucked her truncheon back under her skirts and was keeping her head down, doing her best not to draw attention. Then at last they were at the stairs, and Eslingen braced himself to drag Rathe up and into the hall. The actors gave way, and from somewhere in the shadows Gasquine said, "Philip? What's going on?"

"No time," Eslingen said. He looked at Sohier. "You go, you don't want to get any more involved in this."

"What are you going to do?" Sohier let him take Rathe's full weight, and drew her truncheon again.

"Keep anyone from calling a point tonight," Eslingen said. *Or ever*—but that didn't need to be said right now. "After that, we'll see." She nodded and turned away, and Eslingen looked at Gasquine. "Matthie, if you love me, find Aconin."

"And there's words rarely spoken." Gasquine nodded to a woman at her side, then beckoned them further into the hall. "Backstage. That's the safest place."

"I can't carry you," Eslingen said, in Rathe's ear. "Nico, you need to walk." For a moment, he thought Rathe was past hearing, but then he felt the other man straighten, taking some of his own weight again. "Good man. This way."

The actors fell back, letting him half carry Rathe deeper into the theater. Behind him, he thought he heard Jhirassi say, "Lock the door, and don't let anyone in."

That would buy time, and a part of Eslingen was grateful, but mostly he was focused on getting Rathe to put one foot in front of the other. Rathe's eyes were mostly closed, his head lolling against Eslingen's shoulder, and Eslingen said, "Don't sleep. You can't sleep, Nico, you have to walk—"

"You wanted me?" That was Aconin, emerging from one of the dressing rooms. He stopped, eyes widening as he took in the scene, and Gasquine answered quickly.

"Yes."

"I need a low-flyer," Eslingen said. "Quick and quiet as we can."

"Rathe's hurt?" Aconin shook his head. "No, I see. He needs a doctor, Philip."

"Which he won't get if we stay and they call a point," Eslingen said. "I need your help, Chresta."

Aconin stared, and for a moment Eslingen thought he was going to refuse. Then the playwright shook himself, and gestured toward a narrow corridor. "Down there—it's a servants' entrance. I'll fetch a low-flyer."

"Chresta," Gasquine began, but Aconin had vanished through another of the painted doors. She looked at Eslingen, worry writ plain on her face, and Eslingen forced a smile.

"I've known him a long time, Matthie. And if he doesn't help, he knows I'll kill him."

She smiled then, and Eslingen turned Rathe toward the servants' corridor. They had gone perhaps a dozen steps when he heard Rathe make a sound that was almost laughter.

"She doesn't know you mean it…" His voice was barely a whisper, but that was an improvement.

"Chresta does," Eslingen said, and kept them moving.

The corridor was barely lit, the widely-spaced mage-lights turned so low that all color was drained from the walls and the narrow strip of carpet. There were half a dozen doors at irregular intervals, but when he tried the first one, it was locked. The second opened onto a tiny room crammed with bits of furniture and costume fabrics, and he abandoned the attempt. He would have to trust Aconin, as unnerving as that thought was. *And if he does betray us, I will kill him*: Rathe would not approve, but the playwright would have earned it.

They reached the end of the hall. The door there was barred, and Eslingen leaned Rathe against the wall, hoping he could stay upright. "Wait here, I have to get the door."

Rathe made a noise that sounded like agreement, and Eslingen hoisted the heavy bar out of its brackets. It took him a moment to figure out the double lock, but to his relief it didn't require a key from this side. He cracked the door an inch or so, peering out into the fast-falling night, and saw only an empty alleyway. There were no shouts, no noises to suggest that the points from Hearts had found this exit, and he risked opening it far enough to step outside.

A shadow moved across the end of the alley, and he straightened, swearing, then recognized Aconin. The playwright saw him and beckoned wildly. "This way!"

Eslingen lifted a hand in answer, and ducked back inside. "Come on, Nico, our ride's waiting." Rathe mumbled something, but Eslingen got one of Rathe's arms over his shoulder and his own arm around Rathe's waist. "This way—"

They staggered down the alley, and to Eslingen's relief there was indeed a low-flyer waiting. The driver looked down from her box, her scowl deepening, and Aconin said hastily, "My friend's had a bit to drink—"

"And the sooner he's home, the better," Eslingen said, with his best smile.

The driver made a skeptical noise, but didn't whip up her horse and drive away. "Where to, then?"

"Dreams," Eslingen said. He wasn't sure exactly where in Dreams, or if he dared bring Rathe to the station there, but it was at least safer on that side of the river.

"The Demean Baths," Aconin said. "We can sober him up there."

The driver snorted again. Eslingen wrenched open the carriage door and Aconin climbed in, then reached back to drag Rathe into the compartment.

"The Baths?" the driver asked, and Eslingen nodded, swinging himself up after the others.

"Yes. That was a good idea."

"I thought so," Aconin said sweetly, and the low-flyer lurched into motion.

RATHE RESTED HIS head against Eslingen's shoulder, a light flashing at the edge of his vision in time with the throbbing pain. They were in a low-flyer, he could feel and smell it, and as the vehicle lurched again he swallowed hard against the taste of copper in his throat.

"Don't sleep," Eslingen murmured, and Rathe grimaced.

"I'm not." He wanted to say he was all right, but he couldn't manage to speak with conviction. "Where are we going?"

"The Demean Baths," another too-familiar voice said.

Rathe couldn't hide his scowl. "Aconin?"

"He's helping us," Eslingen said, his tone a warning.

"Helping?"

"We need to get you to a doctor," Eslingen said. "You've had a nasty blow to the head."

"I knew that." Rathe tried to straighten, but lights flashed across his vision, and he sank back against Eslingen, swearing silently. "What happened?"

"There was a riot at the Lilies," Eslingen said.

"I remember that." They'd come into the courtyard with the fight already in full swing, and then there were people behind them—had they come to join the riot? Did they attack? His memories wavered like glass seen through the furnace's heat. "Where was Hearts?"

"They put it down," Aconin said. "With their usual efficiency."

There was something in his voice that didn't ring right, and Rathe tried again to straighten.

"Stay still," Eslingen said. "I'll give you all the details once we get there."

"Get where?" Rathe knew he'd been told, but the name slipped away, dissolving into darkness.

"The Demean Baths," Aconin said again. "Pay attention, Nico, honestly."

"Chresta." Eslingen's voice was a warning, and Rathe saw the playwright shift uneasily.

"Sorry."

"What did Hearts say?" Rathe frowned, struggling to remember. They had come into the courtyard, into the fighting, but he hadn't seen anyone from Hearts, just the actors and bully-men presumably in the Lilies' pay. Or had he? Had some of them held truncheons?

"I'll tell you when we get there," Eslingen said again.

The low-flyer tipped sideways and then back, wheels jolting on stone rather than cobbles: the approach to the Hopes-point Bridge, Rathe guessed, but didn't dare turn his head for fear he'd be sick or fall into a faint. He might have fainted before, he couldn't remember. Certainly there were gaps in what he knew—and why they were going to the baths instead of the station at Hearts was beyond him. Unless—Eslingen had mentioned a doctor? But there would be no doctors at the baths...

He came to himself, uncomfortably aware that time had slipped again. The low-flyer was crossing cobbles now, and even as he registered that, it turned onto a side road, wheels settling into well-used ruts. It slowed, the driver reaching back to brush aside the curtain that separated the body of the low-flyer from the driver's seat.

"Are you sure this is where you want me to leave you? You're right on the edge of the Court."

"It's fine," Aconin said, too cheerfully, and Eslingen shifted his hold on Rathe's shoulders.

"Come on, Nico, we're here."

It took both of them to get him down out of the low-flyer, and he leaned hard against the nearest wall, fighting down nausea, while Eslingen paid off the driver and then came back. "You'd better know what you're doing, Chresta."

"You trusted me this far."

"I didn't have much choice."

Rathe pulled himself upright, still clinging to the wall, and Eslingen moved quickly to take his weight.

"Do you think you can walk a little? Chresta swears it's not far."

"Where are we going?" Rathe asked.

"Somewhere safe," Eslingen said. "Somewhere you can lie down and we can get a doctor for you."

"But we probably shouldn't hang about," Aconin said. "The driver's right, we're right by the Court here."

The Court of the Thirty-Two Knives, Rathe knew. Aconin lodged there, or at least on its borders, but why they would be going there…

"Up you get," Eslingen said, and Rathe managed to take a step without stumbling. "There, that's right—"

It took all his concentration to stay upright, even with Eslingen's support, and his feet felt numb and graceless on the rutted street. His vision blurred and faded, the shadows deepening to full night even though he knew the winter-sun should be shining, and then he stubbed his toe against a wooden step. He looked up, blinking, found himself at the bottom of a flight of stairs that looked vaguely familiar, and in the same moment, Aconin said, "You'll have to carry him."

"I can walk," Rathe said, and managed to take two steps before he lost his balance. Eslingen caught him, bracing him against the wall of the building.

"Go ahead of us, get the door open," he said. "Then—will you go for a doctor, or is there someone you can send?"

Aconin didn't answer, already starting up the stairs. Rathe suppressed a groan, and managed another step, and then another. It was as if he was on an endless treadmill, step after step without an end, and then quite suddenly he was at the top and a door opened ahead of him. Aconin had lit a lamp and a branch of candles, and was motioning to a battered divan.

"Set him here."

Rathe let himself be lowered to the thin pillows, grateful to no longer have to hold himself upright. The world revolved slowly around him, and he couldn't seem to focus; the flashing lights were back, beating in time with the throbbing pain at the back of his skull. He raised a hand to touch it, and a stab of pain shot from the nape of his neck to his toes.

"A doctor," Eslingen said again, and Aconin straightened from lighting a second branch of candles.

"I can fetch one, but do you think that's wise?"

"He needs to be looked at."

"Do you want everyone to know where you are?"

"There must be someone in the Court who'll keep her mouth shut," Eslingen said.

"Not so many that I'd trust," Aconin answered. "Well. Maybe—she's an alchemist by training, and an apothecary, but she knows her business. She doesn't love the points, though, and that's a double-edged sword."

"Nico has a reputation—"

"And don't I know it." Aconin sighed. "She'll come, I think. Probably. Or at least she'll send me with something for him, though if she goes that route, I wouldn't swear you could trust her."

"Just bring her," Eslingen said, and Aconin sighed again.

"All right, I'm going. Bar the door."

"I wouldn't have it any other way," Eslingen said.

Rathe heard the door open and close, and then the solid thump of the heavy bar slotting into place. He managed to look up as Eslingen came to kneel beside him, looking worried.

"You heard, Aconin's gone for a physician."

Rathe knew better than to nod. "Yes." He could almost bring the woman's name to mind, knew he should know her, but the words eluded him. "Why are we here? We ought to be at Hearts."

"Hearts wanted to call a point on you," Eslingen said.

"What?"

"Sohier said there were Levelers there, and one of the adjuncts from Hearts was swearing you were in their lead." Eslingen's face was grim. "You were in no condition to argue, so I brought you out of there."

"It wouldn't stand," Rathe said. Eslingen looked confused, and Rathe went on. "The point, I mean. We should have answered it."

"Sohier thought it would stand," Eslingen said. "She said you'd be in the cells at least overnight, and I wanted you in a proper bed under a doctor's care." He paused. "There was something wrong about that fight anyway."

"What do you mean?"

"Why would Levelers go after a resort-house?"

"Noble women frequent them," Rathe said.

"All right, but not that early in the evening," Eslingen answered. "If they'd been after Aconin, now, that would have made more sense—d'Alamenon's people are still after him, when they think they can get away with it. And I thought I saw some of her knives in the crowd."

Rathe frowned, trying to summon up memories, but could manage only chaotic fragments, movement and noise and color that made no real sense. "Trijn would have backed me. Bailed me, if need be."

"I daresay." Eslingen sat back on his heels. "Look, Nico, the man from Hearts was willing to lie about you—probably fee'd to lie about you, if it comes to that—"

"And we'd have proved it was a lie," Rathe said.

"If he was paid to lie about you, there's no knowing what else he or anyone else might be paid to do," Eslingen said. "I wasn't—I'm not willing to take that chance."

"They—whoever 'they' are—they can't have bought the entire station," Rathe said.

"The carts," Eslingen said.

"Smuggling's not murder," Rathe said, "and it's flat murder you're talking about."

"There's something very wrong here," Eslingen said stubbornly. "This riot—why did it happen? And we were followed and the men following us attacked as soon as we were in the Lilies' courtyard. None of that makes sense except to get rid of us—of you in particular."

Rathe shook his head, and hunched his shoulders against the pain. "This riot is more of Aconin's poisoned pen. And I can't believe you brought us here, to his lodgings. The rest—Philip, we don't know anything that would provoke an attack. You should have let me stand the point."

"That I'll never do."

"Then how can you say you serve the law?"

There was a long silence, and then at last Eslingen shook his head. "I can and I do. But not when the law's being twisted against an innocent man."

"Even then," Rathe said. "I can take my chances better than most."

Eslingen's voice was heavy. "I did what I thought was right."

"You were wrong." Rathe leaned back against the cushions of the divan, his head throbbing.

Eslingen didn't answer, still kneeling on the floor beside the divan. Rathe closed his eyes to shut out the room's slow spin. You had to follow the law, even when it was against you, otherwise you had no standing, no right to challenge it. He'd learned that early on. A part of him was treacherously grateful to be here in Aconin's rooms, in the quiet dark with Eslingen at his side, but he pushed that sternly aside. His comfort didn't matter; what mattered was finding the truth, and if that meant standing the point, he would do so.

He drifted off then, roused sometime later to the sounds of movement and Eslingen saying his name, and opened his eyes to a new and painful light. He blinked hard, and it moved away, revealing a middle-aged woman in a drover's coat, hennaed hair tucked untidily under a dark cap. She looked vaguely familiar, but her name was lost somewhere in the swirling clouds that filled his mind.

"Both eyes move and react," she said, and behind her Eslingen looked momentarily relieved. "Can you lean forward for me?"

Rathe fumbled with the pillows, managed to tilt himself forward. He bent his head, wincing, and she prodded gently at the swelling and then at the bone around it. Rathe caught his breath, pain jolting through him, and she pressed again, frowning, before she had him sit back again.

"Have you got that water hot yet, Chresta?"

"Almost boiling," Aconin answered, and she nodded.

"When it boils, make a tea with this." She produced a small bag and Aconin took it warily. "You should take a small glass of the decoction four times a day—in the morning, then with your meals, and then again before bed. It'll help your wits settle again. Your skull's not broken, at least not that I can see, and I don't see any signs that you're bleeding within the skull. But that was a nasty hit, and you need to rest and let yourself recover."

"I can't," Rathe began, and the attempt to move made the room spin badly enough that he sank back against the pillows again, closing his eyes.

"You don't have much choice," the apothecary said briskly. "You won't be walking straight for a day or three, maybe more. You need to lie down, rest, sleep when you can—"

"We were always taught to keep a head injury waking," Eslingen said.

"Until someone could see to them," the apothecary said, "and I've seen him. He's a lucky man, it's knocked the sense out of him and upset his wits and his balance, but those will both heal. Take the decoction I've made, and if he's still in pain tomorrow, you can give him willowbark. But not before then, just in case he's bleeding. Here, sit forward again."

Rathe did his best to obey, and Eslingen moved quickly to support him. The apothecary snapped her fingers at Aconin. "Water, please, and a cloth if you have it."

To Rathe's surprise, Aconin did as he was told, bringing a basin and a reasonably clean-looking towel. The apothecary set the basin on the floor at her feet and began carefully to wash the area around the wound. Her touch set off more flashing lights, and Rathe bit his lip, leaning hard against Eslingen's shoulder. The apothecary gave him a sharp look.

"What are you feeling?"

"That hurts. And I see lights."

Her hands stilled. "Flashes of light?"

"Yes."

"But otherwise your vision's good?"

Rathe lifted his head, peering blearily past Eslingen's arm. "Yes."

"No blind spots, double vision, shapes that won't stay still?"

"No." Rathe paused. "You asked me this before."

"Yes, but I'm surprised you remember." The apothecary motioned for him to lean forward again, and began dabbing at his scalp, more gently this time. "You'll be vague about a lot of things, from a bit before you were hit to a day or so after. The more you rest, the more chance you have of remembering, or at least of not forgetting anything more."

"Especially if you're not doing anything to remember," Eslingen said.

Aconin brought over a small cup of the tea. The apothecary sent him back to pour out half of it, then looked at Eslingen. "You see how much to give him?"

"I do," Eslingen said, and steadied the cup. Rathe managed to swallow the bitter mixture, though there was a bad moment when he thought it would come back up, and the apothecary pushed herself to her feet.

"Put him to bed, and keep him there for a day or two. Not too much light, and keep him still. Keep giving him the decoction, and he can have willowbark after dawn tomorrow. No spirits, though."

"That'll be for me," Aconin said, and she rolled her eyes.

"You owe me, Chresta. And I don't just mean in coin."

"Let me get him settled," Eslingen said, "and I'll see to that."

Rathe let himself be pulled upright, managed to stumble into the narrow room that held Aconin's bed and not much more. Eslingen lowered him onto the mattress and deftly removed shoes and stockings, then tucked a blanket around him. It was good to lie down, after so much pain and effort; the apothecary's drink was soothing after all. He closed his eyes, meaning only to rest for a moment, and fell into darkness.

SEVEN

Eslingen paid the apothecary's fee without argument: she clearly knew what she was doing, and Rathe was already better for the dose she had given him. She listed the reasons to send for her—*if he can't wake fully, if his vision goes blurry, if his speech slurs or he stops making sense*—and then Aconin let her back out into the night. Eslingen glanced into the bedroom again, saw that Rathe was sleeping, curled on his side to protect his sore head, and lowered himself onto the divan.

"Here." Aconin held out a small glass near filled with an amber liquid, then pulled a chair around so that they sat facing each other. "I told her I'd keep the brandy for us."

Eslingen accepted the glass and downed half of it in a gulp. It was better than he'd expected, and he sipped more carefully the next time, saying, "Can we trust her?"

"Not to give you up to the points?" Aconin cocked his head to one side. "She doesn't have much dealing with the law, so I'd say it's not likely she'd talk."

"She seemed to know what she was doing."

"The knives all rely on her," Aconin said. "She's seen most things that can happen in a fight."

"What in Seidos's name was that all about, anyway?" Eslingen finished his glass, and started to set it aside but Aconin flourished the bottle in his direction, and he allowed the playwright to refill it.

"I wish I knew. The whole mob came boiling around the corner, they practically flattened that poor fish of a gatekeeper, and then some of them came for us and the rest of them started shouting the old Leveler slogans. Can you believe it? They picked the wrong house for that, anyway."

Aconin's indignation looked believable enough, and Eslingen sighed. "What do you mean, the wrong house?"

"Oh, Bonamy has a reputation for holding Leveler views—almost as much of one as our Nico, come to think of it." Aconin topped up his own glass. "Not that you'd know it from his clientele, they're all twelve-quarter nobles from the Ile'Nord these days."

"Nico said there was a rumor that he was involved with the Broadsheet Poet some years back."

"That was before my time," Aconin said. "Do the points think she's back? These broadsheets don't strike me as her work, at least not what gets quoted."

"No?"

Aconin shrugged. "Not that I've seen all of it, of course—as I said, I wasn't here then. But people still talk, and one or two of her sheets circulate privately. She was—I'd call it more specific and angrier than the current broadsheets. They're blunt instruments: burn it all down, and not much more."

Eslingen considered that, sipping his brandy carefully. He'd trust Aconin's literary assessment, though he wasn't sure what difference it would make. The broadsheets were still proposing bloody riot, even if they were written by different women. "So some of the mob came after you? You personally, or the actors in general? Did you recognize any of them?"

"They tried to rush the theater door," Aconin said. "I admit, I took it personally but that mayn't have been justified. And, no, I didn't recognize any of d'Alamenon's people. If I had, believe me, I would say so."

Eslingen didn't doubt it. He leaned back against the divan's cushions, feeling his own bruises for the first time, and wondered what Rathe would say when he found out Eslingen had killed one of their attackers. *Nothing good*, he thought, and Aconin said, more soberly, "What now? Is Hearts serious about calling a point on Nico?"

"Sohier thought they were," Eslingen answered. "But who knows, they may have thought better by morning. And in the meantime, Nico needs to rest."

"Well, it's the only way I'll ever get him in my bed." Aconin sighed. "Don't look like that, you know I'm not serious. And yes, he can stay—you both can stay—at least until you think of something better."

"Thank you." Eslingen blinked at his empty glass, but shook his head when Aconin would have refilled it. "No, I'd better check on Nico and then get some rest."

Rathe seemed to be sleeping normally when Eslingen opened the bedroom door. He stood for a moment in the dark, listening to Rathe's breathing—steady, with none of the rasping that you sometimes heard after a blow to the head—and accepted a bundle of pillows and blankets from Aconin.

"Because I know you'll want to stay with him," the playwright said softly, "and I would be more comfortable on the divan."

He closed the door before Eslingen could thank him again. Eslingen stood for a moment, letting his eyes adjust to the dark—there was a single window, shuttered against the night, a dim outline to his right—then made himself a pallet at the foot of the bed. Time enough in the morning to deal with whatever else would come.

He woke a little after the first sunrise to hear Rathe shifting uncomfortably in the bed. He rose quickly, and touched Rathe's shoulder, gently at first, then with more force. Rathe gasped and woke, opening his eyes to look around with confusion. "Where..."

"We're staying with Aconin," Eslingen said, and Rathe's frown deepened.

"Why—oh. There was a riot. My head hurts."

"Someone hit you," Eslingen said.

"Yes." Rathe sounded vague, but then his expression sharpened. "Did you tell me Hearts wanted to call a point on me?"

Eslingen nodded. "Sohier said their adjunct said you were leading a pack of Levelers."

"Why would they—" Rathe started to shake his head, and winced. "I'll need to talk to them."

"When you're allowed out of bed," Eslingen said. "The doctor left a drink for you, I'll fetch a dose." He slipped out into the outer room before Rathe could answer, and found Aconin stirring up the fire on the stove. The apothecary's brew was already warming; Eslingen waited until it was hot, then carried the cup back into the bedroom and held Rathe upright until he'd drunk it all. The effort seemed to exhaust him, and Eslingen settled him back among the pillows, watching uneasily until he was sure the other man was asleep. He retreated to the outer room, hoping for a breakfast of his own, and accepted toast and a few slivers of strong cheese.

"I've willowbark if you want it," Aconin said. "And there's honey, too."

"If he needs it later." Eslingen huddled close to the stove, grateful for its warmth while he tried to work out what to do. He needed to talk to Sohier, that was certain, find out what she knew; there was still a chance that the adjunct at Hearts had simply been mistaken, and everything could be resolved easily. And if not… he'd need to warn Coindarel, explain why he'd disappeared, though that would have to be handled carefully, given the dead man he'd left behind.

Aconin said, "I could take a note for you. Since I assume you'll want to talk to people."

Eslingen hesitated. "No offense, Chresta, but I'd rather nobody thought of you in connection with Nico." *Or me, for that matter*—but that seemed unnecessarily hostile.

Aconin rolled his eyes. "Oh, yes, of course I was going to walk in the door of Dreams—or Hearts—and say, hello, I've a message from Nico Rathe. I thought more that I'd go to the theater, I need to do that anyway, and find a runner to take a note to whoever you thought would be best."

"That's not a bad idea," Eslingen said, "but perhaps not today? I don't want to have to move Nico if anything goes wrong."

"Also not unreasonable," Aconin said. "I do need to show myself, though— and refill my larder, if you could spare a few demmings."

Eslingen rummaged in his purse and came up with a few coins. "Also, any news—"

"Of course," Aconin said, and Eslingen tried to pretend a confidence he didn't feel.

Aconin left shortly after the neighborhood clock struck nine, and Eslingen returned to the bedroom to sit with Rathe. The pointsman was restless, but not fully awake; Eslingen felt the skin of his forehead, and managed to rouse him enough to take a dose of the willowbark. That seemed to settle him, but he drifted in and out of sleep for the rest of the day. Eslingen woke him at noon to take another dose of the apothecary's remedy, but couldn't persuade him to eat. He wouldn't starve in a day, he told himself, and wished he'd thought to ask Aconin to buy broth somewhere.

Aconin returned in the evening with a basket of supplies that included a small jug of beef tea. Eslingen managed to get Rathe to swallow a few mouthfuls, but he tired quickly, and Eslingen tucked him back into the pillows. He seemed in less pain, just drowsy, and when questioned denied any vision problems or ringing in his ears. The cut on his head was no longer bleeding, though his scalp was still swollen and bruised: all good signs, Eslingen knew, but it was still hard to leave him even long enough to snatch a meal for himself.

The riot, Aconin said, was the talk of Dreams, with most of the theater folk speculating merrily about what had set it off. Everyone had heard the rumor that the Levelers were involved, and that a pointsman had been their leader, and nearly everyone was able to connect that with Rathe. He was sought after, though it wasn't clear whether there was an actual point called yet; Hearts was also asking after Eslingen, and the Guard was reported to be gravely displeased. Sohier had been recalled from Hearts and was restricted to Dreams in disgrace, and Trijn was said to be in a particularly filthy temper. A few people said the Surintendant himself had been seen in Dreams, but that, Aconin said, could not be confirmed. None of it was good news, Eslingen thought, but his attention was on Rathe.

The second night was worse than the first, with Rathe wakeful and complaining of pain behind his eyes. Eslingen sat up with him, feeding him more willowbark and wondering if he should send for the apothecary again. If she hadn't lived in the Court itself, he would probably have gone himself, but he didn't dare risk the streets, and by morning Rathe was better again. The swelling had gone down, and the apothecary's decoction seemed to help; at noon he was able to persuade Rathe to drink a cup of the beef tea, and that night he ate a little bread before saying he felt sick. Eslingen had seen head injuries before, and knew this was good progress, but there was still a part of him that scrutinized every movement for signs of disaster.

The next morning was better, though Rathe still had a worrisome tendency to forget things he'd been told. Aconin reported that Sohier was still under watch at Dreams, and Eslingen reluctantly put aside the idea of talking to her. He needed desperately to know what the points were doing about Rathe, but there was no way they could meet safely. A written message would be worse, left hard evidence, and he mulled over the problem as he tended to Rathe through the course of the long day. It seemed increasingly likely that his best option was to go to Coindarel, but Eslingen found himself hesitating. It wasn't that he didn't trust the Prince-Marshal; he knew Coindarel would protect him, if pressed, and he was sure Estradere would press him. Instead, he had to admit that he didn't want to leave Rathe alone. At least not yet, not until Rathe could stand without help, and remember in the afternoon what he'd been told in the morning. Eslingen still wasn't sure how well Rathe understood what had happened, and he was hesitant to try to explain until he was sure Rathe could follow him. And until he was sure Rathe wouldn't insist on turning himself in: he didn't trust the people at Hearts, and he wasn't going to see Rathe locked up in their cells if he could prevent it.

He was still mulling over the question when he brought Rathe his evening meal, and was aware, abruptly, of Rathe's sharp gaze.

"We're in the Court," he said.

Eslingen nodded warily. "These are Aconin's rooms." He'd said that at least three times a day since Rathe had been hurt, but so far it hadn't seemed to stick.

"Yes." Rathe sipped carefully at the beef tea. His hands were steady today, Eslingen noted; this was the last of the beef tea, but with a little luck Rathe would be able to eat solid food tomorrow. "If there's trouble—Mikael knows me. You can always ask for him. There's a place called Acke's"

Mikael was the aging knife who dominated the fraternity of fighters-for-hire who made the Court their base. Eslingen nodded again. "All right."

"Hopefully there's no need." Rathe frowned at his cup as though wondering what it was, then drank some more. "Hearts called a point?"

"They wanted to," Eslingen said. "I brought you away before they could find you."

There was a long silence, Rathe still frowning slightly. "I'll have to talk to them sometime."

"Not until you're better," Eslingen said.

RATHE WOKE TO the sound of a neighborhood clock striking seven, lay for a moment frowning at unfamiliar bed curtains and badly plastered walls before he remembered where he was. These were Aconin's rooms, and there had been a riot in Hearts… He still couldn't remember much of that beyond a blur of movement and shouting, though now that he considered it, he thought he remembered someone shouting an old Leveler slogan. That might explain why Hearts wanted to blame him—or had Eslingen told him that already? He frowned, the headache beginning to throb again behind his eye. He shifted cautiously, trying to find a better position among the lumpy pillows, and instantly Eslingen was beside him.

"Nico? Do you need anything?"

"I'm all right," Rathe said, and tried to push himself into a sitting position. Eslingen grabbed a pillow, swept it into place to support him and Rathe managed a crooked smile. "You're not bad at this."

"I've had some practice," Eslingen answered. "Do you want the pot? Something to drink?"

"Yes." He managed to get to his feet with only minimal help, Eslingen doing his best not to hover. When he'd finished, Eslingen turned toward the bed, but Rathe shook his head. "Let me sit up for a bit, I've been lying down too long."

Eslingen hesitated, then nodded, easing Rathe into the room's single chair. "I'll fetch your medicine. And some bread?"

Rathe wasn't particularly hungry, but he knew he needed to eat. "Yes, all right." He managed to swallow the thick tea without gagging, and was grateful for the bread and butter to take the taste away. Eslingen offered a second slice, but Rathe shook his head, wincing as the movement set his head aching again. "Maybe later."

"Willowbark?"

Rathe hesitated, but there was no reason to refuse. "Please."

Eslingen brought a small cup with the bitter liquid as well as a slice of bread for himself. Rathe swallowed the willowbark with a grimace—all the honey in the world couldn't sweeten it—and Eslingen settled himself on the end of the bed.

"Where's Aconin?"

"Gone out somewhere," Eslingen answered. "He's still got work to do on that damned review—no, they're not canceling it, despite the riot."

"What does Hearts have to say about that?"

"I've no idea."

Rathe grimaced. "No, of course you don't. And—I think you told me Sohier's in disgrace?"

"Confined to Dreams, last I heard," Eslingen answered. "I'd like to have a word with her, but I haven't dared get too close."

"No one wants to call a point on you," Rathe said. "Do they?"

"Not that I know of," Eslingen said, patiently, "but they know I got you away."

Of course they did. Rathe started to shake his head again, annoyed by his own stupidity, and thought better of it. "We can't stay here."

"No." Eslingen hesitated. "I thought I might try to get a word with Estradere, he should have some idea what's going on."

"Not a bad idea." He was starting to feel light-headed again, sweat prickling on his brow.

Eslingen said, "I thought I might try this afternoon, since you're doing better. Once Aconin gets back."

"Yes." Rathe closed his eyes, and heard Eslingen heave himself to his feet.

"Back to bed with you. The medicine will make you drowsy."

That had better be all it is, Rathe thought, but let himself be settled back into the grubby sheets. He would just rest a little, he thought, and fell into a dreamless sleep.

When he woke again, the shutters were open, letting in a chill breeze and a bar of watery sunlight, and Eslingen was waiting with another dose of the apothecary's brew. Rathe swallowed it, and was relieved to find that it didn't make him sleepy this time. In fact, he was hungry, and Eslingen was more than happy to bring him a slice of a cheese and onion tart. To his surprise, he felt better for having eaten, and sat up carefully, propping himself up against the bedstead. "You said they accused me of leading the Levelers—was that right?"

"That's what Sohier said."

"That doesn't make sense."

"You have a reputation," Eslingen began, and Rathe waved his hand.

"No, that's not what I meant. We weren't—we were behind them, we never made it to the steps, did we?"

"We did not," Eslingen said. "But if their adjunct is willing to lie and say you did—well, he must also have witnesses lined up to lie for him. And I'm wondering why. It's not like we've found out anything."

"Presumably someone thinks we have," Rathe said.

"I wish I knew what it was," Eslingen muttered. He glanced toward the door. "That's Chresta. I told you, I want to try to talk to Estradere—"

"Go," Rathe said. Eslingen gave him a wry smile, and disappeared.

Left to himself, Rathe settled himself more comfortably on the pillows, trying to make sense of what had happened. From what Eslingen had said, it didn't seem likely that it was a mistake, or at least not an honest one: he might have a reputation for Leveler tendencies, but no one had ever heard him support this kind of riot. And in any case, there had to be dozens of witnesses who could swear that he'd been struck down before he got anywhere near the Lilies' door. Even if Hearts was well fee'd, it would be hard to keep him locked up for very long.

It had to be something to do with the carts. Hearts was clearly being fee'd to look the other way while the cargo was smuggled into the city, and if it was gunpowder, that meant something serious was being planned. If Eslingen was right, and the Ile'Nord nobles were planning a private war, that was dangerous enough. And if they were intending something else… This wedding brought nearly every important noble into the city—more than that, it brought every possible claimant to the throne into close proximity. It was generally acknowledged that the Metropolitan of Astreiant would be the queen's heir, but after her… Rathe frowned, trying to work out the line of succession. The Palatineur de Galhac would be the next most likely candidate, except that he was a man; that was presumably one of the reasons that the queen was marrying her great-nephew to the daughter. After them would be the rest of the de Galhac family, a healthy pack of cousins and cross-cousins, and then… After that, it was a tangle, half a dozen women whose families could claim kinship with the royal line, and who were themselves competent enough to be plausible candidates. Most of them had gone quiet once the queen had made her preference clear, but the wedding seemed to have stirred things up again.

He heard Aconin moving in the other room, and then a knock at the door. He sat up, looking automatically for a place to hide—under the bed, there were no other options in the narrow space—and made himself relax. He could hear voices, Aconin's and then a lighter treble, someone's runner paid to carry messages, and the door closed again. He heard the snap of the bolt shooting home, and then the thud of the bar going into place as well. A moment later, the bedroom door opened.

"Trouble?"

"Would you expect anything less?" Aconin asked.

"Chresta…"

"Hearts wants you badly," Aconin said. "They've gotten the Surintendant to allow them to search in Dreams, and now that they didn't find you, they're starting to cast their net among your friends. Among whom they apparently count me. That was a warning from Mirremay: she hasn't agreed to let Hearts search yet, but she may have to."

Mirremay was the head of the not-quite-equal station at Point of Knives. She had no particular reason to like him, not after he'd prevented her from getting her hands on a chest of stolen gold, and Rathe took a careful breath. "Did she say how long?"

"She did not. Which to my mind means you—we—should start thinking of somewhere else for you to go." Aconin paused. "Assuming you're well enough to move?"

"I'll have to be," Rathe said, grimly, and dragged himself into a sitting position.

ESLINGEN CROSSED THE Sier by way of the Queen's Bridge, crossing the square where the gallows stood empty. He had left his hair down, and borrowed an ill-fitting coat from Aconin, and with that and the wooden-soled clogs he looked like a dock-worker on holiday. Even so, he kept an eye out in case he was being followed, but so far he'd seen no sign of it. Or else they were better at it than he had reason to expect, but he put that thought aside.

He took the long way to the Guard's barracks, skirting the edges of the New Fair and then taking the back roads through Manufactory Point, and finally fetched up at the stable gate. The alley was empty, the rutted mud stiff underfoot, and he cautiously tested the latch. It was locked, as it should be, but as he started to turn away, the door swung open, and Martine Faraut looked out. She had a slop bucket in her hand, and Eslingen took an instinctive step back, but she stopped, seeing him.

"Captain. Coindarel's been looking for you."

"And I need to talk to him," Eslingen said.

Faraut nodded. "Inside." She emptied her bucket into the gutter and closed the gate behind them, glancing warily around the courtyard. Luckily it was the middle of the day; most people would be either on patrol or busy with exercises, and Eslingen was unsurprised when Faraut waved him toward the tack room. "Wait here, it'll be private."

Eslingen did as he was told, shutting the door behind him so that he was enclosed in a shadowed space that smelled strongly of leather and oil and brass polish. He fumbled for the lamp, but failed to find it, and instead cracked open one of the shutters, giving him a sliver of light and a narrow view of the courtyard. He watched Faraut replace her bucket and head whistling into the former merchant's house that now served as Coindarel's headquarters. After a while, Patric Estradere emerged, dressed for riding, and disappeared into the stable block. A few moments later, the tack room door swung open, and Estradere said softly, "Philip. We've been—concerned."

So have I, Eslingen thought. He said, "Rathe was hurt. I couldn't let them call the point, not the shape he was in."

"He's hurt?"

Eslingen nodded. "Struck in the head. He'll be all right, but it's knocked his wits astray."

"That's unfortunate," Estradere said. "Unless—but I assume it's shaken his memory?"

Eslingen nodded again. "I'm afraid so."

"It would have been useful to hear his testimony," Estradere said. "There are three men dead, and a lunar dozen injured."

Eslingen grimaced. One of those dead men was his, but he wasn't sure this was the time to admit to that. "Did we learn anything useful from any of them?"

"The dead men were all knives, and known to the points," Estradere said. "The injured are mostly from Bonamy's house, or among the actors, with a handful of hangers-on from the households of the visiting nobility. We've been hearing some very strange stories from them." Estradere perched on the edge of the harness chest. "What's all this about it being Levelers?"

"Sohier—she's one of Rathe's people at Dreams—she says the adjunct at Hearts said Rathe was leading a gang of Levelers to attack the Lilies. By all accounts the gang was shouting Leveler slogans, but I can't swear to that."

"He has a name for espousing Leveler views," Estradere said.

"He thinks the laws ought to apply equally to everyone," Eslingen said. "Which is not the same thing as wanting to murder the nobility."

"Granted," Estradere said. "And for what it's worth, I've seen no signs of sedition from him. But the women at Hearts are very insistent."

"Something isn't right in Hearts," Eslingen said. "Between d'Alamenon's people going after Aconin, and de Castiat arresting herself there, and the carts with gunpowder—and now this."

"They can't all be connected," Estradere said.

"If not, it's quite a coincidence," Eslingen said, and Estradere lifted a hand.

"A touch. All right. What do you want from us?"

"I need to know what the charges are against Rathe," Eslingen said. "And how serious they are about pressing them."

"Very," Estradere said. "Go on."

"Are they calling a point on me?"

"Not yet, but they are looking for you." Estradere paused. "The charges against Rathe include sedition. I gather that the chief point at Dreams has objected, and it's all being argued out before the Surintendant, but so far Hearts won't budge, and there doesn't seem to be much Fourie can do to stop her. Coindarel has not yet been asked to produce you, which is why I'm here instead of him."

So that Coindarel could swear with perfect honesty that he had neither seen or spoken to him. Eslingen nodded. "Can we shelter here? In the barracks?"

Estradere hesitated. "You could. But Rathe—he's not our man. If we refused to give him up, Hearts could—would—go straight to the Surintendant, and Fourie would have no choice but to back them. I'm sorry."

Eslingen could imagine that argument all too clearly, and winced at the thought of undoing everything they'd done to arrange things so that Guard and points could work side by side. Rathe would never forgive him. "No, I understand."

"We're arranging with the queen's court to start patrols in Hearts," Estradere said. "The chief at Hearts objects, of course, and Fourie is reluctant, but I think we can persuade him. I wish they weren't all related."

"Who?"

"De Galhac, d'Alamenon, de Castiat. They're all close cousins. Which is one more reason her self-arrest is so galling to the crown." Estradere slid off the harness box. "But that's another matter. We'll do what we can to protect you, Philip. I only wish it was more."

And I wish it included Rathe. Eslingen nodded reluctantly. "Then I can send for help if I need it?"

"And we will come," Estradere said, and reached into the pocket of his coat to bring out a well-filled purse. "Coindarel wants you to have this."

Eslingen accepted it, feeling the square shapes of at least half a dozen silver pillars through the thin leather. It was enough to keep him and Rathe sheltered and fed for weeks; more than that, it would buy them passage out of the city if they couldn't prove Rathe's innocence. That was obviously also Coindarel's intention, and he was both grateful and chilled by the realization that the Prince-Marshal thought it might come to that. "Thanks."

"I hope you don't need it," Estradere said, and let himself out of the tack room.

He made his way back across the Sier, wondering what their next move should be. Rathe still wanted to answer the point, though as he came back to himself he seemed more willing to accept that it wasn't a good idea. Maybe if they went to Trijn first, or, better still, to the Surintendant, one of them might be able to ensure that Rathe didn't end up locked in the cells at Hearts. But Trijn was equal in status to the chief at Hearts, and Fourie seemed determined not to do anyone any favors… And in any case, Rathe locked in the cells at Dreams was only marginally better: he would be safer there, but he'd still have no chance to disprove the point.

And now that Coindarel had made his position clear, Eslingen couldn't think of anyone else with enough influence who would be able to help. b'Estorr was only one Fellow among many at the University, and a Chadroni and a necromancer to boot; the actors at Dreams and his old colleagues among the Masters of Defense would be willing, but there was nothing they could do that would help. The cap'pontoise Euan Cambrai was Rathe's friend, and a good man, but there was no way that the case could be considered to fall under his jurisdiction. However… Eslingen paused, automatically scanning the square to be sure he wasn't being followed. Rathe counted one of the judge-advocates as patronne; that wasn't the highest rank among the judiciary, but she might be able to use her influence to keep Rathe out of the cells. He lengthened his stride, eager to put the idea to Rathe.

At the edge of Point of Knives he paused again, drawing a drink from the fountain that stood at the center of the narrow square and checking again for pursuit. It would be faster to cut directly through Knives, but that road dipped into the edges of the Court, and he'd been warned often enough of the dangers there. Another day, he might have taken the chance, but not with Rathe hurt. He shook the water from his hands and turned onto the street that curved north around the neighborhood's bathhouse.

The houses were taller here, most of them four stories, and the street itself narrowed, throwing everything into shadow. There were deeper shadows in the alleys that ran between the buildings: too convenient for an ambush, and he wished he was carrying a longer knife. But no one had followed him, and no one seemed to be watching, either from the alleys or the half-shuttered windows.

Then there was movement ahead, and he stopped abruptly, his hand going to his knife. A cloaked man stepped out of a doorway two houses ahead, not quite blocking the road. He was heavily dressed even for the weather, and the cloak hid any weapon. Eslingen drew breath, ready to challenge him, and a woman's voice came from behind him.

"Vaan Esling. So glad to have found you."

He spun to face her, stepping sideways in the same moment so that his back was to the nearest house, and saw the woman grin. She looked familiar, tall and heavily-built, graying hair pinned up under a flat cap and a crooked tooth that showed at the corner of her smile. She wore a plain russet skirt and bodice trimmed with bands of black braid, only that wasn't quite how he remembered her. And then he had it: the neat suit should be topped with a pointsman's jerkin. Chaudet, her name was, one of the adjuncts at Knives.

"Adjunct Point." He let his eyes slide sideways at the same moment, looking for an escape route. The alleys tended to end in locked gates or garden walls: not worth the risk. But he could dodge past her, cut back through the square, and head into the Court. There was at least a chance they wouldn't follow him there.

"I'm glad we found you." She lifted her hands, showing them empty. "No, there's no point called on you, and anyway I'm not on duty."

"And your friend?" Eslingen tipped his head toward the man, and was rewarded with another grin.

"No more is he. We're here—well, call it a favor."

"A bit of in good standing?" Eslingen couldn't keep the irony from his voice.

"If you like. Mirremay's being pushed to let Hearts search premises in her district, to which she strenuously objects."

"Understandable," Eslingen said, when it became clear Chaudet wasn't going to continue. "Do I know those premises?"

"Very likely. Aconin's a Leaguer himself, for all he acts like an Astreianter born and bred."

Eslingen swallowed a curse. "So he is."

"And not generally loved, I grant you," Chaudet said. "But he is one of ours, more or less. The thing is, Mirremay's not sure she can hold out. The Sur's making a decision, but it hasn't come through yet."

"That's useful to know," Eslingen said, dry-mouthed.

"Mirremay hoped you'd think so," Chaudet said.

"I won't forget it," Eslingen answered. Out of the corner of his eye, he saw the other pointsman melt back into the shadows, and took a steadying breath.

"Glad to hear it," Chaudet said. "And now, being as we're off duty—well, I'll wish you a good afternoon, vaan Esling."

She turned away without waiting for an answer. Eslingen watched her go, then started for Aconin's lodgings, hoping he could get there and find someplace else to go before Mirremay was forced to give in.

EIGHT

THERE WERE FEWER things to gather than Rathe had feared—mostly, of course, because they had arrived with the clothes on their backs and nothing else. Aconin found a flask to hold the rest of the apothecary's decoction, and a bag for the powdered willowbark, and packed them together with an uncut loaf of bread into a shabby basket. Rathe managed to pull on shoes and stockings, though bending over to fasten the laces left him sick and dizzy. He straightened slowly, resisting the urge to lie down and close his eyes, and after a bit the nausea passed. He made himself look around the bedroom, seeing nothing more that would betray his presence, then pushed himself to his feet and made his way cautiously into the outer room. Aconin was busy folding blankets into a cracked leather hamper, but looked up long enough to wave him toward the divan.

"Sit down before you fall over. Are you sure you're well enough to move?"

"It depends on where I'm going." Rathe sank into the corner of the divan, grateful for its support.

"Well, that would be the question." Aconin slammed the hamper's lid. "I don't suppose you have any friends in the Court."

Not the sort I'd want to ask for help, Rathe thought. *I can't go to Mikael like this, and there's no one else I'd come close to trusting.* And you'd have to be desperate to trust the Court's senior knife. But then, if this wasn't a desperate situation… He shoved that thought aside. "Did Philip say when he'd be back?"

"He did not. He went to talk to Coindarel, and who knows how long that will take?" Aconin crossed to the window that overlooked the Main Street and pulled back the shutter just enough to peer out. "I don't think it would be wise to wait."

Probably not, Rathe thought, but he wasn't sure how well he could manage on his own. Not well at all, if he had to go any distance, and his skin crawled at the idea of going deeper into the Court without being able to protect himself. "Is there someplace you'd suggest?"

"There are one or two places that don't ask questions," Aconin said. "They're not cheap, though, or they won't be for you." He paused. "And of course I'm guessing you don't have coin on you."

Rathe could feel the weight of his purse in the waistband of his breeches, knew to the demming just how much should be there. "Some, but not a great amount. Surely a room in the Court can't cost that much."

"It's not the room, it's everything else, including discretion," Aconin said. "You're well known, Rathe, and not precisely well loved."

Rathe winced. He'd known it would come to this, and still didn't like it, had no desire to stand in debt to the leader of the Court's knives. "If I can borrow pen and paper, I can send a note to Mikael."

"What *interesting* friends you have, Adjunct Point," Aconin said. "All right, I can arrange that."

He brought a sheaf of paper and a pen and good ink, and Rathe balanced a writing board on his knees, frowning over the words. He waited long enough that the ink dried on his pen, and he had to clean it and start over, but finally managed to form what he hoped would be an acceptable message, or at least one that would buy Mikael's forbearance.

Mikael—am in the Court, need to speak with you about various matters. Rathe. He hesitated, then added, *I'll owe you.* That admission would do him no good, if the note fell into Hearts' hands, but it needed to be said if he was going to earn Mikael's support. He found a wafer, folded the note and sealed it, and held it out to Aconin. "Can you get this to Mikael?"

Aconin nodded. "Not that I'm ever comfortable dealing with the man. But, yes, I can."

"Thank you." Rathe leaned back against the cushions, setting aside the writing board. Aconin made an annoyed noise and rescued ink and pen before they could spoil the paper, then lifted the bar from the door.

"I won't be long. If there's trouble, there's a back way out, through the bedroom window—it overlooks the neighbor's woodshed, you can get down on the roof and out through their yard. If you're sure you're up to it?"

"Do I have a choice?" Rathe asked, and Aconin made a sound that was not quite laughter.

"Not noticeably. But we'll hope it won't come to that." The door closed behind him.

Rathe sat for a moment, wondering if he should bar the door, and then if he should investigate Aconin's back door, but his head was pounding again. Moving like an old man, he made his way to Aconin's table and found the bag of willowbark, then mixed himself a dose. It was bitter enough to turn his stomach, and he sat hunched over on the divan for a long moment before he was sure it would stay down.

And if he could barely walk across the room, how in Tyrseis's name was he going to make it from Aconin's rooms to a new hiding place? If Eslingen were there—but he wasn't, and Rathe couldn't count on him returning in time. He'd have to get himself to wherever he was going, and probably he should be worrying about that before he worried about how he was going to get there. Could he trust Aconin's recommendation? Probably; the bigger question was whether he could trust Aconin. He and the playwright had been at odds for years, but he had to admit that Aconin had a sort of honor. And he and Eslingen were friends. He might not love the points—might make fun of them when he could—but he liked Hearts even less than he liked Dreams. Still, it might be wise to find a different place to stay once Eslingen joined him.

He heard footsteps on the stairs, and started upright, ready to find Aconin's back door, only to realize that it was one person. Definitely not the points, then, and the door opened to admit Aconin.

"It's only me," he said, and Rathe let himself sink back onto the divan. "I've sent your message, though it may take some time to get there. Oh, don't worry, no one will dare try to read it, not when it's going to Mikael, it's just a question of where he might be today. And anyway, I've had a thought."

Rathe felt his eyebrows rise. "Oh?"

"What's the first thing everyone knows about Nicolas Rathe?" Aconin paused. "Well, all right, the second thing, Philip isn't exactly relevant here. Or maybe it's the third thing, since everyone also knows you don't take fees."

"Could you get to the point?"

"It's the way you dress," Aconin said. "Oh, it's the uniform, but under it… You dress like out-of-work day-labor even when you could afford better. If I put you in a decent coat and a proper shirt, no one will know you."

"Clothes don't sit right on me," Rathe muttered.

"That's because they don't fit you," Aconin said. "If you spent a third of what Philip spends on his clothes, you could get your coats made over—but that's not the point. My point is, if you wore a decent coat, or, better still, a fancy one, with a well-tied stock and a shirt with lace, no one will look at you and say, 'Isn't that Adjunct Point Rathe?'"

It wasn't a bad idea, much as Rathe hated to admit it. "And where would I get these nice clothes?"

"From me," Aconin said. "We're not so far off in build. And, much as it pains me to admit it, I'd rather not see you arrested. Particularly not in my rooms, but we're going to avoid that, aren't we?"

"If we can," Rathe said. "All right, I'll try it."

"Please try not to destroy them," Aconin said, and vanished into the bedroom. He returned a moment later with an armful of fabric and another, larger basket, and set them all down on the divan beside Rathe. "Your shirt, please."

Rathe undid the strings at wrist and neck, aware for the first time of just how thin and worn the fabric was. Maybe Eslingen was right, and he should buy another shirt instead of sending this one out to be mended yet again. He put the thought aside, and accepted the shirt Aconin handed him. It was definitely of better linen, discreetly darned here and there but still considerably better than anything he owned himself. There were thread-worked buttons at the cuffs, and two tiny white-work diamonds where the collar closed. He fastened them all, then tucked in the shirt, and Aconin made an approving noise.

"Not bad. Now the stock."

Rathe accepted the length of linen and wound it carefully around his neck. "I need a shave."

"You'll pass," Aconin said, frowning. "But not—don't you know any other ways to tie a stock?"

"This is perfectly fine."

"No, it's not." Footsteps sounded on the stairs, and they both froze. "The bedroom," Aconin hissed, and Rathe caught up his own shirt and the basket of his belongings. He ducked into the other room, closing the door behind him, and heard Aconin say, "Who's there?"

Rathe hovered by the window, unable to hear the answer, but then Aconin sighed loudly.

"Right. You've come home betimes."

"I've brought news." Eslingen's voice was grim.

"That Hearts wants to search my rooms?" Aconin asked. "Yes, we've heard, actually."

Rathe came back into the main room, setting down the basket, and Eslingen gave him an appraising glance. "You're looking better."

"I'm feeling better," Rathe said. It wasn't quite a lie.

"That might be the clothes," Aconin said. "Can you tie his stock for him? Something conservative but elegant."

"Nico does know how to dress himself," Eslingen said mildly. "What's all this about, anyway?"

"It's a disguise," Aconin said, with emphasis. "No one will recognize him if he's not dressed like a stevedore."

"It's not a bad idea," Rathe said, reluctantly, and Eslingen nodded.

"All right, then. Shall I do your stock?"

"Please."

Eslingen stepped in to unwind the strip of linen, standing so close that they might as well have embraced. Rathe closed his eyes for an instant, all too aware of Eslingen's scent, sweat and shaving soap and the herbs that kept his coat moth-free. He could feel Eslingen's movements, wrapping and tying, and opened his eyes again to find a knot of linen pressed under his chin. He grimaced, and Eslingen said, "You'll get used to it. And it does make you look different."

Rathe made himself relax, and accepted the coat that Aconin held out to him. It was peach-colored wool trimmed with lilac braid, colors he would never choose for himself, and he couldn't help wincing as he shrugged it on. Aconin made a disapproving noise and tugged deftly at the shoulders and the waist. That loosened several tight spots, and the playwright nodded.

"Not your color, but not dreadful, either. You see, Philip?"

Eslingen nodded. "You're right, it's not a bad idea. I don't suppose you have something more like Nico's usual wardrobe that I could borrow?"

Aconin laughed. "Try Nico's coat—it won't fit right, and the color's terrible for you. Take off your stock and leave your hair down. And—wait." He vanished into the bedroom, and returned with a battered broad-brimmed hat that had gone out of fashion a decade before. "Here, wear this."

Rathe sank back onto the divan as Eslingen changed, going from disheveled to downright shabby. "You'll pass for a knife."

"I daresay," Eslingen said, with some distaste.

"You'll pass as his knife," Aconin said briskly. "And Rathe can pass for someone who's come to do business in the Court—one of Caiazzo's friends, perhaps."

"That's a game I'm not playing," Rathe said. His connection with Caiazzo was equivocal enough without reminding anyone of it just now. He looked at Eslingen. "Do we know where we're going?"

"Not yet," Eslingen said, and Aconin sighed.

"There's a house called the Lizard. It's only three streets over, but it's well inside the Court. Hearts won't go there—even Knives would think twice. Dame Ellender rents rooms by the day as well as by the hour, I doubt she'd mind having a couple of knives on the premises."

"Right, then." Rathe braced himself, and managed to stand without swaying. "Let's go."

THEY MADE THEIR way slowly down the street that ran deeper into the Court, Eslingen with one eye on the alleys and shadowed doorways, and the other on Rathe. Aconin had found a heavy stick for Rathe to lean on, but he still moved with painful slowness, and Eslingen refused to think about what might happen if they were set upon. Aconin had promised it wasn't far to the Lizard; he hoped that was true, and that the landlady would in fact be willing to take them in. The money tucked into his belt should be a sufficient inducement, but he didn't want to spend too much of it before he had to. Although this was likely to qualify as a necessity. And if they had to leave the city… The safest choice would be to book a passage on a ship heading downriver. It might even be possible to hole up in Ostolas, the port town at the mouth of the Sier, where the points' jurisdiction didn't reach. Technically, though, the Guard had rights there, but he doubted Coindarel would encourage any of them to look too hard. But of course he'd have to persuade Rathe to leave first, and he wasn't at all sure that was likely. He glanced again at the other man, seeing stark lines carved in his face, the slow, shuffling step that made him look twenty years older: a good disguise, but if anything the injury had made Rathe even more stubborn than usual. He was more likely to insist on giving himself up than to agree to run.

And that did not bear close consideration. He glanced over his shoulder, saw no one except a boy scuttling from one doorway to the next, an empty bucket in his hand. Ahead, the street narrowed, the buildings to either side adding extra stories that jutted out over the passageway and cast deepening shadows to either side. He slowed in spite of himself, shifting the covered basket in his left hand so that it could become an improvised weapon, and Rathe said, "I can see it. It's just ahead."

Eslingen looked again, and spotted the sign, a carved lizard hanging above the doorway of the house four doors down. It had been exuberantly colored once, but badly needed a fresh coat of paint. He hoped the landlady was in better repair.

Something moved in the shadows beyond the Lizard, and suddenly there were half a dozen strangers in the street, blocking their way. Eslingen swore under his breath, reaching for his knife. All right, there were five, not six—there had never been a sixth, thank all the gods, but five on one was bad enough—and at his side Rathe drew himself up abruptly.

"Looking for something?"

"We might want a word with you," one of the men answered. He was a big man, barrel-chested, his face half-hidden by a feathered hat. One of the others laughed. "Or with your purse."

"I'm here on business," Rathe said. "You don't want to interfere."

"It's not your place to decide that," feather-hat said.

Eslingen drew himself up, trying to look as menacing as possible. He'd go for feather-hat first, hit him with the basket to drive him back, and then use the knife—take him as quickly as he could and hope that discouraged the rest.

"Fair enough, but I don't think Mikael would appreciate the inconvenience," Rathe said. Somehow he contrived to sound bored, and Eslingen saw feather-hat hesitate for a second.

"I don't believe it," one of the others said, and feather-hat shook himself and spat on the dusty stones.

"Folk like you don't deal with Mikael."

"But I do," Rathe said, and there was a note of silky menace in his voice that Eslingen had never heard before. "I've dealt with him for years. And you know he won't take kindly to having his connections interfered with."

There was a moment of silence, and Eslingen saw one of the trailing men take a quiet step backward. Rathe didn't move, didn't shift his weight off his stick, just kept staring at the man in the feathered hat as though he was just waiting for him to make his move.

"If you're lying, we'll know," feather-hat said, and nodded to the man next to him. Eslingen tensed, but in the next moment the entire group had disappeared back into the alleys between the houses. He hesitated, all too aware that this was the perfect setup for an ambush, but Rathe took a breath and started forward, his stick suddenly loud on the stones.

"Are you sure?" Eslingen asked, careful to keep his voice low.

"It's a risk we have to take." Rathe's voice was equally soft, though Eslingen could hear the tension in it. He braced himself, shifting the basket again so that he could swing it freely, and followed. He looked sharply to both sides as they passed the alley mouth, but the other knives had disappeared. Then they had reached the Lizard, and he followed Rathe through the open door, resisting the urge to swing it shut behind them.

The main room was small, but set up as a tavern, with tables and stools and a serving counter against the back wall, with another open door that presumably led into a kitchen. The tables were all empty, and Eslingen couldn't decide if that was reassuring or alarming. Rathe glanced behind him, and reached back to shake a string of harness bells that hung from the door. There was an answering clatter of wooden-soled shoes from behind the counter, and a heavy-set woman appeared, wiping her hands on her apron.

"We're not serving yet, sorry."

"Dame Ellender?" Rathe said.

She nodded once. "Who's asking?"

"I was told you rented rooms."

"Who told you that?"

"Aconite." Rathe gave a thin smile. "Though of course he often lies."

The woman hesitated, then shrugged one shoulder. "As it happens, I have a room available. At a price."

"And that is?" Rathe tipped his head to one side.

"A seilling a day for each of you just for the room. Two apiece if you want the ordinary, three if you want it in your room."

"In the room," Eslingen said quietly. Rathe shot him a look, but nodded.

"Agreed. Pay the woman, please."

Eslingen set down the basket, and reached into his purse to come up with a handful of coins. "Four days?" Rathe nodded again, and Eslingen handed over the payment. Ellender examined them quickly—the ring on her forefinger was a touchstone for counterfeits, Eslingen saw—then stowed the coins beneath her skirts.

"This way."

She led them down a hall that ran beside the kitchen. It opened onto a muddy yard that gave access to the privies and the midden; a staircase was built against the rear of the kitchen, and she started up without looking back. Eslingen gave Rathe a quick look, lifting his eyebrows in question, and the other man grimaced.

"Go ahead."

That was not the answer Eslingen wanted, but this was not the time to argue. He climbed after her, and emerged on a narrow landing. It had a door, though that was propped open at the moment, and there were four closed doors leading to what were presumably the guests' rooms.

"Front or back?"

"Front," Eslingen said. He wanted a view of the street, particularly if their only way out was the back staircase.

Ellender nodded, and brought out a bundle of keys. She carefully detached two of them and stooped to unlock a front room door. Eslingen watched her, not wanting to look away, and heard Rathe reach the top of the stairs behind him. She got the lock to work and pushed the door open for them.

"There. Does this suit?"

The room was unexpectedly clean, not even dust in the corners, though the only furniture was the bedstead and a table and benches against the wall beneath the shuttered window. Eslingen crossed to pull open the shutters, glancing out into the still-empty street, then looked back at Rathe, who nodded.

"It'll do."

"Right." Ellender crossed to the bedstead, pulled loose the curtains that had been knotted up against the posts. Eslingen opened his mouth to demand the keys, but she was already holding them out. Rathe took them.

"Thank you, dame."

"Send your man down for sheets and blankets," she said, and disappeared, closing the door softly behind her. Eslingen looked quickly at Rathe, and was unsurprised to see him sag, dropping ungracefully onto the nearest bench.

"Are you all right?"

Rathe nodded, and winced. "Tired. And, before you ask, yes, still sore."

Eslingen set the basket on the table and rummaged in it for the apothecary's decoction. "Here. You're due for a dose."

"Not yet," Rathe said. "Willowbark?"

Eslingen looked quickly around the room. "No water. And no pitcher, either. I'll fetch some."

"Get it when you get the bedding," Rathe said.

"You need it now," Eslingen answered, but to his surprise Rathe waved him over, a wry smile on his face.

"I'm all right, I tell you." He paused. "Sit with me a minute, will you?"

"Of course." Eslingen settled cautiously beside him, not sure whether he should be frightened or not. This wasn't like Rathe; normally they asked each other for practical things, or hid their needs in a joke. But Rathe did look more tired than ill, and Eslingen warily put an arm around his shoulders. He felt Rathe resist, and then felt him sigh and lean sideways, letting his head rest on Eslingen's shoulder.

"I wish this would go away."

"Give it a couple more days," Eslingen said. "You're already better than you were."

"True." Rathe didn't sound particularly convinced, and Eslingen hurried on. "And we should have that now that we're here."

"Assuming Aconin keeps his word."

"He will," Eslingen said, and was mildly surprised to find that he believed it. "This sort of thing—he won't give us up, even if it's purely to be contrary."

He felt Rathe laugh. "That I'll believe."

They sat for a moment in silence, Eslingen with one ear cocked for noises from the street. He could still hear the chill in Rathe's voice as he faced down the would-be ambushers: not at all like him, and even less like him to have kept it up talking to Dame Ellender. He couldn't think of a way to ask, said instead, "What do we do now?"

Rathe grimaced. "Wait. I need to talk to Mikael—I'd like to know what he can tell us about that lot who tried to stop us, along with everything else—and I'd like to talk to Sohier if I could figure out how. And at some point I will have to turn myself in."

"But not yet," Eslingen said, in spite of himself.

Rathe grinned. "No. Fair enough, not yet."

He was sounding better, and Eslingen allowed himself to relax a little. "I'll fetch the bedding," he said, and pushed himself to his feet.

LEFT TO HIMSELF, Rathe leaned back against the nearest wall, turning his head to protect the bruise and cut at the back of his skull. He felt better than he had the day before, though the walk had been hard, and if they'd had to fight—that was a thing he didn't really want to think about. He was just glad he'd been able to convince them that he was one of Mikael's contacts. Of course, he'd have to make good on that, but he'd sent the note to Mikael, and he was sure Mikael could find them if he wanted. And that might buy them another day or two, and surely by then he'd be able to function again...

That was another thing he didn't want to think too much about. If he could barely walk from Aconin's rooms to the edges of the Court, he was in no shape to return to Dreams, and in no shape to talk his way out of whatever Hearts claimed against him. Which meant Eslingen hadn't been wrong, and that was something he'd need to say sometime soon. But first—first they had to figure out who had attacked them in the first place, because even his hazy memory couldn't convince him that any of that had been random. And then they needed to figure out why. Turn the events as he might, he couldn't see why it was worth anyone's while to act: it brought them into the open, at a time when the points had no idea who they were or what they wanted. Unless there was something they'd overlooked, but that was the stuff of bad theater. Maybe Sohier had found something, but it was going to be hard to contact her.

And if he couldn't... He shied from the thought, then made himself face it. If he couldn't figure out what had really happened, he was going to have to give himself up and take his chances. The only other choice would be to leave the city, but that would mean abandoning everything he'd built for himself. He'd been with the points since he was twelve, first as a runner, then an apprentice, then a full-fledged pointsman; the thought of ending that made his head throb again, his eyesight flickering in time with his heartbeat. There was nothing for him outside Astreiant; outside the points he'd be just another knife, wiser than some, perhaps, but still outside the law.

The door opened again, Eslingen saying in the same instant, "It's only me." He looked nothing like his usual elegant self: Rathe's coat fit badly, and there was a laddered hole in his left stocking, running down from the knee. He looked like a knife, like the men who'd accosted them in the street—and that was what they could have been, if their stars had been different, Rathe thought. He himself was nothing more than a southriver rat, when all was said and done; he could too easily have become someone's knife, hunting and hunted. At best, he'd have found work with someone like Caiazzo, who at least kept his word. At worst, he'd have been a tavern-keeper's bully, rousting drunks for the meager contents of their purses.

"Nico?" Eslingen set the pitcher on the table, and fumbled in his coat pocket to produce a chipped pottery cup. "I managed to persuade the dame to loan me a cup, but only one. I'll make you some willowbark, but then we'll have to share."

"That's all right." Rathe accepted the cup and tossed back the bitter drink.

"I'll try to find honey tomorrow," Eslingen said.

"It doesn't matter."

Eslingen shrugged. "Up to you, but there's no need to suffer."

"There's no need to draw notice," Rathe said sharply.

"No." Eslingen rinsed out the cup, realized there was no slop jar, and tipped the water out the window. Rathe winced, expecting to hear some protest, but there was no reaction. "So. What do we do now?"

"I want to talk to Mikael," Rathe said. "He'll have some idea who's hiring knives, or at least of what they're being hired for."

"You think he'd tell you?" Eslingen asked.

"He might, since it's likely to cause him more trouble in the long run."

Eslingen nodded thoughtfully, and settled himself on the bench at Rathe's side. "It'd be a help. If he knows anything."

"Then Sohier," Rathe said. "Or someone else I can trust. I want to know if anything's changed in Hearts."

"If you try to go back to Hearts, they will call the point on you," Eslingen said. "And Chresta said Sohier's been confined to Dreams." He paused. "I don't know why they're so worried about you, Nico, but it might be a good idea to get out of reach."

"We're safe enough in the Court."

"I meant leave the city," Eslingen said. "We wouldn't have to go far, just downriver to the port—"

"I'm not leaving Astreiant," Rathe said. *Not like this, not accused of leading a riot. Not ever, if I can help it.* He swallowed the words, went on more carefully, "I can't help thinking that we know something, or someone thinks we do. We need to figure out what."

"That's fair enough," Eslingen said. "I didn't have a chance to say, before, but Chaudet—from Knives—spoke to me on my way back from the barracks. It seems Knives isn't particularly interested in helping Hearts with this business."

"Can't say I'm surprised," Rathe said. "And Mirremay doesn't meddle with the Court, either."

"So we've got some time," Eslingen said. "You can recover, and maybe we can make some sense of this mess."

Rathe allowed himself to relax a little. Eslingen was right, he did need to rest, much as he hated to admit it, and they had bought some time. "All right," he said, and let himself lean against Eslingen's shoulder.

The next few days passed quietly. Dame Ellender was good as her word, sending their meals upstairs by way of the moon-faced boy who worked in the scullery, and gradually Rathe felt the worst of the weakness recede. The swelling went down, the headaches and nausea eased, until he felt almost normal again. After some discussion, Eslingen risked a note to Aconin, asking for news, but the answer was a scrawl on a scrap of paper saying that nothing had changed and the playwright was being watched. That was no surprise, Rathe felt, and did his best to stay patient. Eslingen offered to try to talk to Coindarel again, but that would involve leaving the Court, and neither of them could see a safe way to manage it. That left Mikael, and Rathe professed himself well enough to arrange the meeting. Eslingen gave him a doubtful look, but said only, "If you're sure."

We have to do something. Rathe managed a smile. "I'm sure."

Dame Ellender provided a runner, and a few hours later a note came back, scratched this time on a sliver of slate in crude letters that left no clue to the writer: *Arkadie, 4 o'clock.* Rathe nodded and flipped the runner a demming, and Eslingen raised his eyebrows.

"You're not going to negotiate?"

"I don't have much to bargain with," Rathe said. "Besides, Mikael likes the Arkadie. If he kills somebody there, he'll lose the use of it."

"I'm not sure I'd rely on that," Eslingen said.

"We can," Rathe said, and hoped it was true.

It was a quarter-hour's walk to the Arkadie, through narrowing, uncrowded streets that finally opened onto a long plaza. It was busier there, a handful of women gathered at the decrepit fountain, other people, men and women both, mingling in the shadows beneath the arched arcade on the southern edge of the plaza. The Arkadie was on the opposite end, toward the center, marked only by its larger windows and the red-painted door. Eslingen eyed it warily.

"I don't suppose you know if there's a back way out."

"I imagine there has to be," Rathe said. His head was starting to hurt again, just a faint pulse of pain behind his temples, and he thought he'd be glad of the shadowed interior.

"I'd prefer a bit more certainty than that," Eslingen muttered, but took his place at Rathe's side as they approached the door. It opened at their approach, and a woman stepped out. She was better dressed than Rathe would have expected, and she looked faintly startled when she saw him, but she held the door with absent courtesy. Eslingen caught it neatly and Rathe stepped past him into the Arkadie's main room.

It was dark, after the thin sunlight of the streets, but Rathe could see that it wasn't particularly crowded. There was a group of half a dozen in the corner to his right, and another three or four scattered across the rest of the room, but all of them gave a wide berth to the table in the back corner where a large man sat alone beneath a hanging mage-light, a pitcher of wine and a tray of cups in front of him. In the distance, a tower clock struck four.

Rathe took a breath and started toward the back corner, feeling the weight of eyes on him. Eslingen murmured something that might have been a curse, and matched him step for step. Rathe stopped an arm's length from the table and said, "Mikael. Thanks for seeing us."

The big man waved to the stools that waited to either side. "No trouble. Though you've been getting yourself into plenty."

"Not on purpose," Rathe said.

"And I never knew you were that much of a Leveler."

"He's not," Eslingen said.

Mikael gave him a sharp glance, and a smile that showed teeth. "Always good to have a loyal leman."

"I didn't lead that riot," Rathe said, and managed to keep his voice almost bored. "Though I suspect you already knew that."

Mikael's smile widened briefly. "Now, now, you know I don't play politics." He pushed the pitcher toward them. "Here, help yourselves."

Rathe shook his head, but Eslingen poured them each a glass, then topped up Mikael's without being asked. Mikael nodded his thanks, and Rathe said, "None of the knives in the Court do business without you knowing. I'm wondering just how many of them were behind that bit of trouble."

"And what do you plan to do about it?" Mikael asked.

"At the moment?" Rathe shook his head. "Nothing. There's nothing I can do, not until we get this straightened out. But unless you want to be playing politics, I think you'll want to get this sorted."

Mikael's gaze flickered. "Like that, is it?"

"There's politics involved," Rathe said. "Bringing back the Levelers, that's politics, and it's politics that's set d'Alamenon's bullies onto Chresta Aconin—for something that, for once, he hasn't done. And I'd be curious what you know about that bit of business, too."

"You don't want much, do you?" Mikael asked. "Particularly when you haven't got much to trade."

Rathe waited, and after a moment, Mikael sighed.

"I hate politics. Money and merchantry, that's my business. But, yes, I've heard that someone in d'Alamenon's service was looking to hire additional knives to help out her household bullies—looking for people who knew the city, or so I heard. D'Alamenon was offering solid coin, so I imagine she got her choice."

"Anyone I'd know?" Rathe asked.

Mikael shrugged. "Probably one or two. I'm not entirely certain myself, it didn't seem a matter I should concern myself with."

That was likely enough, and Rathe nodded. "Have you heard talk about smugglers' carts passing through Hearts? They have knives on board, and I wondered if they were hired here."

Mikael blinked as though the question had surprised him. "There's been talk. Though if it's smuggling, it's not any of the regulars. I told them that asked that I didn't know the woman, not that she gave her real name, I'm sure, but there's always those who need coin badly enough to take a chance. Though this doesn't seem to have blown up in their faces—yet."

"There's a metaphor for you," Eslingen murmured. Mikael gave him a quizzical look, and Rathe cleared his throat.

"I don't suppose you'd share that name? Real or not."

"For what it's worth," Mikael said. "The name I heard was Desria Lejanne."

It wasn't a name Rathe knew. "Did she say what she wanted?" Rathe rested his elbows on the table, felt it tip slightly. Mikael gave him a disapproving look, and put his own arm on the table to rebalance it.

"What I heard was, she wanted guards for a chancy cargo. She'd fee'd the points there in Hearts—sorry, Nico—but there were other folk she was worried about."

None of that was a surprise, and Rathe nodded. "What about the riot and these new Levelers?"

"That's a different thing entirely," Mikael said. "It was a quiet word, more a hint than a promise, a woman looking for someone who wouldn't be averse to starting a fight, or finishing one that someone else started. One of my boys made an inquiry, and got as far as meeting at the Lilies and being ready. He backed out— Bonamy's a decent man, no reason to trouble him—but then I heard whispers that the same woman was spreading Leveler talk. I warned my people, but clearly some of them had already taken the job."

Rathe knew better than to ask for those names. He said, "Any idea who the woman was?"

"She called herself Aliez Allera, for all the good it will do you," Mikael said. "I'd lay good money that's not the name her mother gave her nor the one she's using today. And before you ask, my boy said she was fair, average height, somewhere between thirty and forty and dressed like a decent shopkeeper. Blonde hair, painted hands, ordinary face."

"Not much to go on," Eslingen said.

"It's the best I can do," Mikael said. He paused. "For what it's worth, my boy said she might have been someone's upper servant, just from the way she talked, but he couldn't swear to that. She might just have been careful with her words."

"Every bit helps." Rathe drained his cup, momentarily surprised that the wine was decent. But then, Mikael cared for his comforts. "Thanks, Mikael. I owe you."

"I'll hold you to that," Mikael said, and Rathe nodded.

"You can."

NINE

T HE WALK BACK to the Lizard was uneventful, though Eslingen still kept an eye on the shadowed alleys. Either Rathe had frightened the local knives badly enough, or Mikael had put out the word to leave them alone, and Eslingen was grateful for the quiet. He could tell that Rathe was tiring, and by the time they'd climbed the steps to their room, Rathe seemed glad to sink onto the nearest stool.

"Why don't you lie down?" Eslingen said, and wished he'd bitten his tongue instead when Rathe shook his head.

"I'm fine."

"Suit yourself." Eslingen made an effort to keep his voice casual. He should have known better than to call attention to the other's weakness. "I'm just going down to see what I can beg from the kitchen."

He made his way back down the stairs, poked his head in at the kitchen door, and managed to persuade the skeptical cook to part with a loaf of bread and half a crock of soft cheese in lieu of butter. He brought them back upstairs, and was relieved to see that Rathe had mixed himself a dose of the willowbark and was just downing it. He knew better than to say anything, though, and simply set his finds on the table. Rathe nodded his thanks.

"You know, if you did find some honey, I'd take it."

And that was more of a concession than Eslingen had expected. "I'll see what I can do," he said, and drew his knife to hack the bread into rough slices.

They ate in silence, in something closer to content than Eslingen had felt since the riot. He leaned his shoulder gently against Rathe's, wishing they could stay like this just a little longer, but knew they couldn't afford it. They'd already wasted too much time in hiding—not wasted, Rathe had needed the time to recover, but they needed to decide now what they were going to do.

As if he'd read the thought, Rathe sighed and straightened. "We need to talk."

"We do." Eslingen took a deep breath. "So. What next? And for Astree's sake, don't say 'go to the points.'"

To his relief, Rathe grinned briefly. "Maybe not, no. I'm not liking the way things are run in Hearts."

That was probably as close to an apology as Eslingen was going to get. He nodded, saying, "We could leave the city, at least until this is sorted out. I've got money—"

"No." Rathe shook himself, made an effort to speak more calmly. "We need to figure out what's going on."

"How?" Eslingen made himself stop, take a breath and then another, controlling his own instinctive anger. "Hearts wants you under lock and key—and given everything that's been going on, I wouldn't bet that someone doesn't want you dead."

"That's an exaggeration," Rathe said.

"Is it?"

Rathe glared, and Eslingen swept on.

"Someone certainly didn't care if you were killed at the Lilies, and the adjunct at Hearts was willing to lie about your leading the riot. At the very least someone wants you out of their way."

"And that's why I can't leave," Rathe said.

"Are you saying Sohier can't handle it?" Instantly, Eslingen wished the words unspoken, and felt Rathe shift away from him.

"Not fair." Rathe's voice was taut with anger.

"No," Eslingen said. "I'm sorry." Rathe nodded, and Eslingen took a breath. "But—"

"Philip."

"Hear me out."

There was a moment of silence, and then Rathe nodded again.

"If we stay, what do we do?" Eslingen asked. "Hearts has all the points stations looking for you, which leaves the Court as the only place where we're—I hesitate to call it 'safe.'"

"Yeah, I know," Rathe said. "But look, turn it around. We must be close, we must have gotten close, or no one would be going to this much trouble to get rid of us. We need to figure out why."

Eslingen made a face, but had to admit the other man was right. "How?"

"Let's start with what we have." Rathe held up a hand, counting his ideas on his fingers. "First, Levelers and Bonamy."

"Though it certainly doesn't look as though they're friends anymore," Eslingen said. "If they ever were."

Rathe nodded. "Second, carts carrying gunpowder. Which is, unfortunately, all we know about them. Third, d'Alamenon and her knives and her feud with Aconin."

You're leaving things out, Eslingen thought. He said, "De Castiat. And Annechon."

"She's a friend," Rathe said, but the protest was automatic.

"But if she's courting de Castiat, or letting herself be courted—and I grant you there are reasons she might not have wanted to say that to you, she still might know something about de Castiat that would help." Eslingen paused, his eyes on Rathe's face. At least the other man was listening, not rejecting the idea out of hand, and he went on carefully, "And de Castiat is connected to d'Alamenon, and d'Alamenon is connected to de Galhac and the royal wedding, and that makes it about politics, whether or not any Levelers are involved."

Rathe nodded slowly. "All right, I'll buy that. But it can't be the succession again."

"I wouldn't think so," Eslingen said, remembering his meeting with de Galhac. "The palatineur is getting what he wants, his daughter marrying a scion of the royal line. Their children would have a double claim. After the Metropolitan, of course."

"And she doesn't have children yet," Rathe said. "Not that she couldn't still."

Eslingen nodded, trying to remember everything he'd learned from the broadsheets about the twists and turns of the royal lineage. "Even if she did, Feramis—the Castellan, de Galhac's daughter. She could still make an argument for her children if not for herself."

"And I could see the Metropolitan making that bargain if she had to," Rathe said. "You thought well of de Galhac."

"I did," Eslingen said. *Not that I saw much of him, but what I saw, I liked.* "He was willing to lean on d'Alamenon."

"Sounds like there was no love lost there," Rathe said.

"No." Eslingen frowned, trying to remember broadsheet scraps and comments from Estradere. "I think—I was told d'Alamenon made a play for the palatinate herself, when his older sister died. But the family went with his claim. If he hadn't had a daughter himself, it might have been another story."

"So d'Alamenon's got a grudge against him," Rathe said.

"May have," Eslingen said. "Though I will say he didn't sound particularly fond of her."

"And she's got a grudge against Aconin, for something that's for once actually not his doing." Rathe cocked his head, considering. "She's a busy woman."

"She's de Castiat's cousin," Eslingen said. "And in regular contact with her. Busy indeed."

"I'd still like to know if she's involved in the salt trade," Rathe muttered. That wasn't the best connection they had to the woman, Eslingen thought, but waited. Rathe would come to it in his own time, he was too honest a pointsman not to, and it would be easier on both of them if he wasn't pushed. Rathe sighed. "And, yes, that means we need to talk to Annechon. You were right, she wasn't saying everything she knew."

"The question is how we manage that," Eslingen said. "If she'll even talk to us without turning you in."

"She won't do that," Rathe said.

That was probably true, Eslingen thought. He didn't particularly like her, but he thought he could trust Rathe's judgment. But that still left the problem of getting across Astreiant without being spotted by the points. Knives and Sighs and Dreams and Hopes might all look the other way, though when he spelled it out it seemed less likely, but Annechon lived in Hearts, and Hearts would be glad to stop them. The disguises they had used might turn a casual glance, but if anyone was actually looking for Rathe, they wouldn't be enough. "Could we send for her, ask her to meet us somewhere?"

"I'd rather meet her in her own house," Rathe said. "She'd be able to hide us there if we needed it."

Rathe believed she'd do it, Eslingen thought. That would have to be enough. "So how do we get there?"

To his surprise, Rathe gave a crooked smile. "We're in the Court, we might as well take advantage. There are women who sell charms that strengthen a disguise."

"That can't be legal," Eslingen said, and Rathe's smile widened.

"No, but I think we're beyond worrying about that."

And that was unlike Rathe as well, but there was no point in arguing. Eslingen said, "Do you know someone? Possibly more pressing, is she someone you called a point on?"

"There's someone who owes me," Rathe said. "But we'll talk to her tomorrow."

"Fair enough." Eslingen paused. "We also ought to take a low-flyer."

"No way out if we're stopped," Rathe said, without conviction.

"And no reason for anyone to stop one," Eslingen answered.

The next morning dawned clear and cold, the sort of day that anyone might wrap themselves up in cloak and scarf: a perfect day to try to make it to Annechon's house, Eslingen thought, gathering their meager belongings into the basket. He longed for clean linen, for clothes that fit—but none of that mattered unless they could get Rathe to safety. Instead, he pulled on the limp shirt and ill-fitting coat, tied his garters gingerly to keep the hole in the stocking's knee from getting any larger, and braced himself to face the day.

The magist lived deeper in the court, Rathe said, as he led the way through the dirty streets. Technically the shop sold paper goods, pens and inks and sealing wax as well as tablet-and-stylus sets and other writing supplies, but Eslingen doubted there was great demand for those goods in the Court. He said as much, only to earn another of Rathe's sidelong smiles.

"There are always forgers who need gear. Her leman does a brisk business matching inks, and the brother can make a custom seal, no questions asked. And that's not counting what can be done with magistry." His smile faded. "I hate begging her for favors."

There was a note in his voice that made Eslingen stop in his tracks. "Then— don't? We could take a low-flyer, there are plenty of them with closed boxes, no one would see—"

"I don't want to see you arrested," Rathe said.

"I don't want either of us to end up in the cells," Eslingen said. "But if this is more than you can do…"

"It's the sensible thing to do," Rathe said. "I just don't like it."

"Then we don't have to," Eslingen said. It mattered that Rathe kept inside the law, just as much as it mattered that he didn't take fees; it was part of what made him the man he was, the man Eslingen loved and trusted. He hated the idea of Rathe doing something that shamed him, that made him less than himself. "I want you safe, yes, but not if it costs you—not if it's more than you can do." He felt himself flush, the words at once too much and not enough, but Rathe gave him a startled, grateful look.

"That's—yes. Thanks."

"Very touching," a woman said behind them, dry-voiced.

Eslingen whirled, his hand going to his knife, then realized that Rathe had turned more slowly, as though he recognized the voice.

"Regisse."

"Adjunct Point." The woman made no particular effort to keep her voice down, and Eslingen winced.

"Might we have this conversation somewhere more private?"

"But would your leman approve?" The woman was laughing at both of them, her hands tucked into the waistband of her neat shopkeeper's apron. "Oh, very well, let's step inside."

Eslingen glanced at Rathe, received the slightest of nods in answer, and fell into step behind them. Rathe said, "I did want a word with you, Regisse."

"We'd heard you were in trouble," Regisse answered. She was only of average height, but strongly built, broad in hip and shoulder beneath the plain dark wool of her skirt and bodice. "What's Hearts got against you, anyway?"

"I wish I knew," Rathe said. They had reached a door carved with a quill and inkwell, and the woman pushed it open.

"Word is, they're throwing their weight around, even to the point of claiming the right to search here in Knives. Mirremay's not pleased."

"Nor would I expect it," Rathe said.

Eslingen looked around the narrow shop. It was smaller than he'd expected, with a scribe's slanted bench off to the side, no papers visible, but the shelf above it crowded with an impressive array of bottled inks. On the other side of the room, shelves were stacked with reams of cheap paper and boxes marked with blobs of colored wax or wafers of various colors. The more expensive goods were behind the counter, which also guarded the single door that led deeper into the building.

There were none of the jars of herbs or bottles of mysterious liquids that he associated with magists' shops, but of course that part of the business would be kept carefully secret even in the Court.

"No one's happy," Regisse said. "I've even heard it said that Caiazzo is taking an interest."

"That was all this needed," Rathe said.

"We'd all prefer that he kept to his own business," Regisse said. "I've no desire to find him meddling in mine."

"Do you think that's likely?" Rathe cocked his head to one side and Regisse shrugged.

"Let's say he's been known to demand an interest in businesses that are useful to him. And I've been helpful in the past."

That was true enough, Eslingen thought. Hanselin Caiazzo made no secret about wanting full control of his many enterprises, legal and illegal. Rathe said, "Mirremay might have a thought or two about that."

"I'm not getting between Caiazzo and the points," Regisse said, and Rathe shrugged.

"Suit yourself."

"I was going to offer you my help," Regisse said, scowling.

"And we'd gladly accept it," Eslingen said.

Regisse snorted. "Does he say so?" She jerked her chin at Rathe.

"Yes." Rathe nodded. "Since you're offering. But you're still better off going to Mirremay."

"You don't know her." Regisse shook her head. "What were you wanting, Rathe?"

"You make the best no-see-mes in the city," Rathe answered. "And I need to go back to Hearts. Are they good enough for that?"

"You don't ask much, do you?" Regisse shook her head again. "You know the charms have limits, they won't stand up to someone who knows you're there and is looking for you."

Rathe nodded. "I know."

"Then yes, I can make some for you. It'll take a bit, mind."

"We can wait," Rathe said, and Eslingen nodded.

IT TOOK THE better part of three hours to craft the small wax disks. Regisse shooed them into the barren back garden, saying they were bad for business, and Rathe settled himself on the bench against the wall beneath a straggling grape vine. He was feeling better, but it was still sensible to take all the rest he could. Eslingen paced for a bit, working off nervous energy, then came to sit beside him. The bench was shaded, but out of the wind, and if they sat close, they could share a bit of warmth. And comfort: Rathe leaned against Eslingen's shoulder, and was rewarded by the glimmer of a smile. Just for an instant, the tight bands that had shortened his breath—he wouldn't call it fear, not even to himself—eased, and he let himself lean harder, drawing comfort from the touch. Eslingen shifted to accommodate him, but said nothing. He didn't need to say anything, Rathe thought, and that was a gift he had never expected.

Too soon, the house door opened, and Regisse's journeyman appeared, the gray disks wrapped in a napkin, a scrap of ribbon dangling from each. Rathe took his, the wax oddly cold to the touch, and the journeyman said, "Regisse said you know how to use them. Just remember, they don't make you look any different, they just discourage anyone from looking too closely at you." She nodded toward the gate in the corner opposite the privy. "You can leave that way."

Rathe grinned in spite of himself. Regisse might be polite enough, but the journeyman was more what he expected in the Court.

"Well, I don't know how to use this," Eslingen said. He looked dubiously at his disk, and the journeyman heaved a sigh.

"Fasten them somewhere where they'll touch bare skin. Under your stock is fine, or around your wrist, but it has to touch your skin. And, like I said—"

"It doesn't change our looks," Rathe said. He knotted the ribbon around his neck and tucked it under the neck of his shirt, the wax still unnaturally cold against his skin. Eslingen hesitated, but did the same, adjusting his stock to hide the ribbon. "Tell Regisse I owe her."

"Oh, I will," the journeyman said, and vanished back into the house.

"I don't think that young woman cares for us at all," Eslingen said. "Are we sure these will work?"

Rathe smiled. "She doesn't, but Regisse keeps her word. We'll be all right."

"Then we'd better find a low-flyer before Hearts wakes up," Eslingen said.

They made their way through the Court, Rathe all too aware of the eyes watching their progress. Even if they were merely noted as strangers, it was unnerving, but no one confronted them. They reached the Round Market without incident, and Rathe led them in a winding circle through the shabby stalls before they found a low-flyer with a closed box. The driver was shrunken and skinny in her layers of coat and cloak, but the horse was well-groomed, and Rathe saw Eslingen give it an approving glance as he approached the driver.

"Can you take us to Point of Hearts?"

The driver grinned, showing missing teeth. "It's a bit early for that, my lad. Unless you're heading home."

Rathe couldn't suppress a scowl, but Eslingen gave an easy laugh. "We've an errand to run, that's all. Nothing to excite anyone."

"Too bad," the driver said, but reached back to swing the coach door open. "Where in particular, then?"

"Blue Orchids," Rathe said, naming a resort-house that shared a back alley with Annechon's new house, and the driver's eyebrows rose. She didn't say anything, however, and Rathe climbed into the low-flyer, Eslingen following. The driver closed the door, and they lurched into motion.

The streets were crowded in Hopes and Sighs, and even more so on the bridge into Hearts, but once they were into Hearts proper, the traffic thinned out and the driver urged her horse to a jolting trot. Rathe winced, and Eslingen gave him a quick glance.

"I'll tell her to slow down."

"I'm fine," Rathe said, and after a moment, Eslingen relaxed. "We're almost there, anyway."

He was glad, though, when the low-flyer slowed and stopped, brake grinding against the metal-shod wheel. Eslingen opened his door, and visibly relaxed when he saw the street empty. He jumped down, and Rathe followed more carefully, looking to either side. Blue Orchids was closed, its shutters still up from the night before, but a boy came whistling out of the side alley, dragging a grocer's cart behind him. A maid was scrubbing the stone steps of the house opposite, just as maids did in more respectable neighborhoods; further along, a teahouse was newly open, and another woman was returning home with what looked like a load of bread from the neighborhood baker. Eslingen paid off the driver, and the low-flyer jerked into motion, the driver flourishing her whip in hopes of attracting a customer.

"Where now?" Eslingen asked.

"This way." Rathe started down the alley where the grocer's boy had come from, hoping the kitchen workers had gone back inside, and grimaced to see another tradesman trudging toward them, a basket over his arm. The no-see-mes should keep him from looking too closely, Rathe knew, but he kept his head down as they passed. He could feel Eslingen tense beside him, ready to respond to any threat, but the tradesman merely nodded back and kept walking. Eslingen let out his breath in a quiet sigh, but said nothing.

The alley gave onto a service road, ruts worn deep in the packed clay. The nightsoil men had been and gone, for which Rathe was grateful, but it took him a few minutes to pick out the door that led into Annechon's garden. Unsurprisingly, it was locked, and Rathe tugged the bellrope, hoping whoever answered was someone he knew. It seemed to take forever before someone responded, and he looked up and down the shadowed road, hoping that no one would appear. But then at last the shutter slid back and a woman looked out through the bars that protected the little window.

"We're not buying."

"I'm here to see Annechon," Rathe began.

"She's not seeing strangers." The woman started to close the shutter.

"It's urgent," Rathe said. "I have a message."

"Two of you? Not likely."

Rathe reached into his pocket, came up with a folded piece of paper. It was blank, but he hoped she wouldn't be able to tell that. "If not Annechon, tell her woman Lianne. It's from her friend Nico."

"I'll take it to her."

Rathe shook his head. "I'm to give it into her hand, one or the other of them." Beside him, Eslingen stirred uneasily, then did his best to look unthreatening. They were both thinking the same thing, Rathe knew: they couldn't afford to stay in the service road much longer, not without drawing more notice than Regisse's tokens could avert.

The woman grimaced, but then Rathe heard her draw back the bar. "You can wait in the yard. Put the bar up behind you."

Eslingen did as he was told, still trying to look harmless, and the woman scurried away. The yard itself was largely barren, just a few half-grown trees in pots that Rathe guessed Annechon had brought from her previous residence. Grass straggled by the fences, but it was trampled to extinction over most of the space. There had been a gravel path to the privy, Rathe thought, but it hadn't been replaced in some time and was mostly mud now: another sign of Annechon's declining fortunes. A short flight of steps led up to the main level, but the door was shut fast. On the floors above, the shutters were still closed against the morning light. Beside him, Eslingen stirred again, but held his silence.

Then at last the door opened, and a stocky woman in powder blue came down the stairs, holding her skirts above her ankles to keep them from the mud. "You said—oh. It's yourself. She didn't say." She paused, looked hastily over her shoulder. "You know Hearts is looking for you."

"I know," Rathe said. "I need her help, Lianne. I think she knows something that will clear me."

"If she did, she would have told them already," Lianne said.

"If she knew it mattered," Rathe said. "And she may not—probably doesn't. But I need to talk to her."

Lianne looked from him to Eslingen and back again, then flung up her hands. "Very well. I'll bring you to her. But on your head be it if she throws you out."

"Thank you, Lianne," Rathe said, meekly, and followed her up the stairs.

The house was quiet still, only a single woman busy in the kitchen as they passed the open door. Lianne took them up the main stair—less likely to meet other servants there, Rathe thought—and then tapped softly on the door of what was surely the largest bedroom. There was a muffled reply, and Lianne opened the door, letting them into a darkened anteroom. "Wait here."

She slipped through an inner door without waiting for an answer. Rathe glanced around the dimly-lit room, picking out the clothespress, its doors half open, skirts spilling out, and on the opposite wall the delicate table that held Annechon's cosmetics. There was also an expensive satin gown, in a shade of lavender that wouldn't flatter Annechon, and he hoped she hadn't had an overnight guest. But surely if she had Lianne would never have admitted them this far.

The door opened again, and Lianne beckoned to them. "Come in. She'll see you."

The bedroom itself was more brightly lit, a branch of candles on the table beside the bed and a trio of mage-lights hanging from the ceiling. Annechon herself was sitting up amid her tousled sheets, a scarlet wrap thrown over her shoulders and her hair pulled back in a simple braid for sleeping. "Nico. You were the last person I expected to see here."

"I need your help," Rathe said. They had known each other too long to play games; either she would help, or she would send them on their way, but she would never betray him.

"It's not safe."

Rathe ignored her word. "There were things you didn't tell us before. I need to know, Anne."

For a moment, he thought she was going to deny it, waste time on a dance of evasion, but then she looked away. "What are you talking about?"

"De Castiat," Rathe said. "You've been visiting her, you know her better than you said. Is she courting you?"

Annechon hesitated. "In a way."

"She's up to her neck in what's going on." It was a risk, without proof he didn't have, but he saw from Annechon's face that he was right. "Putting aside the salt smuggling."

Annechon grimaced. "For Oriane's sake, sit down. I want my tea."

"Talk first," Rathe said, and she shook her head.

"I'll talk, but I need tea to do it. I've—I haven't made the wisest choice here, Nico." She reached for the bell that sat beside the candelabrum without waiting for an answer, and when the door opened, sent Lianne for her breakfast tray. Rathe looked around, found an empty chair, and drew it closer to the bedside. Eslingen copied him, automatically arranging his borrowed coat as though it fit him properly, but Annechon didn't seem to notice. "Yes, Amariel has been courting me. We've been friends for a few years now—and by that I mean friends, not some euphemism. But once she put herself under arrest, she invited me to visit, and made it clear she was interested in more. She also made it clear she couldn't afford to keep me, which—I regret. So I've been enjoying what I have for now."

It was not a stable situation, nor an uncommon one, though Annechon had always been mildly contemptuous of other women who could not balance feelings and practicality. The door opened before Rathe could decide how to respond, and Lianne set the little table beside the bed. She poured a cup for Annechon, ostentatiously ignoring the men, and slipped away again. Annechon sighed.

"Lianne thinks I'm taking too many risks. She may not be wrong."

"She may not be," Rathe said. "What's de Castiat up to, Annechon?"

"I don't know," Annechon said. "Not exactly. It's something to do with d'Alamenon. She calls the tune in that house."

"Do you mean to say this surrender was her idea?" Rathe asked.

"No." Annechon shook her head for emphasis, then hesitated. "No, I'm certain it wasn't. Amariel was different before the nobles started arriving for the wedding."

"When you say d'Alamenon calls the tune," Rathe began and Annechon sighed again.

"She's paying some of the expenses—they're cousins, I gather. And she's always sending her stewards over. I think they're spying on Amariel, or they might be giving orders. Amariel always sees them, no matter what else she might be doing, and the stewards always leave looking contented."

Eslingen was frowning, spoke before Rathe could intervene. "That's not much to go on."

"If I'd known more, I would have spoken," Annechon said. "Or at least I'd have considered it."

"And the carts?" Eslingen asked. "Are they hers?"

Annechon hesitated. "I don't know."

"Your best guess," Rathe said.

"I really don't know," Annechon said. "I don't think so. She wasn't surprised, but she isn't behind them."

"But she knows more about them," Rathe said, and Annechon nodded reluctantly.

"More than she ought. But she doesn't approve, and she's not happy about them, I'm sure of that." She straightened, drawing her gown closer about her shoulders. "And that's all I can tell you, Nico, I swear it. "

"It's useful," Rathe said. Except that it meant he somehow needed to talk to de Castiat again, and the woman was currently under guard in her own house…

"One other question," Eslingen said. "You said Bonamy was the same man who had a connection with the Broadsheet Poet. And now there's been a Leveler riot at his house. What are the odds he'd be willing to discuss that with us?"

It was a good question, though the arrangements wouldn't be easy, and Rathe nodded in agreement. Annechon blinked. "He might. Though you're not in a position to be much help."

"For the moment," Eslingen said mildly.

Rathe said, "If there is Leveler involvement, we need to know. And sooner rather than later."

"I see that," Annechon said. "I could invite him for an early tea. Would that help?"

Rathe nodded. "And I promise, we'll be discreet."

"That would be appreciated," Annechon said.

ANNECHON OFFERED THEM the use of one of her lesser guest rooms. It was tucked under the eaves, with a bed broad enough for three and a fragile-looking table set beside a gable window. From the look of it, it got little use, nor did Annechon's servants spend much time cleaning. There were cobwebs in the corners, and when Eslingen ran his finger curiously along the window sill, he left a track in the dust. Rathe lowered himself onto the foot of the bed.

"The person we need to talk to is de Castiat. And I don't see how to get to her."

"Surely Sohier's people would look the other way." Eslingen turned away from the window and seated himself beside Rathe.

"Sohier would," Rathe said. "And one or two of the others. The rest would at least report to Trijn, and she'd have to take action."

"By which time, we should be gone," Eslingen said.

Rathe went on as if he hadn't spoken. "Not to mention that Hearts must have their own people keeping an eye on the house. I certainly would, if I was Orlandi."

"But she's not you," Eslingen said. "In fact, she's been doing her best to stay out of this, from the very beginning."

"And she's been fee'd to look the other way, on the carts and Tyrseis knows what all else," Rathe said. "I know. But she'd be a fool not to keep her eyes on the people from Dreams."

Rathe wasn't wrong about that, Eslingen thought. Each of the points' stations jealously guarded their territory, and resented any intrusion from other stations, maybe even more than they resented the presence of the Guard. And it was also true that some of the women from Dreams would not mind an excuse to see Rathe brought down a step or two, with his uncomfortable beliefs about fees and the rule of law. It wouldn't even count as betrayal, just doing their duty and reporting to their own superior. Sohier could be trusted, but the others… It was better not to ask them to take the chance. But that meant either they had to find a way in to de Castiat's house, or persuade her to come to them, and neither one seemed like a good option. "Do we really need to talk to Bonamy?"

"It was your idea," Rathe said, but his smile took some of the sting from the words.

"I know. And now I'm wondering if I was wrong."

"I think now's the best chance we'll have," Rathe said. "Sooner would have been better, while he was still shaking from the riot. But I want to know why he thinks he was a target."

It was what Eslingen had been thinking himself, and he nodded. "Let's hope he'll talk."

They spent the rest of the day in the narrow room. Annechon herself brought them their midday meal, and then Rathe slept. Eslingen settled beside him, wishing he had some of the most recent broadsheets. Or any broadsheets at all: he needed something to distract him from the nagging fear that they would be better off making a tactical retreat. And yet. If they left the city, they'd have to rely on the Guard and Rathe's allies among the points to prove that Rathe wasn't involved, and that left the question of what was really going on in Hearts worryingly unresolved. No, Rathe was right that the best way to prove his innocence was to figure out why anyone was moving cartloads of gunpowder through the district, and there was no one else to do it. The thoughts chased themselves through his head until he found himself mentally reciting ballads to drown them out.

Annechon returned at last, and Rathe sat up, instantly awake. "News?"

"Bonamy's on his way," she answered. "Come down, and we'll talk."

They followed her down to the main floor, using the servants' stair this time, and she let them into a narrow room behind the private parlor. It was fitted with a narrow counter and shelves stocked with painted pottery, and Eslingen guessed it was normally used to ready food before it was taken into the parlor.

"Wait here," Annechon said, and left without pausing for an answer. She left the door partly open behind her and Eslingen stepped closer so that he could see out without being seen. Rathe joined him, frowning. Eslingen glanced at him, lifting his eyebrows in question, but Rathe shook his head, and Eslingen turned his attention to the parlor. If there was trouble—if Bonamy had brought the women from Hearts—they could duck back down the servants' corridor, make their escape through the backyard. Though Hearts would have to be stupid not to watch the service road; better perhaps to try to get through between the houses. The far door opened, and he braced himself, then relaxed, seeing only Annechon and Bonamy.

"You need to tell me what you want," Bonamy said. "I've obliged you this far, but I have enough on my plate right now—"

"And don't we all know it," Annechon answered. "You're bringing trouble down on all of us."

"It's not my doing." From his tone, that wasn't the first time Bonamy had said that.

"It's your house that's hosting the review," Annechon said. "And your hand protecting Master Aconite. But that's not my main concern. What you have done to upset the Levelers? You were one of them not so long ago."

Eslingen saw Bonamy stiffen, and then relax, shaking his head. "Very long ago, Annechon. Too long ago to be worth remembering."

"Sit," Annechon said, impatiently, and Bonamy drifted toward a chair. "But it is remembered, and not just by us in Hearts. And that riot was directed at you alone."

"If that's what you wanted, I've nothing to say." Bonamy turned toward the door, but Annechon put her back against it. "There's nothing I can tell you."

Rathe took a breath and pushed the door open. "I wanted a word with you, Master Bonamy."

Bonamy spun, his eyes widening, but got himself under control. "Adjunct Point. And of course Captain vaan Esling."

"That's right," Rathe said.

"The women at Hearts are looking for you," Bonamy said. There was no sign that he was armed, but Eslingen took a few steps further, placing himself where he could easily intercept the other man if he tried for Rathe, or for the door.

"So I've been told." Rathe managed to sound amused. "For leading a riot, I understand."

"It's what they said," Bonamy answered.

"And what did you say to that?" Eslingen asked, in spite of himself.

Bonamy gave him a sharp glance. "The truth. That I didn't see him—or you—anywhere in the mob. Not that they listened."

"And you don't find that a bit odd?" Eslingen lifted his eyebrows.

"The points make the case that suits them," Bonamy said. "Present company excepted." He paused. "Though I hear there are reasons to think you might support a Leveler riot, Adjunct Point."

"It's no secret," Rathe said. "I believe in the law and that the law applies to everyone, noble and common alike. But I don't favor murder and riot."

"Who said anything about murder?" Bonamy sounded genuinely alarmed.

"The Broadsheet Poet, for one," Rathe answered.

"That was a long time ago." Bonamy looked away.

"Not so long as all that," Rathe said. "And it was her slogan they were shouting outside your door."

"You were her friend," Eslingen said, and Bonamy flinched.

"The Poet is long gone." There was a note of bitterness in his voice that suggested all the stories were true. "I give you my word on that."

"We need more than that," Rathe said, almost gently.

There was a moment of silence, then Bonamy shook his head and dropped abruptly onto the nearest chair. "Yes, I knew the Broadsheet Poet. I knew what was written. But the Poet is gone."

"Dead?" Rathe cocked his head.

Bonamy looked genuinely surprised. "No. Not that I know of, anyway. But gone. Gone from the city and from politics altogether."

"Put a name to her," Rathe suggested.

"No. She's left the city, and that's outside your jurisdiction." Bonamy managed a fleeting smile. "Should she come back, I'd—rethink that answer. But she hasn't. These latest broadsheets aren't her work."

He sounded very certain. Eslingen looked sideways, and saw Rathe nod. "All right, grant you that. Then why did these Levelers attack you?"

There was another silence, stretching longer than the first. Eslingen heard a clock strike five in one of the other parlors, and Bonamy flinched again. "It was a hired mob. I've no idea."

His voice carried no conviction. Eslingen said, "You brought up the carts." It was a thrust at random, but Bonamy's mouth tightened.

"What's that got to do with anything?"

"You tell me," Eslingen said.

Rathe said, "They're carrying gunpowder, Bonamy. Barrels full of it, enough to arm a small company, or so Philip tells me. That sounds very much like the war the Poet wanted."

"That's not—" Bonamy shook his head. "No one wants that."

"Whoever's writing these broadsheets wants it," Rathe said. "And barrels of gunpowder mean they have a way to get it. What do you know about the carts?"

Bonamy buried his head in his hands. "I didn't have a choice." Eslingen took a step forward, but Rathe caught his wrist. Bonamy looked up at them, a grimace that was not a smile twisting his face. "They stored them in my cellars. The barrels."

"Why didn't you warn somebody?" Eslingen demanded.

"Who would I tell?" Bonamy answered. "Hearts? Orlandi was part of it, and half the station with her. And they were watching me too closely for me to try elsewhere." He looked at Eslingen. "That's why I tried to get you to look into the carts, but that came too late."

"Who's they?" Rathe said, cutting across anything Eslingen would have said.

"Hired knives." Bonamy shook his head. "One or two of them I could put a name to, but they're hirelings, and I'm sure they've been well paid to keep their principal a secret. It was they who led the riot, that was to put you off the scent. And to ensure I kept quiet."

Eslingen took a breath. "What were the barrels for?"

"I don't know. I swear it." Bonamy ran his hands through his hair.

At least there should still be time to stop the plan, whatever it was, and figure out the rest after they'd made sure there would be no attack. Eslingen said, "If we send someone—the Guard, maybe—to seize the barrels—"

"But you can't," Bonamy interrupted. "They're gone. They took the last of them away overnight."

"Where?" Rathe's voice rose dangerously.

"I don't know," Bonamy said again. "I wasn't part of their plan."

"Why didn't you tell someone?" Rathe asked. "Annechon, any of your friends in Hearts. They could have passed the word."

"They knew," Bonamy said. "Tyrseis, you don't understand any of it. They knew."

"Knew what?" Eslingen said.

"I was the Broadsheet Poet," Bonamy said. "They said they could prove it, and—well, it was true, I don't doubt they could."

"You? The Poet?" Annechon's voice was sharp with disbelief. "You've made your living off the nobility."

"And paid for it, every step of the way," Bonamy said bitterly. "Over and over, I thought someone cared for me, and every time, I was sent away without even a parting gift to sweeten the sting. Five years I was with her—she was the worst of them—five years at her beck and call, her secret lover. I was willing, I admit it, I loved her and I did what she wanted. She bore two sons, and then she said I was no use to her if all I could get was boy children. She threw me out, said I'd failed to honor my contract, and when I complained, she set her people on me to drive me out of the house that was supposed to be mine. Set it on fire so I couldn't claim it."

"And the children?" Eslingen said, after a moment.

"I don't know," Bonamy said. "She didn't keep them with her household, being boys, there was no need to claim them. I would have taken them, I told her so, but she said no child of hers would be raised by a hobby-horse."

Eslingen flinched. He was a motherless man himself, left for his father to raise, but at least he'd had a father to claim him, and an aunt who'd taken them both in. He'd never doubted that his father had loved him, whatever his mother had chosen.

"Who was she?" Rathe asked, and Bonamy shook his head.

"What does it matter? She has a name and lands in the Ile'Nord, and she'd just call me a liar." He sighed. "I came to Astreiant because she couldn't touch me here. But that was why I wrote what I did. I wanted them hurt. I wanted my boys. I wanted them all to burn."

"But you stopped," Rathe said.

Bonamy drew a deep breath. "That winter, when the riots broke out—we were all starving, and the fighting didn't feed anyone. I was working in a resort-house then, not that anyone wanted us, and I learned I'd crawl to anyone to keep my friends fed. I was too ashamed then to keep writing. So I kept on with what I knew, and made my peace with it. Eventually I had a patronne who supported me— she might even have loved me—and it didn't seem to matter so much anymore. And—I suppose I grew old. I have my own house, that was her parting gift to me, and I make sure my own people are safe. That's all I can hope for."

Eslingen looked away, unable to bear the pain on the other man's face. It made all too much sense, in a terrible way, but there was still something missing, some piece that didn't quite fit. "How did they know? The knives who threatened you. How did they know you were the Poet? No one else did."

Bonamy blinked as though the thought hadn't occurred to him. Rathe said, "Who did know? This patronne, the one who gave you the Lilies?"

"She's dead," Bonamy said.

"Who might she have told?" Rathe asked. "A sister? A daughter?"

"She had no sisters," Bonamy said. "And, as I said, she's dead."

"But she could have told someone," Rathe said. "And we need to find whoever's behind this—sooner rather than later, or you will get to see everything burn. I swear we'll keep your secret. If we possibly can."

Bonamy closed his eyes. "The Palatine de Galhac."

TEN

D*E GALHAC*. R*ATHE* closed his eyes for an instant, the pieces of the puzzle shifting into new patterns. Not the palatineur, but his sister, the one who died childless—despite Bonamy's efforts, it seemed. And whom he had loved, if the pain in his voice was anything to go on.

Eslingen said, "What about the palatineur? Did he know?"

"Martin?" Bonamy blinked again, sounding genuinely surprised. "I suppose he might have—yes, we were friends, I didn't make any effort to keep things from him, nor did she."

"And the soeuraine? D'Alamenon?" It was taking an effort for Eslingen to keep his voice calm and unthreatening, and Rathe laid a hand on his arm.

"I never told her," Bonamy said. His mouth twitched. "But she might have. They were close, more like sisters than cousins, Dariela was fond of her almost until the end."

"But not at the end," Rathe said.

"D'Alamenon wanted to be palatine," Bonamy said. "And Dariela wouldn't put Martin aside, not when he had a daughter who was everything you'd want in an heir. They made it up before the end, or so I thought."

"Or seemed to," Eslingen said. He looked at Rathe. "Coindarel says d'Alamenon tried to make the claim after the palatine died, but the family went against her."

"D'Alamenon seems to turn up everywhere," Rathe said. "She wanted to be palatine, that's no great surprise, but then she's also de Castiat's cousin, and her stewards are there to call the tune, you said, Annechon."

Annechon nodded thoughtfully. "I'd say so. Not that Amariel likes her particularly, but—" She stopped abruptly. "Nico. D'Alamenon is hosting a ball for the Castellan and her husband-to-be. She rented a house just for that, here in Hearts. Amariel was complaining about it, that d'Alamenon wanted all her kin to contribute to the expense."

"What sort of ball?" Eslingen asked, and Annechon shrugged.

"What you'd expect. Dancing and dinner and a late supper at the end before everyone goes home. Good wine in lavish quantities, apparently the house has a deep cellar already stocked and it comes with the price. Oh, and the queen was to make an appearance, and maybe the Metropolitan. But I only know what I hear, it's not a thing I'd be invited to even if Amariel and I had an arrangement."

The queen and the Metropolitan, Rathe thought. And presumably de Galhac and his closest kin, as well as the bride and groom. Dozens of other nobles—maybe a hundred or more, and certainly everyone who might stand between d'Alamenon and a claim to the throne. And a cellar already filled with barrels, among which a dozen or more barrels of gunpowder could go unnoticed. "When? When is the ball?"

Annechon frowned. "Tomorrow—no, I have the days wrong. It's tonight."

The breath caught in Rathe's throat. It was already late in the day, and he was a wanted man. He couldn't just send word to the Surintendant, or the Prince-Marshal, claiming that d'Alamenon intended to assassinate half the nobility, he would need to send proof as well...

"That can't be right," Eslingen said, but his tone was less certain than his words.

"Can't it?" Rathe's voice was grim. "Can you put the pieces together a better way?"

"I can't," Eslingen admitted. "But it's thin, Nico. Gods, it's thin."

"We need proof," Rathe said.

"Coindarel would take my word," Eslingen said.

"Would the queen listen?" Rathe asked. "And even if she did, what about the

Metropolitan? And de Galhac and all the rest? We need proof solid enough to stop them." He paused, imagining the preparations for the ball, dozens of servants busy in the kitchens and the ballroom, in the yard and in the stables, all of them going about their business with no idea that the cellar was filled with powder, ready to bring the house down about their ears. "We need to defuse the barrels. She's bound to have them on some sort of clock, or a long fuse, she can't want to be there when the house blows up."

Eslingen nodded. "There are ways, yes. And a timer would be proof, at least enough to get everyone's attention."

It was a risk, Rathe thought. Even if they found a timing mechanism and brought it to the queen's court, d'Alamenon could still deny it. She could call them liars, say they were part of some Leveler conspiracy to sow dissension among the great and good, or to spoil the royal wedding—and that might just be what d'Alamenon had intended when she fee'd Hearts to accuse him of leading a Leveler riot. But they could at least save the lives of the people hired to work in the house, and that counted for a great deal. "Annechon. Do you know where the house is?"

"I don't." Annechon shook her head. "But it shouldn't be hard to find."

"I know it," Bonamy said. "I can take you there."

Out of the corner of his eye, Rathe saw Eslingen start to say something, then stop, grimacing. He could guess what the other man would have said: why would Bonamy help, after all this, and met Eslingen's eyes with a grimace of his own.

"I owe Martin this much," Bonamy said. "And Sylla. They were…kind, after Dariela died. More than kind. They let me see her buried, they acknowledged my right to that. I don't want anything to happen to them."

"It would be a help," Rathe said, as much to Eslingen as to Bonamy, and Eslingen sighed.

"How far is it? Bearing in mind that Hearts is still after Nico."

"It's part of that row of houses that back onto the old city wall," Bonamy said.

Eslingen looked blank, and Rathe nodded. "I know it. A quarter hour's walk, maybe a bit more if we go roundabout."

"Hearts doesn't go there much," Annechon said. "The householders take care of their own."

Rathe nodded again. That was no surprise—Hearts had always given the nobility more leeway than they deserved—but at least this time it would work in their favor.

"I know a way that should avoid the points," Bonamy said, and this time Rathe nodded.

"All right. And thank you."

Bonamy was as good as his word, though Rathe was careful to replace the no-see-me against his chest, and made sure Eslingen did the same. Even the lesser streets were busy, Hearts coming to life as the evening approached, but somewhat to his surprise, no one seemed to pay any attention to them. In fact, most people averted their eyes, even though he would have thought Bonamy to be well-known.

"Not that I'm complaining," Eslingen said as they passed through an empty plaza, "but people are going out of their way not to look at us. What's waiting for us?"

Bonamy looked momentarily startled. "Nothing."

"Forgive me if I have doubts," Eslingen said.

Rathe put a hand on his sleeve, bringing them all to a stop. "It's a fair question, Bonamy."

"What question?" Bonamy asked. "I don't understand."

"Why is everyone ignoring us—ignoring you?" Rathe asked.

"We value discretion in Hearts," Bonamy said stiffly. "They assume I'm escorting you to an appointment. And given the direction we're going, it's likely to be someone important."

Eslingen laughed, and after a moment Rathe joined him. "I wouldn't have thought we were the type to appeal to a noble lady."

"She would be choosing between two different types," Bonamy said. "It's not uncommon."

Rathe paused, caught between offense and embarrassment. He'd read the chapbooks, of course, there wasn't an apprentice in Astreiant who hadn't bought at least one of the crudely printed stories of what happened between women and men in the houses of Hearts, but it had never occurred to him that he might be taken for a lady's-friend. Eslingen laughed again.

"It's good to have an excuse."

"I suppose," Rathe muttered, but followed Bonamy without further complaint.

The house was where Rathe had expected it would be, one of five built on ground that sloped gently down away from the wall that had once enclosed the city proper. The queen's court had always been outside those defenses, and had walls of its own; these were the houses of nobles and the wealthiest of the merchants-resident, close enough to reach the queen's court with ease, but far enough apart to assert their own importance. Each was different, one built like a small castle with a tower at each end, another tall and narrow and surrounded by immaculate gardens, a third with multiple round windows cut into the slates of its roof. It was obvious which of the houses was their destination: its gates were open and long banners hung from the eaves, gold and scarlet stripes quartered with a blossoming tree on a white ground. Torches stood in the brackets beside the gate, ready to welcome the guests, and two boys hauled an empty handcart out from an alley, its sides badged with the flame of the Bakers' Guild.

Bonamy nodded to them, and led them down the alley. "The house belongs to the landame Vignet, she's loaning it to the soeuraine. They're cousins."

"Aren't they all?" Eslingen murmured.

"I know her cook," Bonamy went on, as if the Leaguer hadn't spoken. "If d'Alamenon has any sense, she'll have kept her on."

They were almost at the kitchen door. It stood open, spilling noise and lamplight into the alley, and a pair of girls were sitting on the broad stone step, methodically trimming a bushel of long beans. They scooted to either side without a word, and Bonamy leaned into the doorway. "Saire?"

"I'll fetch her," someone called from within, and a few moments later an older woman appeared in the doorway, wiping her hands on her apron.

"I love you, Amorin, but I haven't got time for you."

"It's important, I promise," Bonamy began, but she was already looking beyond him.

"Who are these?"

"They just need a brief word," Bonamy said.

"That's Rathe, isn't it? The one they say started your riot."

"It wasn't my riot," Bonamy said, "and he didn't do it."

"It's important," Eslingen said, with his best smile, and Rathe interrupted.

"More to the point, we won't take up your time. You've had any number of barrels added to your cellar lately." It was taking a chance, and he relaxed slightly as he saw her puzzled frown.

"Yes, wine for the ball."

"More than you thought necessary," Rathe said.

Saire nodded again. "Yes. Why?"

"We need to look in your cellar," Rathe said. "I think someone's brought something that shouldn't be there, that's a danger to all of you. I hope I'm wrong, but I can't take the risk."

"Hearts is looking for you," Saire said. From her tone, she neither approved or disapproved, was merely stating a fact. "To call a point for the riot."

"They're well fee'd to do it," Eslingen said.

Saire gave a sideways smile. "They're fee'd to do most things—Captain, is it? All right, you can look. But you mayn't touch anything, and I'll go with you. And you'll come, too, Amorin, I want your witness. You can have a quarter hour, no more."

"That'll be enough," Rathe said, and hoped it would be true.

Saire made a sound of disbelief, but beckoned for them to follow. "Claire! Keep an eye on things, I'll be back in a minute or two."

There was an indistinct answer from deeper in the kitchen, crowded with cooks and assistants busy at the worktables and tending the great range beside the fireplace. Rathe caught only a glimpse of the controlled chaos before Saire had brought them through to a pantry lined with racks of jarred spices and staples, and then to an ironbound door at its end. She fished under her skirts and brought out a bundle of keys, then unlocked the door, pushing it open on well-oiled hinges. Stairs led down into the dark, and she reached for a mage-light lantern hanging just inside the door. "This way."

She started down the stairs, holding the lantern high, and Rathe followed, Eslingen on his heels and Bonamy slower behind him. The cellar was much as he'd expected, long and low, the ceiling held up on arches as roundly curved as barrels, wooden racks stretching into the darkness. Closer to the door, the racks were filled with an array of bottles, each one daubed with the cellar-keeper's mark, but beyond them, wider racks held an array of barrels of various sizes, from the small firkins that would hold the most expensive wines to the great hogsheads stacked under one arch. "We'll need to look at some of them," he said.

"You can't broach them," Saire said, instantly bristling, and Rathe shook his head.

"No, no need." He moved down the main aisle, not entirely sure what he was looking for. "Where did they put those new barrels?"

"They were supposed to put them here," Saire said, frowning now at one of the middle racks. "But these are maseigne's, that's our mark on them. The fools must have taken them all the way to the back, that'll be more work for us serving."

All the way to the back would bring them toward the front of the house, Rathe thought, following her gesture. And that would put them under the parlor and the ballroom, exactly where you'd want to place gunpowder to kill as many of the guests as possible.

"There," Saire said, and pointed to a rack of barrels that bore none of the painted markings. "That must be them."

"May I?" Rathe took the lantern from her and brought it closer. There were more barrels than he'd expected, half a dozen in this rack alone, another half dozen in the rack opposite, and as many more stacked outside the racks against the wall of the cellar. Eslingen rapped sharply on the nearest barrel, cocking his head at the sound, then shrugged one shoulder.

"Dame," Rathe said. "I need to tap one of these barrels. Only one, and you'll have to open it anyway for the ball. There's no harm in doing it now, but I need to be sure what's in it."

"Poison?" Saire sounded sharply alarmed.

"No. Not that, but not what it should be," Rathe said. "And I still hope I'm wrong."

Saire hesitated for a long moment, then reached beneath her skirts again to bring out a wooden spigot. "One of you fetch me the mallet, it's by the door."

Eslingen moved to obey, came back quickly with the heavy mallet. She handed him the spigot, then braced herself and swung the mallet hard against the bung. The blow sounded thick and dead, without a liquid echo, and the bung barely moved. She frowned and hit it again, and this time drove the bung fully into the barrel. She reached instantly for the spigot, then froze. Instead of a gush of liquid, there was a whispering like sand, and a thin stream of black grains spilled out into the lamplight.

"Quick, dame, stopper it," Eslingen said.

Saire obeyed, then stooped to examine the spilled powder. "What is this?"

"Gunpowder," Eslingen said.

"Impossible," Saire said, and shook her head. "In my cellar?"

"All or most of these new barrels," Rathe said. "Bar one or two to serve the guests before they were set off."

"Set off," Saire repeated. "Like fireworks."

"Worse," Rathe said. "I told you, it's a danger to everyone here."

Eslingen had been examining the barrels, and now moved to the back of the racks. "Nico."

Rathe came to join him, and saw that the ends of the barrels were wrapped in cording, strands running between the barrels and into a tapped hole in the head.

Another strand ran across the stone floor, dirt scuffed over it to dull its color, and connected to another web of cord that linked the barrels against the wall. A third strand led to the barrels on the opposite rack. "Slowmatch?"

"Fuse cord." Eslingen was already searching behind the rack, then moved to examine the barrels against the wall. "They must intend to fire it themselves, I don't find a clockwork. Or even a candle fuse, though I wouldn't want to trust that myself. I suppose they want to be sure everyone is here before they light it." He stooped and drew up a thicker length of cord about a foot long. "Here's the actual fuse. I'd say that would give them half an hour or so to take themselves out of harm's way."

"Can you undo all this?" Rathe waved at the barrels.

"I can pull off all the cord and spoil it," Eslingen said, "but all they'd have to do was bring more. They'd really only need to put a fuse to half of them, a third, even, the rest will go up when the others do."

Rathe swore. "We can't just leave this—"

"No," Eslingen said. "We need to send to Coindarel, and to the queen's court, tell them what's been done here."

"And to maseigne," Saire said sharply. "She'd never be part of this."

She was d'Alamenon's cousin, Rathe thought, but at least Saire seemed certain the woman wouldn't agree to killing her own people. "Right. Send notes? While you, Dame, take your people out of here."

"I can't do that, we're pledged to serve the ball," Saire began, then looked at the barrels again. "That's enough powder to bring down the entire house, isn't it?"

"And the walls next door," Eslingen said grimly.

"Demis in chains." Saire covered her mouth with her hand for just a moment, then straightened. "Swear to me you had nothing to do with this."

"I promise," Rathe said. "As I hope to keep my place at Dreams, I swear it. This is none of my doing, nor Philip's—vaan Esling's."

"From you I'll take that," Saire said. "What do we do?"

"Clear the house," Eslingen said. "The houses next door, are they occupied?"

Saire shook her head. "They're empty, both of them, and the staff lives out. Some of them are working for us, though."

"Tell everyone to leave," Rathe said. "Send them all home—tell them why if you have to, there's no point in keeping it secret now. Tell them to stay well clear until tomorrow." *Or until everything blows up in our faces, but hopefully it won't come to that.*

"We still need to warn the court," Eslingen said.

"I know," Rathe said. "But we can't leave this unwatched, either."

"We can send a message—messages." Eslingen didn't sound convinced, and Rathe shook his head.

"Someone needs to go in person. You need to go, Philip, no one's trying to call a point on you, and you've got the rank and Coindarel to back you if you need it."

"He's on the other side of town," Eslingen said.

Saire lifted her head. "The Prince-Marshal? He's to be a guest tonight so he'll be at the queen's court with the rest of them."

Rathe nodded. "That's the first luck we've had. Go to him, Philip, tell him what's going on."

"I'll go with him," Bonamy said. "Martin will listen to me. If you'll have me, Captain."

Eslingen nodded, still looking at Rathe. "And you?"

"I'll stay here," Rathe answered. "And make sure no one gets a chance to set these off."

For a moment, he though Eslingen might argue, but then the Leaguer nodded again. "You can bar the door from this side—that should keep anyone out." He drew the knife he'd been carrying since the riot. "Here."

"Thanks." Rathe clasped his shoulder, wishing there were time for more. "Go."

Eslingen hurried up the cellar stairs, Bonamy close on his heels. He plunged through the kitchen, hearing the sudden uproar as the cooks and servers saw Saire's face, checked at her shout from behind him.

"Captain! There are horses in the stable, tell Estinne I said you should have them."

He lifted a hand in thanks, and clattered down the stairs. The groom had heard the commotion and was already leaning out of the wide door. "Here, what's going on?"

"Saddle two horses," Eslingen said. "Quick as you can. Saire's orders."

The groom looked from him to Bonamy, and then ducked back into the stable. Eslingen followed, seeing four horses waiting, and the groom gave him a sharp look. "Fast or far?"

"Not far, but we're in a hurry," Eslingen answered.

"Belstan and Flower, then, and it'll go faster if you help."

Eslingen took the tack he was offered, and brought out the neat bay mare named Flower. Bonamy held the bridle competently enough while Eslingen saddled her, then scrambled into the saddle while Eslingen adjusted Belstan's tack. He swung himself up and gathered the reins, looking down at the groom. "Does your lady have another stable? You'll want to take these horses there, right away." The man started to question, and Eslingen put his heels to Belstan's ribs. "Ask Saire," he called over his shoulder, and urged the horse through the open gate.

He drew up in the open street to let Bonamy catch up, and the older man said breathlessly, "I can lead the way—"

"Go," Eslingen said, and fell in behind them.

The streets were even more crowded now as Hearts opened for business, and it was impossible to move at more than a trot. Bonamy threaded his way through the edge of a market, then pulled up so sharply that Eslingen's horse backed and sidled. "What's wrong?"

"Points. Orlandi herself, unless I miss my guess."

Sure enough, a tight wedge was pushing its way into the market, a mix of women and men in the familiar heavy leather jerkins, truncheons already in hand. Eslingen recognized the woman at their head, and swore under his breath.

"We have to turn back," Bonamy said, and Eslingen instinctively urged his horse closer to block his way.

"No, that'll draw their eye." He nodded toward the next street that led away from the market. "Go there, but don't seem to hurry."

"It's the wrong direction," Bonamy said, but nudged his horse forward. Eslingen copied him, keeping hands and heels still with an effort of will, and they reached the side street together without drawing a shout. It was deep in shadow, the buildings overhanging the street, and Eslingen allowed himself a sigh of relief as he urged the horse into a trot. Bonamy caught up with him easily, and Eslingen risked a glance over his shoulder. There was no sign of pursuit, and he looked back at Bonamy.

"Which way from here?"

"This is the long way," Bonamy answered. "There's not a cross street for some time. We'll take the first one, and work our way north and west."

And from there out of the fringes of the city into the Western Reach, and then to the royal palace that lay beyond: an hour's walk, if not longer, though the horses would speed their travel. And then however long it took to find Coindarel, or de Galhac, or anyone who would listen and believe them, and then close to another hour back to Vignet's house: plenty of time to get Saire and her people safely away, but also entirely too much time for d'Alamenon's knives to come, and there was only Rathe to keep them away from the barrels in the cellar. He could do it, Eslingen told himself. The cellar door opened inward, and it could be barred from the inside; he'd seen no other door or window—and there wouldn't be one, not if that was where the landame stored her best wines. All Rathe would have to do was get inside and shut the door against them. He knew better than to make a fight of it, especially not with his head still not fully healed. It would take sapper's axes to cut through that door, and it would take time to find them, and still more time to cut through the heavy wood. Rathe would be fine.

They reached the edge of Hearts at last, and the street opened out into one of the broad avenues that made up the Western Reach. Bonamy chirped to his horse, and they broke into a faster trot, cutting between two large *mannories* to reach the Royal Road that would bring them to the queen's court. Already Eslingen could see it in the distance, a tower of solid stone that had been added onto over the years, so that now that original fortress was surrounded by three-story brick wings and another set of walls that could be held, Eslingen thought, just long enough for the court to escape to the core of the palace. He had no right to be there, nor any proof of who he claimed to be, and he hoped Saire was right that Coindarel was in attendance.

The first gate was fully open, watched by a couple of men in the livery of the royal household. Eslingen pulled up to a walk, but before he could say anything, Bonamy leaned down from his saddle, hand outstretched. "To see the Prince-Marshal."

The nearest servant took whatever coin Bonamy offered, bowing slightly. "With the queen, sir, I believe."

"Thank you."

Bonamy started forward, and Eslingen followed, uneasily aware of the inner wall and the windows that overlooked this first courtyard. If anyone attempted to attack, a few musketeers could slow any charge with a few well-timed volleys; even small cannon, sakers or serpents, could wreak havoc in the enclosed space, and anything larger, loaded with grape, would be pure slaughter.

But this was not an attack, and they were not the enemy; they were here to serve the queen whether she wanted it or not, and the uniformed men at the next gate were on the same side. Eslingen pulled his horse to a stop, trying to read the embroidered badges on the scarlet coats: scarlet chevron on gold, and a black crescent beneath it, an Ajanine coat of arms, but not one he knew. The two men on duty crossed their halberds in front of him, barring the way, and out of the corner of his eye Eslingen saw a couple of pages scurrying from the stables. That was a good sign, and he swung himself out of the saddle.

"I'm with the Guard. I have an urgent message for the Prince-Marshal."

"One of us will carry it," the older of the halberdiers said.

"I'm to give it to him directly," Eslingen said.

The two halberdiers exchanged glances, and then the older man relaxed slightly. "Lieutenant. This man has a message for the Prince-Marshal."

Eslingen turned, still holding his horse's bridle, to see a tall woman emerge from the narrow gatehouse. Her uniform was no more elaborate than the guards', but there was expensive lace at her wrists and throat, the latter providing a bed for a gilt gorget of rank. "For Coindarel?" she asked, and Eslingen nodded.

"I'm with the Guard."

"And your friend?" She looked at Bonamy, still waiting patiently in the saddle.

"He's a witness. It's urgent, Lieutenant, or we wouldn't trouble the Prince-Marshal here."

There was a moment of silence, and then the woman shrugged. "He's within. Let them through." Bonamy swung down from his horse with more grace than Eslingen had expected, and the pages came to lead the animals away. "Go up to the main gate, they'll direct you from there."

"Thank you, lieutenant," Eslingen said. The halberdiers removed their weapons, and he started for the palace without looking back. Bonamy fell into step at his side.

"If we can't find the Prince-Marshal, we can ask for Martin—the palatine."

"I think we're more likely to get the Prince-Marshal," Eslingen answered.

"True." Bonamy paused. "Will he listen?"

"Yes," Eslingen said, and realized that he did in fact believe that. The question was, could Coindarel convince the queen? But that would be Coindarel's problem—and surely it was within his scope. The queen had always trusted him, and it would be easy enough to prove that he was telling the truth. The main thing was to keep the royal party from going to the house.

The broad steps that led up to the palace loomed in front of them, the polished stone very white in the rising twilight. There were guards lined up along the edges, their coats bright scarlet with gold braid and the queen's sunburst stitched on breast and cuffs. Eslingen nodded to the nearest as he started up the steps, expecting to be called back, but no one said anything until he reached the open door. It was blocked by another young lieutenant, her hair pinned up under a distinctly non-uniform lace cap, who held out her hand at their approach.

"Your invitations, sirs?"

"I'm with the Guard," Eslingen said again. "I have an urgent message for the Prince-Marshal."

"I can take it for you."

"I need to speak with him directly," Eslingen said. "As does Master Bonamy, as witness."

The lieutenant looked from one to the other, visibly contrasting Eslingen's ill-fitting clothes with his military bearing, and Bonamy's neatly respectable suit. "Come with me."

Eslingen followed her into the cool dark of the vestibule, lit only by a pair of hanging lanterns that cast circles of light that did not quite overlap. The walls were painted, he thought, but it was impossible to make out more than gesturing shapes—a woman on horseback, a family group, a battle scene—all the colors blurred and grayed in the shadows. He could hear music ahead of them, and the low hum of voices, and abruptly a door opened, spilling light across the parquet floor.

"What is it, Ferrand?"

"Two gentlemen for the Prince-Marshal," the lieutenant answered. "They say it's urgent."

The woman looked from one man to the other. "Names?"

Eslingen took a breath, knowing he didn't dare hesitate. "Philip vaan Esling. Captain in the City Guard. This is Master Amorin Bonamy."

"Vaan Esling." The woman's voice was flat. She was older, her hair just touched with gray, her satin gown trimmed with lace and only a senior steward's jeweled collar to mark her rank. "We were warned about you."

Eslingen lifted an eyebrow. This was what he had dreaded from the start; he only hoped he had the means to convince her. "By Point of Hearts, I assume. I assure you, maseigne, the matter is urgent."

"We were warned you would attempt to disrupt the ball," the woman said, "and I have been instructed to prevent it. If you are willing to wait quietly, I won't have to have you arrested."

But otherwise, she was quite happy to do so: that was very clear. Eslingen said, "Instructed by who, maseigne?"

"By the queen's chatelaine, Captain." *No one you should argue with*, her tone implied.

"And who spoke to her, I wonder?" Bonamy said. Behind him, Eslingen could see the shifting crowd, dozens of women and men in their finest silks and satins, the colors gleaming in the light of several enormous chandeliers. All nobles, all of the finest families, the twelve-quarter nobles that ruled Chenedolle, but there was no sign of the Prince-Marshal, or even of the queen herself.

"I only need a quiet word with the Prince-Marshal," Eslingen said. "If you'd call him to the door, there won't be any disruption."

"Until he hears what you have to say," the steward said. "We'll have no Leveler nonsense here."

"I'm no Leveler," Eslingen said, with what he hoped was an aristocratic smile. "I serve the queen and the queen's law."

"And yet you're here with a hobby-horse from a Point of Hearts resort-house, demanding entrance." The steward shook her head. "No, Captain."

"Let me speak with the Palatine de Galhac," Bonamy said, his voice taut. "He knows me, he'll speak for me, I swear it."

The steward just barely stopped short of rolling her eyes. "Not likely."

In the ballroom, the crowd was starting to move, forming up into the lines that would allow them to depart in formal order. Eslingen could see more of the stewards moving among them, adjusting precedence, directing groups to one side or the other. He thought he caught a glimpse of Coindarel among the other Enfantes of the royal house, the queen's closest kin, but the man was gone before he could catch his eye. If he said nothing, did nothing now to interrupt, the wedding party would get to Vignet's house and find it empty, just Rathe waiting in the cellar to show the waiting barrels and explain what they'd done. That would still keep the queen safe—unless, of course, something had happened to Rathe, and d'Alamenon's knives were waiting, ready to set off the gunpowder. He'd have to pay for his interference, but that was no price at all, not if it saved the queen and her court. It was what Rathe would do, and with less hesitation. He took a breath, filling his lungs, and let out the shout that was trained to cut through the clamor of battle. "Prince-Marshal! Prince-Marshal, alarm!"

The steward swore, grabbing his arm, and the young lieutenant seized him as well, kicking at his ankle to overbalance him and swing him away from the door.

"Prince-Marshal!"

There was the scrape of steel, and he froze as the lieutenant put her sword to his throat. "Stand and be still." Bonamy took a step away, as though he would have entered the ballroom, and the lieutenant tightened her grip, drawing a trickle of blood. "Try it, and I'll cut him."

"We'll have none of that," a familiar voice said, and Eslingen felt the pressure ease. "Philip, I assume you have a reason for this?"

"Prince-Marshal," Eslingen said, and felt his knees go weak.

"Lieutenant, put your sword away." Coindarel waited, and the woman reluctantly obeyed. "Now, Philip. Your explanation?"

"I've been to the house where this ball is to be held," Eslingen said. "The cellar is stuffed full of gunpowder. I counted at least twenty barrels, and there may be more."

"Enough to bring down the house on top of them," Coindarel said.

"Prince-Marshal," the steward said. "I beg your pardon, but we were warned about this. There is no powder, just a Leveler plot to spoil the wedding."

"It's easily proved," Eslingen said. "Come with me, send troops with me, and see for yourself."

"And who's behind this, do you know?" Coindarel shook his head. "No, you're right, that can wait. Follow me—and who's this?" He pointed to Bonamy, who bowed.

"Amorin Bonamy, Excellency. I—have come to bear witness."

"Then you come, too." Coindarel turned, shoving his way through the gathering crowd. Eslingen followed, ignoring the oozing scratch on his neck, and Bonamy clung to his heels. Abruptly, the crowd parted ahead of them, and a small woman swung to face them.

"Well, Raimon?"

She was tiny, the top of her high-piled hair barely reaching Coindarel's shoulder, but the candlelight glittered from the gold brocade overdress, and the jeweled girdle that clasped her waist. And from the small, delicate crown that was nearly lost in the faded gold of her hair. Bonamy went to one knee at her feet, and Eslingen barely stopped himself from doing the same. Instead, he made his deepest bow, and the queen waved impatient acknowledgement.

"Raimon?"

"This is Philip vaan Esling, majesty, and—Bonamy, was it? Who comes as

Philip's witness. They tell me there is gunpowder in the cellar of Vignet's house, ready to be set off—presumably to kill the guests, though I haven't had all the details yet."

The queen lifted one hand, and a taller, younger woman moved to join her, her unfortunate red hair mostly covered by a jeweled cap. "You'll want to hear this, Metropolitan. Very well, vaan Esling, tell your story."

"Majesty." Eslingen bowed again. He'd never been so close to the queen before, had only seen her from a distance, a gilded doll surrounded by her courtiers. Seen now, at little more than arm's length, her skin was slack with age and deeply lined, kohl and rouge too emphatic, particularly in contrast to Astreiant's Metropolitan, waiting now at her side. "We—the City Guard and the points—have been working together to deal with several matters that seem now to be related." Quickly, he ran through what they had found, from the mysterious carts to the riot to the complaint against Rathe and their attempt to unravel it, culminating in the discovery that the barrels of gunpowder had been brought to the house where d'Alamenon was to host a celebratory ball. "I've seen the barrels myself, majesty, and cut the fuse-cord that linked them. I beg you to stay safe here in the palace."

The queen's painted eyebrows rose. "And are you accusing the soueraine of being behind this?"

"Majesty, I have no proof of it," Eslingen answered, "but also there's no one else I could name."

"Majesty, this is nonsense." A woman a little older than the Metropolitan stepped out from the circle of listening courtiers. Eslingen saw de Galhac behind her, and knew she had to be d'Alamenon herself. "I don't say the captain lies, he may be honestly mistaken, though it's well known that his leman has Leveler sympathies, that's why he was charged with this riot. But none of this is my doing. All I have done is celebrate my cousin's wedding. And where is this Rathe?"

"He remains at the house, majesty," Eslingen said. "To make sure no one can get at the powder until it can be secured."

"Or to put it there himself," d'Alamenon said.

The queen looked thoughtfully at her, and d'Alamenon curtsied deeply.

"Pardon, majesty."

The queen nodded. "Vaan Esling?"

"I saw the barrels in place myself, majesty, as did Master Bonamy." Eslingen held his breath, and relaxed as she nodded again.

160

"Clearly this will take time to unravel. Raimon, this is what your Guard is for. Send them to secure the house—no, go yourself, I want your word on this. Master Bonamy, you will stay with me."

"Yes, majesty," both men said, and Coindarel touched Eslingen's sleeve.

"Come, Philip."

"Let me go ahead," Eslingen said. "I've left Nico there alone, there's no knowing who'll come for him."

"Not alone," Coindarel said. "Not without witnesses." They had reached the door of the hall, and he looked around quickly. "Tarlan!" The junior lieutenant appeared out of the shadows, the Guard's dark blue coat blending into the shadows. "Go with Captain vaan Esling, take the best horses we have. And, Philip—good luck."

"Thank you," Eslingen said, and wished he didn't see the worry in Coindarel's eyes.

RATHE WATCHED THE gate close behind Eslingen and Bonamy, then turned back to the kitchen. The noise was even louder than before, someone shrieking in fear and someone else yelling for quiet, and finally Saire banging a spoon on an empty pot to demand everyone's attention.

"You heard me! The party's off, take yourselves out of here! Go, now!"

"What about our pay?" a woman shouted.

"You'll be paid for what you've done," Saire answered, and there was a rumble of discontent.

"There won't be a ball," Rathe said, pitching his voice to carry. "No one's coming, and the house is dangerous. You need to leave now."

"But our pay," a man said, one of the waiters, from the look of him, and Saire set her hands on her hips.

"You'll be paid tomorrow for the work you've done," she said again. "I'll see to that myself. But the pointsman's right, there's barrels of gunpowder in the cellar, and the captain's gone off to warn the queen to stay away. And you should be gone, too."

Someone shrieked again, and Rathe saw the shock of the words fly round the room. "Gunpowder?" someone said, and one of the women swore loudly. A cook, her hair bound up in a spotless kerchief, called out, "That can't be right. Saire, are you sure?"

"Saw it myself," Saire answered. "And touched and tasted it. Go, all of you, unless you want to be caught up in this."

That was enough to turn the tide. Rathe heard the clatter of knives and spoons and dishes hastily set aside, saw women and men stripping off their aprons and heading for the doors. Only a handful of people, three women and an older man, hung back, looking to Saire.

"What's to do with all of this?" one of the women asked, waving her hand at the array of pots and pans still waiting on the fires. "We can't waste it."

Saire looked at Rathe, who shrugged. "Up to you. When do you expect the guests?"

"The soeueraine's stewards were to come at half past seven," Saire said. "The guests were invited for nine, which means half past."

"There's time, then," the man said.

Saire nodded. "Right. Take everything off the fire, put anything that can be saved in the buttery. If it'll spoil—" She grimaced. "Take it, someone might as well get the use of it."

"It's not so bad," the nearest woman said. "We'd only just gotten started on the dinner things, most of the rest should keep."

"Do what you can," Saire said. She looked at Rathe. "Make sure Estin's got away, will you? And took the horses? Then—keep an eye out for the soeuraine's people. I don't want my people here when they come."

Rathe went back out to the courtyard, relieved to see that it was empty. The stable doors were open and the stalls were cleared: Eslingen had warned the grooms, and they'd had the sense to listen. And Eslingen was well away, on his way to the palace to fetch Coindarel and the Guard: Rathe had never expected to be grateful for that, but he was now. As long as Eslingen could persuade Coindarel to come—but he would. He knew Coindarel, and Coindarel knew and trusted him. As long as he could speak to Coindarel, it would be all right. *And if he doesn't find Coindarel? If Coindarel isn't there?* Rathe shoved the thought away. Eslingen would find a way.

He peered out the gate, seeing the street empty to either side, then checked the back entrance as well. There was nothing there, either, and he went back into the kitchen, shaking his head in answer to Saire's sharp stare. "Nothing, dame. And there's still half an hour before they're expected."

Most of the kitchen had been cleared, the pots removed from the fire and their contents either discarded or stored somewhere safe. The uncut loaves of bread were suspended in nets from the beams, and the man was just disappearing through the buttery door with a crock tucked under each arm. There were what looked like two cheeses wrapped in cloth on one of the worktables, but even as Rathe watched, one of the women collected them and disappeared after the man. A girl not much more than apprentice age was hauling a cone of sugar up to its place below the rafters; she secured the cord and came back to Saire, saying, "That's that, Gran. I don't see anything else."

"Those tarts," Saire said, pointing, and the girl swung around, her skirts swirling. She made an annoyed noise, snatched up a covered platter, and disappeared into the pantry. Saire looked back at Rathe. "They'll be coming soon enough."

"Which is why I want you gone," Rathe answered. "You and the last of your people. No need to put yourself in wrong."

"Put the blame on you, then?"

Rathe shrugged. "It's the truth." And if it came to that, he'd have far more to worry about than a charge of driving honest women from their work, but there was no need to say so.

The women emerged from the buttery, the man trailing at their heels. "That's everything I could see, Saire," their leader said. "It'll keep at least another day or two, and we didn't lose much."

"No, it's well done," Saire answered. "And now, off with you, before you're dragged any deeper in."

One of the women and the man turned away, but the other woman hesitated. "What about yourself?"

"I'll be right behind you," Saire said, and the woman turned away.

"Gran," the girl said.

Saire shook her head. "Don't you start."

"You're not going, are you?"

"I'm going when I'm ready," Saire answered. "And that's not until I have to."

"And that should be now," Rathe said.

"They won't be expecting any trouble," Saire said.

"Even if they're not, they'll still send a knife or two to tend those barrels," Rathe said. "You don't want to face that."

"We could help," the girl said.

"We'd be in the way," Saire said. "That's what you're saying, isn't it?"

Rathe nodded, though a part of him wished he could risk it. It would be easier to watch for the knives if he had someone to cover both doors—but it wasn't safe. "Best you go now."

"Right, then." Saire gave the kitchen a last sweeping glance, then picked up a basket she'd left on the table. "There's bread and wine in the pantry if you want it."

I'm not likely to have the chance, Rathe thought, but nodded again. "Thanks."

He walked with them to the back gate in the growing twilight, and after a moment's thought, barred it behind them. It would be easier to watch the front gate from inside the house, and he could leave the kitchen door barred, force the knives to come in through the main hall. Better to lock that door, then, but leave it unbarred, so that he knew which way they'd be coming. Of course, that would also mean they'd know something was wrong, but with only himself to watch, there wasn't much to be gained by surprise. His task was to keep them from setting off the powder in the cellar, make sure that no one could be harmed even if Eslingen wasn't able to persuade the queen to stay away—though of course he would, surely. He hoped. In the distance, a tower clock struck seven.

He went through the main floor, locking windows and barring the side doors. He wished Eslingen were there to help make the plan: this was the sort of thing Eslingen was good at—had been trained for. But there was no point wishing. Eslingen was the man who wasn't subject to a point, who could speak at the queen's court, and bring the help they needed. And after all, there was a solid chance the knives would come, find the servants fled and the doors locked, and run away themselves. Any of Mikael's knives would have the sense to cut their losses.

It was growing darker out, the main sun almost down and the winter-sun not yet risen. He was hungry, he realized with some surprise, and retreated through the hall to the kitchen, keeping an ear out for noises at the back gate. He cut himself bread and cheese, ate in a hurry and washed it down with a cup of watered wine, still listening, and after a moment's hesitation, slipped the best of the kitchen knives into his belt. The tower clock struck the quarter hour, and then half: any time now, he thought, and cocked his head at the sound of a knock at the back gate. The bar rattled in its brackets, and the knocking came again, more loudly. Rathe checked the bar at the kitchen door, and the heavy shutters that closed the windows, then made sure the cellar door was open for his retreat. Then he returned to the hall, peering out through the gap in the shutters that covered the ballroom windows.

No sign of d'Alamenon's people yet, and he reached into his purse, feeling the smooth cold glass of the thunderflashes he'd taken from Aconin. They might prove useful, depending on what he was facing, and there was stone enough in the hearths and in the kitchen itself to set them off. He saw movement beyond the gate, shadows gathering, and then the scrape of the gate against the hard-packed ground. There were more than he'd expected, easily a lunar dozen, and one stopped and pointed to the house. Rathe flinched, afraid he'd been seen, then realized they were talking about the lack of lights. He could hear querulous voices, a woman complaining that someone had failed, another exclaiming that the souveraine would be furious, and a man's voice rode over the rest, demanding silence.

"Something's wrong. Go back, tell them at the house. We'll go in and see what's to see." One of the women started to protest, and the man shoved her back toward the gate. "Go! You have your orders."

The group split, not eagerly, eight or nine of them retreating toward the gate, the six remaining starting purposefully toward the main stair. That was Rathe's cue, and he slipped back down the hall, ducking under the shadow of the staircase that led to the upper floors. Someone pounded on the door, calling for a name he didn't recognize, and then there was a pause before the lock scraped open.

"Noll? Saire? Where in Tyrseis's name is everyone?"

"Something's definitely gone wrong," another voice said, and the first speaker swore again.

"Keep quiet if you haven't anything more useful to say. Check the ballroom and the parlor."

Rathe waited, turning the first of the thunderflashes over in his fingers. He heard the scuffling of feet on the stone floor, and then a woman's breathless voice, coming back into the hall.

"Nothing. There's no one here and everything's locked from the inside."

"Same in the parlors," a man said. "It's gone wrong, Frantje. We need to get out of here."

Rathe held his breath. If only it could be that simple—they wouldn't have evidence against the knives, but it would ensure the queen's safety, and the safety of her household…

"Don't be a fool," Frantje said. "Move on."

Rathe flung the first thunderflash across the hall, aiming for the stone flags beneath the butler's counter. The first missed, but the second struck home, exploding with a flash and bang as loud as a gunshot. He heard curses and scrambling as the knives ducked into cover, and Frantje's voice rose above the rest. "You there! Come out and face us!"

Rathe didn't answer, sliding backwards into the kitchen instead. He stopped at the cellar door, the last thunderflash ready in his hand. Frantje's voice came indistinctly from the hall—asking if anyone had actually been hurt, Rathe guessed—and then the sudden rush of footsteps toward the kitchen door. He threw the last thunderflash at the stone sill, and hurried down the cellar stairs, slamming the door behind him. He dropped the bar into place and stood listening, waiting for the knives' next move.

Someone banged on the door, shouting something incoherent; a heavy thudding followed, and then more shouts. Frantje's voice rose above the rest, demanding silence, and then there was a more determined knocking. "You in there! Open up, and we'll let you walk away."

Rathe didn't bother answering, felt around instead for Saire's lantern. He found it after a moment, cupped it in both hands to trigger the mage-light, and held it up to illuminate as much of the long room as possible. The barrels of gunpowder were shadows at the far end, the fuses pulled and piled in an untidy heap in the center aisle, as safe as they could be, at least for the moment.

"You!" Frantje called again. "There's no sense sacrificing yourself for your mistress, she doesn't give a printer's blot about you. Open the door! We'll let you go, and no one will ever be the wiser."

That sounded more like a Leveler argument than something d'Alamenon's knives would say, and Rathe frowned. Still, it was better to keep them talking if he could, and he leaned cautiously toward the door. "I know what's down here." He pitched his voice higher than usual, let it waver slightly. "You'd have brought the whole house down on us."

"What do you care?" Frantje said. "These nobles, they're nothing to you—"

"And we're nothing to them," Rathe answered, abruptly furious. "You'd have blown up the house with all of us in it, and I don't care whether it was for politics or principles. You don't care about anyone who works here."

There was a silence, and then someone said something, the words too low-pitched for Rathe to make them out. Frantje answered, then raised his voice again. "Last chance! Open up now, or take the consequences."

"And let you kill the neighbors?" Rathe called. He waited, but there was no answer. He could hear the knives moving on the other side of the door, and then the scrape of wood on stone as something was dragged up against the door. It struck the wood with a resounding thud, but lock and bar held firm. He braced himself, waiting for them to try again, but instead there was silence. Had they given up? It seemed unlikely, but he couldn't think what else they could do. It would take time and a good deal more effort to break down the door; maybe they'd gone for axes, but that would also take more time than they really had. No, if they had any sense, they'd give this up as a spoiled job, and take themselves off before anyone got enough of a look at them to call the point. At least he was fairly certain that was what Mikael would tell his knives to do, but there was no knowing what the soeuraine's men might try instead.

The silence continued. He thought he heard footsteps overhead, moving toward the far end of the cellar, but the sounds faded, and he couldn't be sure. Take down the bar, chance peering out? Probably not a good idea, and yet the silence was unnerving. Eslingen would take the chance, he thought. No, Eslingen would make it as un-chancy as possible, and that meant luring them back in, if they were waiting. He reached for the bar, let it scrape loudly against the bracket, and held it ready to drop if there was the slightest sound from outside. There was nothing, not when he did it again, not even when he lifted the bar entirely away and let it thump loudly on the landing at the top of the stairs. There was nothing from the ceiling, either: maybe they had done the sensible thing, and fled.

He set the bar at his feet, easily in reach if he was wrong, and very quietly turned the lock. The snap of the mechanism sounded very loud in the silence, but there was no movement in response. He took a breath, and eased the door back, bracing himself to slam it shut again.

There was no movement, and no light, either, though he would have expected some twilight still to linger. But there was nothing, and when he pulled the door back a little further, he saw only solid darkness. Solid wood, he realized, and flattened his hand against roughly hewn planks. It was the back of one of the heavy storage cabinets, dragged hastily across the doorway. He closed the door again and locked it, set the bar in place just in case, and sat down on the edge of the landing. It made no sense. Why lock him in, if they were going to run? To buy time? Any sensible person would stay safe in the cellar until the guests arrived and rescued her.

He looked around again, seeing the barrels' shadows leap and waver as he moved the lantern. Still nothing from upstairs, and he made his way down the stairs toward the barrels of gunpowder at the far end of the cellar. Even coming closer, he didn't hear anything, though he caught a faint acrid whiff of something that raised the hairs at the back of his neck. He froze, sniffing, but the smell was gone. He took a breath, and then another, the air smelling only of dirt and stone, and then the smoke was back, stronger than before. He lifted the lantern, looking for the source, but saw nothing.

If the knives had started a fire above, in the ballroom… He was already turning, hurrying back to the stairs. He unbarred the door, unlocked it, and flung it wide. The cabinet had been pushed all the way across the opening, completely blocking the door. A faint line of light showed at the edge of the doorway, a gap not as wide as a finger, but if there was a weakness, that would be it. He found what he hoped was a point of leverage and shoved at it, startled and appalled by the unmoving mass. He threw his whole weight against it, but there wasn't room enough to get a decent start. The cabinet didn't budge.

He swore, looking over his shoulder toward the barrels of gunpowder. If the fire burned through the floor, dropped burning beams and floorboards onto the barrels—it wouldn't be the explosion the knives had planned, but it would be sufficient to do serious damage. It would easily be enough to kill a man in this confined space, even if it didn't bring the walls down on top of him. He looked around, hoping this might be one of the houses that still had a well inside the cellar, but if there was one, it was more likely to be in the buttery. Certainly there was no sign of one in the cellar. There were only the barrels of wine, and they wouldn't do him any good, the alcohol would burn just as well as the wood of the casks. Or maybe it would be better than nothing?

He turned and began searching the aisles, looking for a bucket or a pitcher, anything that would carry liquid and let him wet down the barrels. But of course there were none to be found: Saire wouldn't leave that temptation in her people's way. The smell was getting stronger, and he thought he saw the first thin thread of smoke worming its way through the gaps in the ceiling. He swore and retreated to the stairs, training the mage-light on the ceiling. Eslingen was on his way—he was sure to be, he was Coindarel's man and Coindarel would listen to him, no matter how improbable this might sound. And even if he couldn't persuade them, the guests would see that something was terribly wrong. They would see the fire, and would have the sense to stay back, even if they didn't know he was trapped in the cellar and wouldn't know to rescue him… The smell was stronger now, and he could definitely see smoke at the cellar's end, a thin haze hovering below the ceiling. But Eslingen would come.

ELEVEN

IT DIDN'T TAKE long to claim horses from the stables, Tarlan's sharp orders cutting through the confusion. She ordered the nearest sergeant to join them, picking an older man with the skeptical gaze of someone who'd seen long service: a good witness, with no axe to grind. It was a good idea, Eslingen knew, even as he chafed at the delay. Someone offered a sword and pistols, and he accepted both, grudging even the moments it took to sling the sword belt around his waist. And then at last they were off, charging through the gate and down the long avenue at a canter, only to be forced to pull up as they reached the more crowded streets of Hearts. Tarlan reached into her coat and produced an artilleryman's whistle, sounded a shrill blast. Heads turned, and people scurried out of their way, but even so, they were barely able to make a trot. Better than a walk, Eslingen told himself, feeling his horse fighting the bridle, infected by his own nerves. Better than having to wait for the rest of the Guard. He looked at Tarlan. "What's the fastest way?"

"We're on it," the lieutenant answered.

Go faster, then. Eslingen curbed his first response, and concentrated on following her through the crowd. Ahead, the road widened into a market square, not as busy as he would have expected, and then he saw the barricade drawn up across the central passage. It was a makeshift construction of barrels and boards and one battered pushcart, but there were at least a dozen points in attendance, stopping anyone who wanted to pass. He swore, and Tarlan said, "Do we stop?"

"We don't have the time," Eslingen answered. As he spoke, the market's clock struck the half hour. He cursed again, and set spurs to his horse, aiming for a spot where the barrier was only boards balanced on a set of barrels. He heard Tarlan's whistle shrill again, heard the sergeant shout something indistinct, and crouched lower on his horse's back. Someone shouted for them to stop, to stand down, and the nearest of the points waved his truncheon at him. Eslingen ignored him, gauging his horse's stride. The man dove aside as Eslingen gave the signal, and his horse leaped up and over the fragile barrier, clearing it easily. He heard the others follow, and set off down the market without looking back.

Tarlan passed him at the edge of the market, the whistle still clenched in her teeth, and waved him left at the next cross street. Eslingen obeyed, and she slowed to a trot as they passed into the shadows. There was no sound of pursuit, but she shook her head as she retrieved the whistle. "The points will make us pay for that."

"Blame it on me," Eslingen said.

The sergeant snorted, and Tarlan said, "The colonel won't allow that."

"He'll do what's sensible." Eslingen looked around at unfamiliar buildings. It was getting toward full dark, the street now deeply shadowed, only a few lights showing in the upper windows. "Which way?"

"This way," Tarlan said, and chirped to her horse.

Eslingen followed. "We need to go faster."

"The street's too rough," the sergeant said.

He was right, Eslingen knew, but he still wanted to push faster. And if he did, and his horse slipped, or fell, or came up lame, it would take more time, but even so, he listened for the quarter-hours, heard the clocks strike twice more before they came out onto a street he recognized. The air smelled strongly of smoke, as though every house on the street had lit their fires.

"Where are the grooms?" Tarlan asked, slowing her horse to a walk. "And the lights?"

There were torches in the brackets by the gate, but they were unlit, and the windows were shuttered. That would be Rathe's doing, Eslingen thought, choosing to control the points of entry. He said, "We sent everyone away, no sense keeping them in danger if anything went wrong."

He swung down from his horse without waiting for her answer, slung the reins around the nearest post, and started for the main door, drawing his first pistol as he went. There was no sound from the house, no movement in the shadowed alleys either side, and he started up the stairs.

"I smell smoke," the sergeant said, and Tarlan caught her breath.

"Fire! In the ballroom—"

A light flickered in the tiny gap between the shutters. Eslingen swore, put his hand to the latch, ready to snatch it away, but the metal was cool to the touch. He jerked it open, and smoke rolled out, driving him back a step.

"Fire!" Tarlan said again, and reached for her whistle. She blew a shrill blast, and then another. Shutters opened in the house two doors away, but there was no other response. "Fire, damn it, the house is on fire!"

"Nico's in there," Eslingen said. The first great wave of smoke was past; he could see flames in the ballroom to his right, and in what must be a parlor on the other side, but the hall was clear.

"He won't have stayed," Tarlan said. "Not if there's powder in the cellar."

Probably she was right, Rathe was no one's fool, but Eslingen didn't dare take the chance. He shoved his pistol into his belt and stepped into the hall, drawing his stock up over his nose and mouth against the stinging smoke. The ballroom was well alight, flames leaping up from a pile of splintered furniture in the far corner and another between the windows. The curtains were smoldering, flames licking at their feet, and Eslingen charged across to rip them down, dropping them onto the fire in the hope of smothering it. For an instant it worked, and he stamped on the folded cloth, but then had to leap back again as the flames broke through. They were nibbling at the paneling, and at the elegant parquet floor, and beneath them were dozens of barrels of powder...

"Nico! Nico, are you here?"

There was no answer, and he backed out of the ballroom, nearly running into the sergeant.

"I tried to put it out," the sergeant said, jerking his head toward the parlor. "Where's the well?"

"Kitchen," Eslingen answered. "Tarlan?"

"Rousing the neighbors."

Sure enough, Eslingen could hear the sound of her whistle, and shouts from the street. "Bucket brigade. I have to find Rathe!"

He started for the kitchen, the sergeant at his heels. It was much darker in the back of the house, the air only lightly hazed with smoke, and he wished he'd brought a lantern. "Nico!"

He thought he heard an answer this time, and turned toward the cellar door only to stop dead in his tracks. Someone—d'Alamenon's knives, it must have been—had dragged one of the heavy storage cabinets across the cellar door, its feet leaving splintered gouges in the floor. "Nico, where are you?"

"Philip?" The voice came faintly from behind the cabinet. "Get out, the house is on fire—"

"There's time," Eslingen said. "Sergeant, give me a hand."

They threw their weight against the cabinet, but it barely moved. Eslingen braced himself, back against the narrow side, and shoved with all his strength, but nothing happened. There was more smoke in the air now, and he could hear the crackle of flames. The sergeant looked at him. "Let me try to put out the parlor."

"You can't," Eslingen began, then shook his head. "Go. Do what you can, wet things down, then come back, I'll need you—"

The sergeant was already moving, heading for the buttery and the well that kept it cool. Eslingen wrenched open the doors of the cabinet and began pulled out the contents, heavy crocks, stacks of iron cookware, covered baskets that were surprisingly light for their size. He tried the cabinet again as the sergeant reappeared, a bucket in each hand slopping water on the floor, but the cabinet was still too heavy to move. Through the door, he heard Rathe coughing.

"Philip! You've got to get out of here."

"Not without you," Eslingen answered.

"This isn't a Dis-damned play!"

"I'm still not leaving you."

"Idiot! I don't want you dead!"

Eslingen ignored him, looking around for something, anything that would help him move the cabinet. The wood was solid, inches thick to keep out insects, it had to have taken four or five men to move it in front of the door, and it would take as many to move it away again. The sergeant returned, coughing, his face smeared with soot, buckets dangling empty.

"The lieutenant's roused the neighbors, they've gone for the water-men. More are coming—"

"I'll open the back door," Eslingen said, and the sergeant vanished into the buttery. This wasn't nearly enough, not to stop a fire as well-started as this one, but he hauled the bar out of its brackets and paused for a moment. Would it be enough to lever the cabinet away? No, there wasn't enough space, and the angle was wrong, but if he could pull the cabinet over… There were chains in the hearth, and a heavy hook, meant for holding pots of water. He grabbed them, still hot from the embers, managed to jerk them free and came back to the cabinet. The empty shelves made a ladder of sorts. He climbed it, reaching across to drive the hook into the wood below the decorative molding, then leaned back, putting his full weight on the chain. For a moment, nothing happened, and he braced both feet against the second shelf, pushing himself out and away. The cabinet tilted abruptly, and he leaped clear an instant before it crashed to the ground. "Nico! It's clear!"

There was a scraping sound and the door swung open. Eslingen held out his hand and Rathe took it to lever himself over the fallen cabinet, clung to him for just an instant longer than was necessary before he shook himself free. "The fire—we need to warn—"

"Our lieutenant's done that," Eslingen said. "Are you all right?"

"Fine." Rathe turned toward the kitchen door just as the sergeant staggered in from the hall, thicker smoke billowing behind him.

"Captain! The Colonel's here, and the neighbors brought buckets. The water-men are on the way."

The kitchen door swung open. Tarlan and half a dozen of the Guard tumbled in, followed by women and men in ordinary clothes, a few with outer robes slung hastily over nightwear. All of them carried buckets, and the sergeant pointed them to the buttery.

"We'll need to wet down the powder," Rathe said, and coughed again.

Eslingen patted him on the back, as much to reassure himself as to ease the cough, and looked around for anything to carry water. "There's bound to be a pitcher somewhere—"

"The water-men are here," someone called, and Rathe swung around.

"Over here! There are barrels of gunpowder in the cellar, you need to wet them down."

"So we've been told," a stocky man said. He was dressed in a dark oiled-canvas coat, and there were two more young men at his shoulder. "You two, follow the bucket brigade, call the rain for them. You—pointsman, is it? Show me these barrels."

"Down here." Rathe led the way down the stairs, the water-man on his heels. Eslingen followed more slowly, to see the water-man plant his feet and roll his shoulders like a man about to lift a heavy weight.

"I'd be happier if we were closer to the river," he said, half to himself, and lifted his hands, tracing magists' symbols in the air. The smoke thickened, or perhaps it was something else, and there was a sudden chill. The taste of smoke vanished, replaced by a cold damp, and drops sprang out like dew on the sides of the barrels. "That'll hold them until the boys and I can finish the job."

He turned, brushing past Eslingen to hurry up the stairs. Eslingen watched him go, suddenly exhausted, and Rathe caught his shoulder. "Come on. We'll be needed to haul water. They'll trap the fire, but it's the rest of us who'll finish it off."

Eslingen shook himself. "Right," he said, and followed Rathe upstairs to take his place in the bucket line.

RATHE WAS NEVER sure afterwards how long they worked to fight the fire. Certainly the winter-sun was well up, and the water in the well had dropped far enough that they had to let the rope out to its fullest extent before drawing it up, but at last the flames were doused and the water-men certified that the embers were truly cold. Coindarel had arrived at some point, and the Metropolitan herself, stalking through the wreckage in her court finery. And then she was gone again, and they were standing in the dark with the sweat cooling on them, a clock in the distance striking two o'clock. There was no sign of anyone from Hearts, and Rathe wondered vaguely where they were. Though it was probably just as well they weren't here, or they'd be trying to call a point on him, and he wasn't sure he was ready to face that.

"Nico?" Eslingen put his arm around Rathe's shoulders, and Rathe heaved a sigh.

"Do we dare go home, do you think?"

"You'll go to the barracks," Coindarel said, "where I can be sure you'll be safe. And then her majesty wants to talk to both of you." He paused, his mouth twisting into a wry smile. "And to the Surintendant, alas for me. But it would be best if you slept first."

There was no arguing with that, nor, Rathe found, did he want to. His head was aching again, and he was more than willing to let Eslingen find a low-flyer and bundle them both aboard. The room in the Guard's barracks was small and plainly furnished, but the bed was big enough for two, and the mattress almost achingly soft. He barely managed to strip to shirt and drawers before he fell deeply asleep.

He woke to full sunlight, and a clock striking the hour: ten o'clock. He sat up quickly, wincing in anticipation of another headache, and saw Eslingen seated at the narrow table in his shirtsleeves, reading a scribbled note. Eslingen looked up at the movement, and smiled. "Oh, good. I was going to have to wake you."

"I'm awake." Rathe swung himself out of bed, startled and pleased to see a tray with a teapot and a plate of sausage pastries waiting. "Do I remember we were supposed to see the queen?"

"We are." Eslingen pushed the plate toward him, and Rathe poured himself a cup of tea. It was still hot, and deeply fragrant, and he closed his eyes, savoring it. "There's time yet."

"Do we know what she wants?"

"An explanation, I gather," Eslingen said. "Being as the landame's house nearly burned down, or blew up, and there's all sorts of allegations flying about."

"None of which we can prove," Rathe said. That was a fresh bitterness that turned the taste of the pastries to ash on his tongue. "I could swear to the knives, I saw them clearly, but there's no proof they were hired by d'Alamenon."

"Unless de Castiat knows more than she's saying," Eslingen said, but he didn't sound convinced.

"She won't talk," Rathe said. "Annechon made that clear."

"Bonamy can testify to holding the barrels."

"But only to who delivered them, if that, not to who really owned them," Rathe said. "And even if he did, his word isn't much against a soeuraine."

"He says de Galhac will speak for him."

"And believes it, I'm sure." Rathe poured another cup of tea. "And there's still the matter of the point against me."

"That won't stand," Eslingen said, but Rathe could see the doubt in his eyes. "You should shave."

Rathe rubbed his chin unhappily, but knew Eslingen was right. He managed it anyway, despite the borrowed razor, and borrowed a clean shirt from one of the lieutenants. Someone had brought in a magist to clean their coats, but even so, a hint of smoke still clung about them, and he was all too aware that he was hardly fit to be seen inside the queen's court.

Coindarel had ordered a private carriage, with ample room for all of them, and drawn by a pair of matched bays that drew Eslingen's eyes for a long moment. Rathe braced himself for an unpleasant ride, but to his surprise, the springs were good enough that the jolting didn't wake a headache.

It was nearing noon by the time they reached the palace, the winter-sun sinking behind the roof, the sun itself casting short shadows on the stones of the courtyard as they climbed down from the carriage. The sky was the bright unreliable blue that promised cold to come, and even in the doubled sunlight there was an edge to the air.

Pages were waiting, and hurried them through the vestibule, where they were handed over to a steward in livery, who brought them down a side corridor to another woman, not in livery but bearing the queen's sunburst pinned to the collar of her bodice. She brought them into a narrow parlor where the long windows overlooked a garden, its beds already cleared and tidied for winter. There was no fireplace, but a portable stove had been set by the largest of the carved chairs, and the queen stretched slippered toes to it, while Astreiant's Metropolitan peered out the windows, and another woman in an expensive gown busied herself at the sideboard. An older man sat beside her, Amorin Bonamy standing uneasily at his shoulder. The Surintendant was there ahead of them, Rathe saw, sitting bolt upright in an uncomfortable-looking backless chair, but there were no other points present. Whether that was a bad sign or not, he couldn't tell.

"Raimon." The queen waved a hand, beckoning them closer.

Coindarel swept a graceful bow. "Majesty."

"So this is them." The queen beckoned again, more emphatically. "Eslingen—vaan Esling—and Rathe."

Eslingen bowed, more deeply than Coindarel. Rathe did his best to copy him, murmuring, "Majesty."

"You did well enough," she said, "but I would have liked to lay hands on at least one of these knives."

The Surintendant stirred. "With all respect, Majesty, there were lives at stake."

"One of which was my own, yes, I'm quite aware of that." To Rathe's surprise, she smiled. "And I'm not ungrateful, I assure you, Rainart. I don't need holes blown in the middle of my city. But I also need to be sure it can't happen again, and that's where the problem lies. Unless you two know more than you've said?"

Rathe felt Eslingen's eyes flick toward him, and cleared his throat. "I'm sorry, Majesty. I have an idea of who was behind all this, but I can't prove it."

"And therein lies our difficulty," the queen said. "Tell me what you know, Adjunct Point. Maybe there's something we can use."

"Majesty," Rathe said. He took a breath, hastily marshaling his thoughts, and began to lay out the pieces of the problem, from the sudden upsurge of Leveler broadsheets and the peculiar self-arrest of the Vidame de Castiat to the carts of gunpowder and Bonamy's unwilling cooperation, to the riot and their flight to the Court. "I think that it was staged to make sure we—vaan Esling and I—weren't able to follow the threads we'd found. Even with Hearts not able to call the point, we couldn't come back into the district—"

"He was hurt, badly, and that delayed us," Eslingen said, and Rathe glared at him.

"We weren't able to come back, and so we weren't able to trace where the carts came from, or how they were connected to de Castiat, though I believe they were."

"We think they were the same people she hired to move her salt," the Surintendant said. "And that we will be able to prove."

"Not that it does us any good," the Metropolitan said. "She's already self-convicted, self-fined, and self-imprisoned. There's not much more we can do to her."

"Ban her from my court," the queen said. "She might have a word or two to say to that."

The Metropolitan bent her head. "Worth the attempt, majesty."

The queen waved a hand. "Go on, Adjunct Point."

"There's not much more to tell," Rathe said, and knew he sounded bitter. "Master Bonamy told us where the gunpowder had been, and that it had been moved, and we knew that the soueraine was hosting a ball that night to celebrate the wedding. If this was a move against the crown, and we had every reason to suspect it was, that was where we needed to look first. And the powder was there."

"The fuses were set," Eslingen said. "Laid out ready to go. There was enough powder there to kill everyone in the house, not just the guests but everyone working there, and probably half the neighbors, too."

"It's well this was prevented," the queen said. "But, as you say, there's no proof."

"No one but d'Alamenon benefits from any of this," Rathe said. "And everywhere you look, there she is, or one of her cousins, or both. But no. It's not proof."

"Martin?" The queen looked at the man sitting beside Bonamy, and Rathe realized that he had to be the Palatine de Galhac. "What do you say to this?"

De Galhac sighed. "My sister was fond of d'Alamenon. They were, I thought, good friends. But I knew she would have gladly disinherited me if she could have gotten the rest of the family to support her, and I know she betrayed at least one secret Dariela shared with her." He gave Bonamy a sad smile. "None of us wanted to bring trouble down on you, Amorin. I'm sorry for that."

"It wasn't your doing," Bonamy murmured.

"If we accuse her directly, she'll simply deny it," the Metropolitan said.

Fourie stirred slightly. "We might be able to persuade one of her knives to talk."

"You'll have to catch them first," the Metropolitan said.

"They were her men," Rathe said reluctantly. "Not from the city. Mikael said it wasn't any of his people, and I believe him."

"He doesn't deal in politics," Fourie agreed. "Still, we'll hunt them. With the Guard's help, if we have to leave the city."

Rathe saw Coindarel stiffen, and then relax. "Whatever we can do for you, Surintendant."

"It's a start," the Metropolitan said. "And you might get something that way, you never know. But you won't find the kind of proof you need to accuse d'Alamenon."

"Unless you have anything to add, Martin?" The queen looked at de Galhac, who shook his head.

"If I did, majesty, I would tell you. I'm sorry."

"So." The queen flattened her hands on the arms of her chair. "That leaves me to deal with her, and deal with her I shall. I will request that she leave the court and return to her own lands, until I summon her myself."

There was a little silence, and finally the Metropolitan said, "Risky."

"Do you have a better idea?"

"Sadly, no." The Metropolitan shook her head. "But you're right, it's more of a risk to keep her here. Though I'd like her watched."

"I'm sure that can be arranged," the queen said, and the Metropolitan bowed.

"As you say, Majesty."

Rathe cleared his throat, knowing perfectly well it wasn't his place to speak, but knowing, too, that he owed Annechon this much. "Majesty, maseigne, there's one thing—" Both women turned to look at him, the queen's painted eyebrows rising in a way that made him wonder how he'd ever found Eslingen's expression intimidating. He stumbled on anyway. "The vidame, de Castiat, I don't believe she was a willing party. You might find something useful there."

"A possibility," the queen said, after a moment. "Certainly worth considering."

Rathe bent his head again, and decided it was better to stay silent. To his surprise, it was Eslingen who spoke next.

"I beg pardon, but there's one other matter to consider. A point has been claimed against Rathe, here, and it's clear that the charge is false."

"Philip." Rathe put his hand on Eslingen's shoulder, and Fourie swung around in his chair.

"I have housecleaning to do, Captain, and I assure you, you can leave that to me."

There was a vindictive note in his voice that made Rathe wince. Eslingen said, "Thank you, Surintendant."

"Indeed, I trust you will," the queen said, and Fourie bent his head unhappily. "Now. Captain vaan Esling and Adjunct Point Rathe. I am indeed grateful for what you did, and I am well aware that you saved many more lives than my own and that of my kin. I know that you don't accept fees—your reputation precedes you—but I hope you will accept a gift, a very small acknowledgement of what you did for the city."

She held out her hand, and Rathe came forward reluctantly. He couldn't refuse, but it still felt too much like a fee. She smiled as though she'd guessed his thought and placed a ring in his palm. It was a signet, the gold table a little smaller than his thumbnail; it was old, too, the once-sharp lines of the design worn down, all the edges rounded. It showed Astree's scales and sword, the scales in perfect balance, and he frowned, an old memory stirred. "A judge's ring?" He added, belatedly, "Majesty."

The queen smiled, looking suddenly younger. "Ah, Rainart, you always pick the clever ones. Yes, they were given to the judiciary in my grandmother's day, but the custom has long been in abeyance. It was meant to remind them of their duty to the law." She paused. "Serve the law, Rathe, the rest will take care of itself."

Rathe closed his hand tight over the ring, managed to bow and back away without falling over his own feet, the metal pressed tight into his palm. This, the ring and the words, the queen's order, was the last thing he'd expected, a gift of greater value than any fee. He slid it onto his middle finger, and found it fit comfortably, promise and pledge. He was vaguely aware that the queen spoke to Eslingen, handing him something, and then that the Metropolitan was speaking, but the words washed over him, meaningless as rain.

Eslingen's hand closed on his elbow, and he let himself be led out of the parlor. They made their way back through the tangled corridors, Eslingen steering him unspeaking, until at last they reached the gate. A groom whistled for a low-flyer, and Rathe climbed aboard without complaint, Eslingen scrambling after.

"Home," he said, and Rathe nodded, leaning back against the cracked leather cushions as the low-flyer jolted into motion. He was exhausted, and his head ached, and more than anything he wanted his own rooms, his own bed and Eslingen beside him…

He was still in a daze when they reached the house. Eslingen manhandled him up the stairs and left him on the bed; Rathe closed his eyes, and roused only briefly when Sunflower nosed up against him.

He woke again a little before sunset, Sunflower still tucked against his ribs. The dog snuffled and stretched when he sat up, then leaped away and trotted ahead of him into the main room. Eslingen was sitting by the stove, a pile of broadsheets in front of him, and the teapot swaddled in a towel. "I think it's still hot," he said, by way of greeting, and Rathe accepted a cup gladly.

"Anything alarming?" He nodded to the broadsheets, and Eslingen smiled.

"Less than before, I think. I didn't find any new Leveler sheets, which argues that was d'Alamenon's doing, too."

"We should have had her." Rathe sighed. "If it wasn't for the riot—"

"Nobody died," Eslingen said. "And they would have, if her people had managed to set off that powder. A whole house full, servants and guests and probably half the neighbors." He paused. "There was nothing else we could do, Nico."

"I know." And it wasn't a choice, Rathe thought. If it was between saving Saire and the rest of the household, and holding off in the hope of getting some kind of proof—it was no choice at all. "I just hate to see her getting away with it, that's all."

"She's not gotten away with it," Eslingen said. "She's banished from the queen's court, and that matters a great deal, for somebody as ambitious as her. And she'll be watched. If she puts one toe out of line, they'll have her."

"Yes, but I wanted the point." Rathe allowed himself a snort of laughter. "And now you'll tell me I'm getting above myself."

Eslingen shook his head. "Not you. Never you. If anyone could have... But it would have cost too much."

Rathe smiled, obscurely comforted. "What did the queen give you? I missed that part."

Eslingen held out his hand, fingers spread. There was a heavy silver ring on his third finger, a ring Rathe had never seen before, set with a flat black stone as smooth as a mirror.

Rathe cocked his head. "A signet? Without a seal?"

"She told me I could choose my own," Eslingen said, "and I said I thought I'd leave it blank. To be true to my family, I said, but I think she knew everything I meant."

Eslingen was a motherless man who passed for noble, a Leaguer who served Chenedolle, a soldier who had turned to the law. Rathe nodded thoughtfully. "She's wise. What are you going to say if anyone asks why it's blank?"

"Look mysterious and say I can't answer," Eslingen said, with a grin.

Rathe laughed, the familiar joke driving away the last of his regret. "And no one died."

"No." Eslingen put his hand on Rathe's shoulder, and Rathe took a deep breath. That was a victory, and they were together. He touched Eslingen's fingers, words as always failing him, but Eslingen's hand tightened in answer. That was enough for now.

ABOUT THE AUTHOR

MELISSA SCOTT is from Little Rock, Arkansas, and studied history at Harvard College and Brandeis University, where she earned her PhD in the Comparative History program. She is the author of more than thirty original science fiction and fantasy novels, most with queer themes and characters, as well as authorized tie-ins for Star Trek: DS9, Star Trek: Voyager, Stargate SG-1, Stargate Atlantis, and Star Wars Rebels. She won Lambda Literary Awards for *Trouble and Her Friends*, *Shadow Man*, *Point of Dreams* (written with her late partner, Lisa A. Barnett), and *Death By Silver*, with Amy Griswold. She also won Spectrum Awards for *Shadow Man*, *Fairs' Point*, *Death By Silver*, and for the short story "The Rocky Side of the Sky" (*Periphery*, Lethe Press) as well as the John W. Campbell Award for Best New Writer. She was also shortlisted for the Otherwise (Tiptree) Award. Her latest short story, "Sirens," appeared in the collection *Retellings of the Inland Seas*, and her text-based game for Choice of Games, *A Player's Heart*, came out in 2020. Her most recent solo novels, *The Master of Samar* and *Fallen*, were published in 2023.

ABOUT
QUEEN OF SWORDS
PRESS

Queen of Swords is an independent small press, specializing in swashbuckling tales of derring-do, bold new adventures in time and space, mysterious stories of the occult and arcane and fantastical tales of people and lands far and near. Visit us online at www.queenofswordspress.com and sign up for our mailing list to get notified about upcoming releases and offers. Or follow us on Facebook at the Queen of Swords Press page so you don't miss any press news.

If you have a moment, the author would appreciate you taking the time to leave a review for this book at Goodreads, your blog or on the site you purchased it from.

Thank you for your assistance and your support of our authors.